The Full Moon Murders

Con Shalevski

First published by Busybird Publishing 2022

ISBN:
Paperback: 978-1-922691-83-5
Ebook: 978-1-922691-84-2

Cover image: Photo by Aron Visuals: https://www.pexels.com/photo/full-moon-surrounded-by-clouds-3750779/

Cover design: Busybird Publishing

Layout and typesetting: Busybird Publishing

Busybird Publishing
2/118 Para Road
Montmorency, Victoria
Australia 3094
www.busybird.com.au

*For my son Nicholas, my life partner Annwen,
and my step-daughter Alessia.*

Prologue

The flashing lights illuminate the sky, reminiscent of the Northern Lights in Norway. Police cars have filled the street with authority, ambulance vehicles made useful for what they are meant for. Bodies scattered on the lawn needing attention. The entire town have made their way to the clinic to see the devastation.

Three gurneys are brought out through the front door, making their short journey to the waiting vehicles. Sheets covering the bodies that occupy them. The innocent bystander sees a massacre before them, painting the picture that something dreadful had been brought to their town that will change its land's future.

Media vans parked on the nature strip, police helicopter hovering above, capturing it all from a different angle. Headlines of the event that will be plastered across the front cover of the morning paper.

A reporter shoves a microphone into the face of a detective. The question is asked. A tone of no respect.

'Can you tell us what happened, detective? Who are the victims?'

And so, the story begins …

CHAPTER 1

Annie is on the last train home from her part-time job as a kitchenhand in an up-market restaurant at Southbank. She works long hours most evenings to make enough money to take a trip back home to the States to visit her family. It's not an ideal job, but her boss and colleagues are great which makes work a fun place to be. Plus, she gets paid whilst being happy. The other reason Annie works these crazy hours is to support her studies and lifestyle. She is studying Psychology full time at uni.

The train carriage is almost empty, and it smells of alcohol and urine with a light floating stench of vomit. It's quiet and eerie with only the sound of the train rattling on the tracks. Looking around, Annie can see a young Asian couple holding hands, looking so much in love. An elderly drunk man is wearing clothes that look like they've seen better days. Even from where she is sitting, Annie can smell his dirty clothes. Looks like it's been a while since they've been washed. Also in the carriage are three teens, eyes plastered on their mobile phones, not even noticing that there are others around them. Everyone on the carriage looks tired. Their day must have been busy, Annie can tell by the look on their face. Exhaustion is the fashionable look for the evening.

The drunk man is lying across three seats. Luckily for him it's not peak hour. Otherwise, he would have had a problem finding a seat and staying upright. The Asian couple seem to be unwinding from a night out. Friday nights in the City of Melbourne are always overloaded with people. It's the one night of the week where the city offices come alive and have their end of week drinks. The women let out their hair and the men go a little crazy. There is something happening on every corner that attracts you to it, before it releases you back into the jungle for the next. From buskers to jugglers, painters and palm readers, just to mention a few. For a few dollars you can entertain your overworked mind.

The teenagers seem harmless and keep to themselves, focusing on their phones, not even talking to one another. Phones do that to people these days. They're hypnotised by the frequency in the air and drowned in their text messages and social media, probably Snapchat or TikTok, forgetting how to socialise.

Annie looks out the window and something catches her attention. Flashing lights up ahead. There are three police cars in the vicinity of the apartment she shares with her university friends, Sally and Oscar. They live in Clifton Hill. It's not the quiet suburban area that she is used to, with busy streets at all hours of the day. Ybor City, where Annie was born, is the opposite to Clifton Hill. Ybor was always quiet and rarely anything interesting ever happened.

The train station Annie usually gets off at is closed. An announcement made a few moments earlier confirms that. It's the end of the line for Annie and the other passengers. Something terrible has happened, and she's afraid to find out what.

There are police officers patrolling the platform, forensic staff marking spots of interest with numbered tags. A pain develops in her chest, her heart skips a beat and the thought of murder creeps into her mind. The book Annie is currently reading sits next to her. She picks it up and places it in her bag. It's a murder mystery that has her thinking the worst.

She looks out the window again. Something bad has definitely happened - police are everywhere. Her mind goes into shock. Her body follows and freezes with fear. Annie needs to get home. *What if I can't get home? What if something terrible has happened in my building?* All these thoughts are travelling through her head with such great speed that it's hard to keep up.

She needs to get off once the train comes to a stop. Will all the commuters get off too or will they stay on? She looks around the carriage again and notices the drunk man. He is fast asleep and holding onto his bottle of wine like a mother holding onto her child, making sure they don't fall out of her arms. Everyone is now standing and no one tries to wake him. They just leave him there, snoring away like Lachie the Purple Wiggle. Most likely they're scared. They all want a quick getaway.

The train has stopped and police officers storm on board, making sure everyone gets off. They tell them all to make their way over to the entrance of the platform. Annie looks down at her seat to make sure she has collected everything. She passes the drunk man on her way through. They're going to have had a hard time removing him from the train.

'Head out towards the carpark,' an officer yells out. Annie is caught in the middle of the three teens. She feels an elbow whack into her ribs. She loses her breath and momentum and falls behind the pack. Annie catches the last bit of the officer's sentence while she sucks in some air. 'There is another officer by the police car who will guide you further.'

Guide us where? Now is not the time to be apprehensive; Annie is confused and questions keep flooding in to her head. *What has happened?* is the question that leads the rest.

The path is clearly marked with police officers and paramedics. Annie feels safe with them around for the time being. The media must have got wind of this, and they've brought out the crew trucks and units by the dozen. Cameras flashing from every angle, police helicopters hovering above them like the army patrolling the Gaza Strip. It was like a scene from a movie. *Mission Impossible* or something similar, sweeping the skies above, searching for the culprit, or culprits, down below. Culprits? Annie is amongst them.

The closer she gets to the apartment, the more it seems like a movie unfolding on a large screen before her eyes. She can sense death in the air. Annie picks up the pace and jogs past the last officer, eager to get home to see if her flatmates are okay. She slows down briefly and looks around, noticing a number of officers she hadn't seen earlier. Her mind lapses as time goes by.

I want them to be home, I need to know that they're safe. Annie's mind is racing fast and she can't help but think about Sally and Oscar. Her breathing moves up another level, and it hurts. She has now hit panic mode. *What if something has happened to Sally or Oscar? What if the police are there for them?* Annie can't help but think the worst.

Annie needs to stop thinking irrationally and concentrate on getting home, pronto. Her anxiety shifts into overdrive. She can't recall how long it's been since departing the train when she reaches the apartment block. Police have cordoned off the building and set a perimeter by the entrance. Annie stops abruptly before she gets any closer and looks around. Noise coming from every angle, her heart beating the loudest. In the park opposite the apartment there is someone on the ground, covered with a sheet. The sheet must've been white, but now the blood has turned it red. Whoever is under that bloodied sheet is dead. The body is covered from head to toe; it looks mummified.

It takes Annie a few seconds to realise, but all of a sudden, her heart sinks and her legs give way, unable to stay upright. She drops to her knees; tears begin to form in her eyes and she can't control them from coming out. Annie knows who is under that sheet. There's a handbag next to the body that looks all too familiar. It's a knock-off Gucci Annie had bought for Sally when she went traveling through Bangkok one year.

The fear Annie had been feeling has now turned to reality.

An unmarked police vehicle arrives with a flashing blue light on its dashboard. The car comes to a screeching halt on the nature strip. Two men get out of the car; one short and stocky with three-day growth, the other slightly taller with a boyish look and a cigarette hanging out of his mouth. By the way they're dressed, you would think they had been called out from a cocktail party. A look far from matching the scene.

The two men were Detective Natloz and Detective Petridis. They have been working as partners in Homicide for four years. Now they find themselves leading a new case.

Detective Natloz doesn't look well. He looks like he has just woken up from a deep sleep. There are better looking zombies in TV shows. Despite that, he approaches Annie with care. She is now accompanied by a female officer who looks out of sorts, probably fresh out of the academy. He tells her he will take over and she leaves without a word. Annie watches her go, leaving her with the detectives. Petridis is looking around for any visible clues, or anyone who might have seen or heard something.

Annie is finding it hard to contain her emotions and begins sobbing uncontrollably. A muffled sound comes out that turns out to be words, 'I can't believe Sally is dead.'

The detective looks at her with a confused look, concern creeps in on his face. 'Who is Sally? How do you know who is under that sheet?'

Annie's eyes are fixated, just staring at the bag in the distance. He follows her gaze, then asks again with more authority. 'I said, how do you know who is under that sheet?' as he bends down and gets to Annie's level.

Annie's brain is in cahoots with her words; shock has stopped her voice in its tracks. She wants to answer, but fear won't let her speak. She points to the bag for a few seconds.

'What is it?' he asks in a much quieter tone.

'The bag,' Annie responds. 'I bought that for her.'

'How do you know it's the same bag?'

'The fuzzy die that's hanging off it. She won that at The Show last year. It's missing a dot off the three.'

Natloz gets up, his knees cracking like someone taking a bite into pork crackle, and makes his way over towards the body. The description about the bag given to him by Annie was correct. The fuzzy die is attached to the bag, the number three missing one dot. He looks over to where Annie is still on the ground. *How could she have seen the bag from that distance?*

'Has anyone gone through this bag?' he asks some officers that are close by.

'No, sir,' one of them replies.

There are a few items from the handbag spread out on the ground. Nothing out of the ordinary: lipstick, coins, a brush. There is a diary lying two metres away and a purse by her feet. Blood has been splattered on one side of the purse. He puts on some latex gloves and approaches the purse, slightly tilting his head to one side, looking a little scattered. He doesn't want to contaminate any evidence, but he has to confirm whether she is right. He opens the purse.

Money and cards still sit neatly in position inside her purse, so he's convinced this wasn't a robbery gone wrong. Someone killed this young lady for fun. Could that have been the motive? Did she get into an argument with someone she knew? Perhaps a boyfriend or an ex? She could have been stalked by someone and then attacked before she had a chance to run. Someone might have seen it happen and we need to find that someone. There are so many apartment buildings around here. Surely someone would have seen or heard something.

'Get a team together and start door knocking while things are still fresh,' he tells the officers. 'I want something to work with by the end of the night. Move it.'

As the group deploys for their task, he returns to inspect the body. In the twenty-two years on the force, he has never seen anything like this before, and neither should Annie. Natloz lifts the sheet to take a closer look. His gloves stained red from the blood. The body of Annie's friend Sally is mutilated like it had been chewed up by a crocodile and spat out. Something, not *someone*, has killed Sally. He speculates that this young lady's life has been cut short for someone's thrill. He can feel the long night ahead of him. He covers Sally and returns to Annie.

'How do you know the victim?' he asks.

Annie looks at him with glazed eyes, like she had been crying for days. They're swollen and dark. 'We live together,' she says sadly. 'We share an apartment. Oscar lives with us, too.'

'Who is Oscar?' he replies as he removes a notepad from his jacket pocket.

Annie stares at it. She knows that everything that she says will go down as evidence against Oscar. She is quite sure he had nothing to do with it. But what if Oscar and Sally had an argument? What if he had lost his temper? They did have a small disagreement yesterday but Annie didn't think Oscar would ever hurt Sally. They have known one another since school.

Surely one lie can't hurt? She doesn't want Oscar getting into any unnecessary trouble. What if he had absolutely nothing to do with this? There is a possibility he doesn't even know what has happened. She decides to keep her mouth shut and give the detective minimal information until she hears from Oscar herself.

Her silence is testing Natloz's patience. He has a short fuse and can be abrupt when pushed and poked at.

'I need to know who Oscar is,' he says firmly. 'I also want to know if he and the victim had any arguments in the last few days. Now is not the time to hold back.'

Detective Petridis arrives. 'Witnesses saw the victim walking through the park when she was attacked.'

Annie isn't paying much attention to what the detectives are talking about. Her mind is elsewhere, not in the present; the past is flashing by as she thinks about Sally. Thinking how terrible it would have been for her, whether she saw her attacker or even knew what was about to happen. Uncontrolled tears start to flow down Annie's face once again.

'The witness said he saw the victim tackled to the ground but didn't have a clear view of the attacker from where he was.' The cigarette sticks out of Petridis's mouth while he's talking. 'He was scared for his life and hid behind his car. The witness also said that he heard a noise, like something an animal would make, followed by a yell.'

Quiet falls as they think, so it's easy to hear the sound of a text message alert. The detectives look at each other and then at Annie. She takes out her phone.

'Is it Oscar?' Natloz asks.

It is but Annie is not about to tell the detectives that. The text reads:

> **I didn't do it, Annie. Please believe me. I saw her lying there, dead. But it wasn't me. I didn't do it.**

Natloz reaches over and holds his palm open. He asks if he could read the text. Annie agrees and gives Natloz the phone. He reads the message.

They have their first suspect.

CHAPTER 2

Annie would always tell people that the best days of her life were when she was a youngling growing up in Ybor City. Young and innocent and full of life. Annie's family and childhood were all she ever spoke about. She would talk to complete strangers about all the family secrets, ones that were never supposed to be spoken about. But Annie loved and trusted everyone. Her mother once told her that trusting people the way she did would get her into trouble someday, and so the story goes.

Ybor City in Tampa Florida is a quiet neighbourhood where the new generation moved in to replace the generation of yesteryear. Her family had moved in with one sole purpose, and that was to raise a family in a safe and quiet environment. They say that the grass is always greener in Ybor City. Residents of this town swear by it.

Ybor is a little suburb that lies north of McKay Bay. Funny enough, it has a boulevard called Melburne. It's lively and known for its boutiques and vintage shops. There is also a very strong Cuban and Latin American influence. Most Americans can speak some Spanish. Yborians recommend you close your eyes when walking down Avenida República De Cuba and absorb all the aromas the cafés have to offer. It will drive you loco, making you feel you're in Central America. Annie would always mention to her friends who lived out of town how much she would love to capture the smell in a bottle for safekeeping, and share some with them. Life was great for Annie in Ybor.

When she was young, Annie's mother, Mavis, would always say that if the family hadn't moved to Ybor City, then Australia would definitely have been their home. Mavis loved everything about Australia. Her best friend, Mimi, had a relative in Sydney and they constantly chatted about it. From time to time, she would refer to it as 'Down Under'. She wanted to feel every bit Australian with every opportunity she got. She even tried using the Aussie accent down at the local supermarket.

Everybody loved Mavis and her stories. Some true, most made up. She was a walking encyclopedia of information. She had a plethora of knowledge and an abundance of character. She was a friend to so many and a mother to most.

Mavis was mostly impressed with koalas and kangaroos – two animals she was hoping to see in real life one day. Until then, she stuck to watching them on the Discovery Channel or reading about them in magazines. She loved the idea of having kangaroos live extremely close to humans in Australia. As a joke, Mavis once told Annie that she would send her money to buy a joey and bring it back to Ybor. That story never got old. It's not only the indigenous community who have the privilege of having these marsupials as neighbours. Kangaroos roam the streets of the outer suburbs of Melbourne. Mavis was so excited when Annie told her she was moving there to study.

Mavis and Annie's dad, Ron, made the move from Charlotte to Ybor when Annie's eldest brother was three. She has two brothers and two sisters, making her the fifth and youngest of her sibling clan. Malcolm is the eldest, now thirty-seven years old. He's a civil engineer and has worked the same job since leaving school. He works for a large company called McIntosh Lauber and Sons. He has worked his way up the ranks and is an asset to the company.

Malcolm has always been the fun-loving big brother. Annie could never remember a time not seeing him smile – besides that stormy night during the winter of 2002 when Malcolm's hamster, Roger, had escaped from his cage, never to be seen again. No one knew what had happened to that furry little critter. Malcolm had made posters with a little help from his siblings and went out on his bike and stuck them to poles, shop windows, and on people's cars.

Malcolm was great at sports, especially football. He tried out for the State Championships and nailed himself a contract with UCLA. He had a promising career until he injured his knee, which sidelined him with a reconstruction. Malcolm wasn't the same after that. He never played football again. His dreams of becoming an NFL player were cut short. A big part of him never got over it.

Annie has many fond memories of her childhood but the one she speaks of most is from her Junior High Prom. Bobby Dunn had asked Annie to the prom. He was a track and field super athlete, and the best in the state. He was so fast; he held the 100-metre sprint record for the entire time Annie was at school. He was also the high school heartthrob. Annie knew that any date with Bobby would surely have all the other girls talking. Eyes staring at her, piercing the back of her head. Girls would line up just to watch him enter the classroom. Annie couldn't believe he had asked her. She felt like she was the Prom Queen, and Bobby Dunn her King.

But Bobby's reason for asking Annie to the prom was not the reason Annie hoped to hear. She thought he chose her because he was attracted to her. Boy, was she wrong.

His bright plan was to escort the least popular girl at school to make himself look and feel great. Like he was doing her a favour. He became an instant hero; all the girls were talking about how sweet Bobby Dunn was to take a loser like Annie to the prom.

Bobby had made himself the most wanted boy at school. All the boys wanted to be like him and all the girls wanted to be with him. The other students thought Bobby could do no wrong. Through his eyes, he was the greatest.

The one thing Bobby lacked, though, was brains. He hadn't realised but a lot of kids despised him, the ones with a bit more sense. They saw through his fake machismo and would talk about him behind his back. They called him names and said things about him – words that would be too much for his small vocabulary. Let's just say he wasn't the brightest of students.

Bobby entered the prom like the Emperor of Rome, ruler of the Romans, king of the Colosseum. Luckily for Bobby, he had no lions to contend with. He and the rest of his posse had snuck in some booze that got passed around amongst his inner circle. On this particular evening, Bobby had consumed way too much alcohol and began making a fool of himself.

He entered the girl's toilets looking for Annie when he spots her in there with two of her friends. Bobby pushed his way through and grabbed Annie by the hair. Annie freaked out and started to yell, telling Bobby to stop because he was hurting her. Bobby refused to listen and began to rough her up even more. He thought he was way too much of a man to stop and would not listen to Annie's pleas.

Annie's friend, Veronica, ran out of the girl's toilets and called Malcolm over from where he was playing in the school band. Malcolm dropped his guitar and made his way to the toilets. He entered and saw Bobby abusing his baby sister. Malcolm saw red and turned into a raging bull. He grabbed Bobby by the neck, dragged him out of the toilets and onto the stage. He then proceeded to tell everyone over the speaker what Bobby had done. What Malcolm really wanted to do was drop Bobby's trousers and show everyone he's not the man he claims to be – see if his pecker was happy to make an appearance or would it be too shy and remain hidden from stage fright. One can only guess.

All the alcohol he had consumed couldn't prevent the embarrassment and guilt. Bobby put his tail between his legs and left.

'Ladies and gentlemen, Bobby has left the building,' Malcolm said, and with that the whole school gymnasium bust out laughing. Bobby's popularity deflated and within three months he had left school, never to be seen or heard from again.

Malcolm stood up for Annie that night, but also paved the way for other boys never to mistreat girls. He had made a statement that would last a long time. The day Bobby Dunn mistreated Annie was the day she saw her brother Malcolm as the true King of the Prom.

Darryl is the second eldest and a little less fortunate than the rest. Darryl didn't have the capacity or patience to learn. He suffered a head injury when he was young which caused him to have regular seizures. Darryl had struggled his entire life and didn't have many friends. He was bullied at school which caused him difficulties later on in life. Malcolm had left school by this stage and was unable to be around for his struggling brother. Because of it, he couldn't hold down a steady job and relationships lasted less time than a tennis match. It was due to his anger and frustration that everything around him crumbled.

Annie's relationship with Darryl had been a difficult one when they were kids. Annie found her brother a little challenging at times. He would often pick on her because she was the youngest and the easiest of targets. Annie's ability to condone the abuse has made her wiser but still the frail scared woman she is today. Malcolm had stepped in a few times but an argument was inevitable, and fists were often used to settle the dispute. Annie had decided to keep out of Darryl's way and spent more time with Malcolm.

Darryl currently lives in a small town just outside of Georgia with his second wife and one-year old son, Jackson. Darryl is a Correctional Officer with the county jail and is managing his seizures with medication and the love for his son and the support from his wife.

Melanie and Kimberly are twin sisters born four hours apart. Annie's relationship with her sisters was peachy. They grew up being more like triplets, inseparable and always getting into mischief with neither of them blaming one another. The three girls together were impossible to beat or to compete against. They were known as the Three Musketeers (of course, they named themselves that), one for all and all for one.

They had such a wonderful and happy upbringing. As a family, they would often go on vacation to Fort Lauderdale. The beach was the Carter's favourite family holiday spot. Sitting under the scorching sun, soaking up those rays and tanning to the point of darkness. The local boys would spy on the girls in their skimpy bikinis. The Three Musketeers returned the devilish act, perving on the finely chiselled hunks. Those were the days. All that remain are the naughty memories.

Melanie never married and passed away suddenly three years back. She had a brain haemorrhage while sitting on a park bench reading. They didn't find her until two hours later. It was the hardest time of Annie's life. She not only lost her sister, but a best friend. One of the Musketeers.

Kimberley is doing well and working as a nurse in the Mercy General on the Cardiac Ward. She doesn't have time for a husband or kids, choosing to be married to her job. Kimberley knew that if she ever needed her sister, Annie would drop everything to be there for her. Annie's family is her life and finds it a little hard being so far away from them.

Living in Australia is what makes it hard. She would love to be closer to her family. Annie lives well over 15,000 kilometres away and will take almost a day to get home. That has always worried Annie, but now she has her own problem that she needs to deal with. She's in a foreign country alone, and she's doing it tough. This has knocked all the wind out of her.

She never expected to come home tonight to find Sally dead ...

CHAPTER 3

Annie's apartment is a small place, with only two bedrooms. A wall separating the eerie, dungeon-like rooms. The lighting in the place is minimal, which makes it dark and hard for anyone to concentrate. There's a painting on the back of the front door that is meant to resemble a goat, but it looks nothing like one. There is a musky, stale stench in the apartment; air doesn't seem to travel through these four walls. There is one window that is locked and secured with a piece of wood. Recent burglaries in the building have prevented them from keeping the window open.

The flooring is solid wood with a number of rugs scattered across it. The rugs are old, with large holes. They look like they've been bought from an op shop. There is a dark stain on one of them that sits neatly at the entrance door. Natloz looks over his shoulder towards Petridis and glances down at the stain.

'Take a photo of that, and get Forensics to check it out.'

Petridis takes out his phone and snaps a picture. Natloz moves to the middle of the room and does a slow spin on his toes, trying to get a better view of the room in a quick motion, to picture how things operate in this apartment. He is trying to work out whether Oscar had anything to do with Sally's death; maybe Oscar had an accomplice? Someone to help him trick the police, someone who had pretended to witness the attack outside when what really happened was Oscar had killed Sally in the apartment. Hard to believe, but doable. Natloz has seen enough to speculate any crazy thought that pops into his head.

Natloz is not ruling out anything yet; all of or any of these allegations could be true. So much can be told from a picture, especially if the picture talks to you. He has his eyes and ears peeled. That picture could talk to him at any moment. The apartment could potentially be a crime scene. Only time will tell.

There is an old two-seater couch and a recliner in the small living room, with an abundance of cushions covering the couch. None of the cushions matched in colour or size. There were about twelve in total. The look on his face clearly shows that Natloz is not a big fan of pillows.

'Do you think they have enough cushions?' says Petridis with a smirk.

'Be serious, Pet,' Natloz replies with an even bigger smirk.

Might be odd to some, but not strange at all. There are a lot of people who have a crazy pillow fetish. Just not these two detectives.

The television and VCR seem older than the couch. Teenagers would take one look at this setup and imagine it to belong in a museum, or something so unnatural that it has come from out of space.

Petridis makes his way to the kitchen. He reaches over for the light switch and flicks it on, only to find it's not switching on. His first reaction is to think the globe has blown. He looks over to Annie, who is staring into space. Petridis calls out to her softly so as not to startle her. She looks up at him, responding in an even quieter voice. 'Yeah?'

'The globe?'

'Oh, it's been like that for a while now. We just haven't gotten around to changing the globe yet. We got used to it after a while.

We don't spend that much time in there. There is a little lamp in the corner by the microwave. We switch that on if we need light.'

Petridis is dumbfounded how three grown adults couldn't find the time to change a light globe. It's times like these he wishes he was able to spark up a cigarette. Release some tension before it turns into stress.

While Petridis searches the kitchen, Natloz looks around in the bedroom. It doesn't take long to work out it's the girls' room. Having only two bedrooms in the apartment, Sally and Annie had to share. Two double beds had been crammed into the room, with only enough space for an antique dresser, which they shared. Four large drawers below two small ones on either side, divided by a very dirty mirror. Stains on the glass minimise the reflection of anyone who is looking at it. You would think it had never been cleaned. He doesn't feel that bad about his place after seeing the state of this one.

Annie has tacked photos on the wall above her bed. There are a few photos of what seem to be her family, but most of them are of Oscar and Sally. There is one photo that stands out. It shows Annie and Sally hugging in front of an old tree with Oscar standing behind them. He's looking down at Sally, so much taller than her that it's like David and Goliath. The thing that caught Natloz's attention is the way Oscar is looking at Sally. The expression on his face, the look in his eyes … it makes Natloz feel there was some kind of hatred or unease between the two. Annie had mentioned them growing up together in Perth, but that doesn't necessarily mean anything. Hate makes people do unspeakable things.

He has seen that look before on the faces of criminals he has dealt with. He knows it quite well. The innocent become helpless victims and their attackers become unstable psychotic killers.

Oscar's eyes are directed towards Sally in a trance-like death stare. A look so calm that it would scare even the fearless. A planned victory before the victory is even accomplished.

Natloz takes the photo and slides it into his jacket pocket. It could come in handy at some point. He's hoping Annie doesn't notice it missing. With what's happened here tonight, her mind is preoccupied with other things. He feels safe to take it.

Annie is still in the kitchen with Petridis. He is searching through the cupboards and pantry, trying to find anything that might help them with the investigation. Annie assists where she can.

It seemed like they didn't do much cooking in their kitchen; the pantry and fridge were almost empty of ingredients. A handful of canned items and a loaf of mouldy bread amongst the barest essentials. The fridge had a tub of yogurt, less than half a carton of milk, cheese slices, and other fridge condiments and necessities. Beer and white wine housed on the bottom shelf. The freezer had a number of frozen foods, meat pies being the clear winner. No MasterChef in this apartment.

Natloz enters the kitchen holding the photo. Guilt got the better of him. Natloz feels he can get more from Annie being honest. 'I'm taking this photo,' he says. 'Where was it taken and when?'

'About a month ago. It was taken up in Kallista.'

'Do you have any more from the same day?'

Annie nods and heads towards her bedroom. She wants to be alone for a minute. Talking about the photos has brought on fresh tears. She doesn't want to be followed. A quick glance over her shoulder shows that nobody has.

Natloz pretends not to watch her, but he can see her from the corner of his eye. He senses she has something to hide. Something she doesn't want the detectives to see.

From the angle she is standing, Annie can see the Forensic team at the entrance to the apartment. There's a team member in the hallway and two in the lounge room. Petridis is in the kitchen and Natloz standing in the archway to the kitchen. Now is her chance.

She had noticed a pair of grey gloves on her dresser that belonged to Oscar. The detectives might not have noticed them. She can see red marks on them that look like dried blood. What If it is blood? Oscar would have some explaining to do. Annie needs to make them disappear without being seen. She needs to speak with him first, try to save him from a conviction. She also knows that she is tampering with evidence that could land her in trouble, too. All she knows is that Oscar is innocent. The detectives think otherwise.

Peter Kirby who works alongside Dr Langer with Forensics, enters with great anticipation. 'Detectives, I might have something.'

Peter was dusting for fingerprints at the entrance when he discovered blood under the doormat. It was a partial footprint. What was interesting was that there were no other bloody prints anywhere else, no trail leading to or from the apartment, no prints anywhere else besides under the mat.

'Where the hell does it lead to?' Natloz wonders.

'Nowhere,' Kirby says. 'There is no trail.'

Both detectives are puzzled by the new finding. It's like someone has stepped on some blood and imprinted it onto the carpet. None of this makes any sense because the print is under the carpet.

Natloz looks for Annie, but she is still in her room. That is a long time to be looking for more photos … and alone. Now was his chance to surprise her and walk into something that might give her away. But before he gets to the room, Annie walks out holding the gloves.

'I found these in there. They belong to Oscar. If we're going to be honest with one another, then we should start now. I found a few more photos from the same day, too.'

Annie knew that if the detective had found the gloves, they would have surely found Oscar's DNA on them. Annie contaminated the gloves by touching them and having her prints on them too, knowing too well that they cannot use them as evidence anymore. She's read enough books to know these little cunning tricks.

The disappointment from failing to notice the gloves earlier is written all over his face. Annie had killed any kind of evidence that could possibly have been found on the gloves in one fell swoop. A job well done.

He looks up, like he's about to say something to God. A look of despair. 'Idiot,' he says. Talking to himself, not God.

Natloz is about to ask Annie for the gloves when he hears a voice coming from behind him. It was a man's voice. So soft and angelic, and somewhat hurt. A voice in distress.

'Who is the detective in charge?'

Natloz and Petridis look at him like he had just appeared from behind a magician's cape, or better yet, sent from up above. Could God have listened?

'That would be us,' responds Natloz.

'I'm the guy you might be looking for,' says the young man, who was escorted to the apartment by another officer. 'I'm Oscar Lopez.'

There is a God after all.

CHAPTER 4

Oscar and Sally had been born kilometres apart. 2,239, to be precise. Sally was born in Broome, which is far north of Perth in Western Australia. If you were going to drive from Broome to Perth it would take you 23 hours and 40 minutes, and that's without stopping. It would normally be a two-day trip with plenty of breaks in between to rest. The roads can get repetitive and boring, a venomous candidate for drowsiness that will cause you to fall asleep at the wheel. There are signs up and down the road telling you that. People tend to listen to them.

Sally was raised mostly by her grandparents. Her dad left before she was born and had nothing to do with her upbringing. He never showed any interest until she was ten. He showed up a handful of times during Christmas and on her birthday (which he always got wrong). The fact that he couldn't remember her birthday made it that much more difficult for Sally to have a normal relationship with her father. He was never there when she needed him most.

When she turned twelve he disappeared and no one knew where he had gone. Sally had asked a few friends of the family and relatives on numerous occasions about his whereabouts, but none of them seemed to know. It's like he'd vanished off the face of this planet. Sally never wanted any harm to come to him, but could not love him like a child should love their father. There were days she would get angry and sit in her room with the door closed and cry. She would see her friends with their dads doing all the things dads do with their daughters, but her dad couldn't even be around, and that totally sucked for her. He brought this on himself and Sally was the one that is suffering for it.

As a child, Sally would always get into trouble doing the opposite from what she was told to do. She reminded her mother of herself when she was little. The constant yelling of her name and daily phone calls from her school teacher made her mum realise that the apple hadn't fallen far from the tree. Two peas in a pod.

Sally got pregnant at the age of seventeen to a boy she didn't like. A boy who lied to her to get what he wanted. She realised she was too young to be a mother, so she travelled to Perth to terminate the pregnancy and start a new life. She went without telling her mother the truth about why she was leaving Broome. She just said she was off to find her dad. She might have gotten a better reaction if she told her the truth.

Without fear or regret, Sally set off on a Greyhound bus, dreading the more than 2,000-kilometre journey for a secret she wanted to bury for good. She had no intention of returning to Broome anytime soon. She'd miss her mum the most, but if she had stayed in Broome she would have died an unhappy young mother.

Perth was everything she expected it to be and more. Vibrant, colourful, and liveable. Sandy blue beaches and promenades of shops and beautiful people, Perth was a dream she didn't want to wake up from. Sally had an aunt who lived in Fremantle, a house Sally was welcomed to anytime she chose.

Merri is her dad's sister. Sally had kept in contact with her up until twelve months ago when Sally's mother told her to break the connection. 'Merri is a bad influence', she would say, and that she would ruin any hope of Sally succeeding as an adult. Merri was so much like Sally's dad. She was constantly reminded of the kind of family her mum had married into and the trouble she had to deal with. Stories that would prick the hair up on your arms every time. So, Sally listened to her mother and cut all ties with her aunt.

The cause behind all this was Sally's mother, Raechelle. She was afraid that if Sally had learnt the truth about her father, she would lose her daughter. The truth is, Sally's mother didn't want her husband around. She suffered from anxiety, depression, and severe panic attacks, making her vulnerable and susceptible to a mental breakdown. She constantly fought with herself in her head, and feared that she would eventually meet that dreaded fear of being alone; thinking that one day she was going to end up old and lonely. She often wondered if anyone would stick around to care for her. So, she began spreading rumours about Brian that caused a whole heap of trouble for him: how he had affairs with work colleagues, was involved with a Christian cult that worshipped demonic saints, and had a drinking problem which led to also being addicted to recreational drugs.

Brian was loved by everyone, which made it hard for them to believe these stories and accusations. After a while, Brian did take up drinking and spent lots of time away from his family due to the embarrassment his wife had caused. People were beginning to believe Sally's mother and her theories. Brian ended up leaving to save himself, and most importantly, his daughter.

Some would say an abortion is not the right solution, that a foetus is a living human so an abortion is murder. But it's a decision never taken lightly. Abortion groups have so much to say about these procedures – they make sure they send their message through loud and clear. Sally believed the decision that she made was the right one for her. Either way, she was doing it alone.

Or was she? She decided to make a call.

Sally and Merri met that afternoon at a posh café down from where Merri lived. It was a quiet little pocket of shops that made the meeting that much more secluded. They spoke for hours about the baby and the abortion. Merri wanted to make sure Sally knew what she was doing, and that she had decided to abort this baby herself. They also spoke at length about the hard time Sally's dad had, thanks to her mum, and why he had to leave. As a father, he needed to make decisions based on the current situation he was in, no matter the consequence. Brian made a crucial decision to leave his family, hoping one day he and Sally would reunite and try to mend the fragile relationship between them.

Sally felt that she had made the right decision to go out searching for her dad. So many questions were forming in her head, the ifs and the whys.

Merri leant over a little closer, and gave Sally some news she was pleased to hear. 'Sally, your father is living here in Fremantle and has been asking about you for a decade now. He has never stopped asking about you.'

Sally went numb with excitement. She was frozen to her seat. Her mouth opened like she was about to say something, but couldn't. Everything around her went silent and fragments from the surroundings moved in staggered stages. All she could hear was the sound of waves and her father calling her name. That was all she ever dreamt about growing up as an early teen; for her dad to one day take her to the beach. Waves splashing against the shore, building sand castles even though she'd be too old to do that, and walking a dog along the beach, chatting for hours. Make up for all the lost time they didn't share together when she was young.

So many more questions began to form in her head. She was feeling so overwhelmed with excitement that she forgot to breathe.

'Sally, are you okay?' Merri looked concerned. 'Sally, dear?'

A tap on Sally's shoulder made her flinch. A large male figure stood over her. She stared at him with confusion. She desperately wanted to recognise the face. She knows this man but her eyes are deceiving her. She feels overwhelmed by his looks. Something she can't pin down.

'Hello, Sally,' he said. 'I'm your dad.'

Dreams that had been shattered once were mended in the blink of an eye. The beach was right there; her dreams a stone's throw from being fulfilled.

CHAPTER 5

Oscar is sitting in a tiny interview room back at the police station. The room is lit up like the MCG. It has limited furniture. A metal table that is bolted to the ground with two seats on either side attached to it. The clock on the wall is ticking loudly as everything else in the room remains quiet. Oscar knows it's early Saturday morning. He is normally at work now. Time is all he has left to think about.

There is nothing in that room that could to be used as a weapon. Not that Oscar would try anything anyway. He handed himself in to explain he had nothing to do with Sally's death. He needs to clear his name before things get out of hand.

There is a metal bar on one side of the table, used for cuffing suspects. The room is dull and dingy, colourless and had a really bad smell of fear. The thought of who might have had the unlucky privilege to occupy this room in recent years is troubling Oscar. He can't believe he is sharing a seat that could have had the backside of a notorious murderer or even rapist occupy. Kidnappers thrown into that mix, too. That thought makes Oscar feel degraded and belittled. A thought crosses his mind: he's there because they think he killed Sally. That makes him no better than the others who have sat in this room.

He didn't kill Sally, he is certain of that. He remembers everything about last night. What he got up to and where he was.

He is ready to talk to the detectives. He waits patiently, but the detectives are taking their time; a strategy he assumes they have used on numerous occasions. Oscar can sense them watching him through the two-way mirror. Who else is out there?

That happens often in movies Oscar has watched in the past; suspects being watched through that mirror, discussing tactics on how to deal with the scum on the other side. It feels like he's the lead character in a movie. He looks around the room. Nowhere to go, no windows to escape from, and no one will believe him. Doomed from the moment he presented himself to the detectives. He feels like he might have just sentenced himself.

†

The detectives are watching Oscar, watching his every move, hoping he'll slip up and give them something to work with. Mumble something to himself loud enough for the detectives to hear. Something that might incriminate him and tie him to this murder. Most of the time they get the result they try to fish out of the perp.

Natloz can see that Oscar is tiring, wearing himself out thinking about the events of the previous night. He is hoping Oscar will crumble under pressure and tell them he did it. The hamster is working overtime in his head.

Sometimes you need to be cruel to be kind. He has left Oscar in that room all alone for over an hour with no water and the temperature turned up to 28 degrees. It's a sick tactic that has worked every time.

Petridis gets a call on his mobile.

'Who is it?' asks Natloz.

'I don't know. Private number.'

'Probably telemarketers. Get rid of them and come back. Time to go to work on this kid.'

Petridis takes the call but moves away from his partner for

some privacy, giving Natloz a hand signal that he will be back in a minute. Natloz follows Petridis with his eyes, trying to work out who is on the other end of the call. Petridis has an intense look on his face, like he's receiving important news.

Natloz enters the interview room alone, leaving Petridis to deal with his call. The smirk on his face makes Oscar frown. Oscar thinks the detective must know something. Has a murder weapon been found in the apartment? If so, someone has planted it there – but who? It might not be that at all.

He must have something on me, thinks Oscar. *But what?* It's amazing how thoughts like these can make your mind go a little crazy.

'Hello, Oscar. Sorry to keep you waiting. There were a few things we needed to sort out. Do you know why you're here?'

'Yes, I know why I'm here,' says a scared Oscar. 'You want to know if I had anything to do with Sally's death.'

'That's right. That is why you came back to the apartment. Guilt made you turn yourself in. You killed Sally, didn't you? You mutilated her body to make out that she was attacked by an animal, didn't you?'

'What? No, I didn't do it. I didn't do anything.'

'Yes, you did. You killed your friend. Did you get into an argument with her, hit her over the head to only later realise you went too far? You then dragged her body out to the park to make it look like some beast had killed her when all along, the beast was you, Isn't that right, Oscar?'

'No … no it wasn't me. I swear it wasn't me. I saw who did it, I mean, I saw *what* did that to Sally, but it wasn't me.' Oscar's voice changes, from scared to angry. 'You fucken arseholes. You're holding the wrong guy. It wasn't me, I tell you. The real fucking monster is out there.' He points with his right index finger towards the door. His voice mellows down to almost a whisper. 'I'm not the one you want. It wasn't me.'

Oscar loses his cool and begins yelling and screaming. He's angry and frustrated. His anxiety has caused his temperament to fluctuate. He tries to get up off his chair, placing both hands flat on the table. Natloz moves his body back slightly while still seated. He swings his legs around and stands up, backing a few feet away from the table. His immediate reaction is to grab the can of mace from his belt, his hand moves directly to it, eyes still fixed on Oscar. Natloz knows he is no immediate danger but habit has him doing it anyway. To be on the safe side, Natloz decides to cuff one of Oscar's hands to the table, making sure he has nowhere to go.

'Sit the fuck down, Oscar.'

'I'm telling you, it wasn't me,' Oscar repeats.

Natloz tells him once again to sit down. Oscar doesn't listen. The rage that is running through him seems to have taken over his mind. Visions of his friend's murder come flashing in and out, preventing Oscar from hearing anything the detective is saying. It's all proving to be too problematic. His body and mind have gone into lockdown and he finds himself staring into the abyss, his screams echoing off the four walls.

Petridis hears the commotion from outside and quickly makes his way into the interrogation room, ready to tackle the unknown. He sees Natloz standing opposite Oscar with his hand on the mace. The thought of his partner hurting this kid makes him react quickly, preventing any kind of unfortunate mishaps.

Oscar comes to his senses and notices what Natloz is about to do. He quickly raises his right hand while lowering his head and plants his arse firmly on the seat. His hand remains raised above his head.

Petridis moves in at the same time and stands directly in front of Natloz, stopping this already frightening scene from getting worse. Petridis then takes out his cuffs, placing them around Oscar's other wrist and securing it to the metal pole on the table.

Both hands are now cuffed and secured. Oscar begins to sob like a child, gradually getting louder. Echoes of the crying bouncing off the walls. Saliva drooling down his chin, reminiscent of a Saint Bernard or Rottweiler.

Oscar whispers something to himself. The detectives lean in a little closer to make out what he's saying.

'It wasn't me,' he's saying. 'I didn't kill Sally. It was that …'

'What did you say?' Natloz asks.

Oscar is not responding. He has gone into a vacant state. His eyes are glazed from the tears. From a frenzy of anger to a little kid put into the naughty corner. Eyes still wide open, but nothing ticking in his head.

Natloz moves around the table, leans over, and whispers into Oscar's ear. 'Oscar, what did you see in the park? Tell me so I can catch who did this. Let me help you.'

There's nothing more than a soft breath. Oscar is done for the evening. Exhaustion has kicked in and the lights have gone out. They'll try again a little later on. For now, Oscar needs some rest and a doctor to look over him. Petridis is already on the phone to the doctors asking them to come and check on Oscar. That is the only way the detectives will get anything more from him. A night in a cold cell might get him talking if it doesn't kill him first.

The detectives are interrupted by a knock on the door. The door swings open and Detective Short enters with a piece of paper. 'Sorry to barge in this way, but we've just had a call from dispatch.'

Natloz takes the paper from Short. He reads it and the look on his face changes. Another body has shown up.

CHAPTER 6

The crime scene is flowered with police and showered with reporters who keep their distance behind the red crime scene tape. The media know never to cross that line.

Detectives Petridis and Natloz arrive at the scene not knowing what to expect. The information that was given to them was scarce, with a lack of description of the body and the cause of death.

'Doesn't look like we're going to rest anytime soon. These bodies better not keep popping up or we'll probably need a vacation just to catch up on sleep,' says Petridis.

Saturday was meant to be their day off. Not today, though.

'I'm not sure what's going on, mate,' Natloz says, 'but if this is connected to the body yesterday, then we have a long day ahead of us.'

There's an eerie feeling in the air. An overwhelming butterfly sensation that is creating a bad feeling in Natloz's stomach. There is evil in the air, he can sense it. Something is not right.

'I don't feel the best, mate,' he says to Petridis.

'What are you feeling?'

'Not sure. Just not well.'

'You look okay, mate. If that is any consolation.'

Sweat begins to form in little puddles around his temple, and his skin starts turning blue in odd-shaped blotches. Natloz feels faint and queasy, like he is about to throw up. He hears a voice. The sound is so faint, it's coming from afar. He's hot and dizzy, his vision blurred, sweat pouring profusely now from his skin. Natloz collapses to the ground.

Concerned for his partner, Petridis calls out to the paramedics. They are already on their way, having noticed what has happened.

'Stay with me, mate, don't fucking give up on me now,' says Petridis, holding Natloz's hand while the paramedics try to revive him. His partner has gone blue in the face. He has stopped breathing. Petridis is asked to drop his hand and move away as the paramedics proceed with CPR. Pumping his chest with both hands vigorously. One, two, three, four, five, up to fifteen times before they breathe air into his lungs. This goes on for about three minutes. Natloz is not responding to the frantic work the paramedics are administering. They begin to fear the worst. He needs a miracle. If there is one person Natloz needs right now it's that God who he spoke to not long ago. Now is the time he needs him the most.

The call must have come down the line. Natloz's eyes open suddenly, staring up at the moon shining bright, a perfect circle up in the crystal blue sky. It's a full moon.

'What happened?' he says. He seems dazed and confused, and fighting for breath. An odour had been released from his body that reminds him of death. 'What the fuck just happened?'

Petridis looks at him, opens his mouth to say something, but doesn't seem to have any words to continue with. For a few seconds Petridis is lost for words, unable to answer his partner. He gains composure and lets Natloz know what happened.

'You passed out, mate. You were there with me one minute, then on the ground the next.'

Natloz remembers hearing a conversation that was going on, and a lady's voice in distress from a distance.

'Did you hear that lady calling for help?' he asks Petridis.

'What lady?'

'A lady is in trouble.'

'I didn't hear a thing, mate. Are you sure you're okay?'

The paramedics cut in and ask him how he's feeling.

'I haven't felt this good in ages.'

The paramedics are puzzled with the unexplainable speedy recovery and bizarre response. It's like nothing ever happened to him. A mystery that needs solving.

'We've seen some weird shit resuscitating people but this takes the cake,' says the older of the two paramedics named Ted. He looks like he has seen a ghost. Forty years in the service and for the first time retirement has crossed his mind. 'I really think you should come with us to be examined a little further and monitored overnight. Let the doctors conduct some tests. Make sure everything is okay with you. You really don't look the best there, buddy.'

'I am not going anywhere with you guys. I feel fine and I have a lot of work to do here. If you morons haven't noticed, we have a fucking crime that has been committed and you want me to go to the hospital and get tested? Are you for real? Get the fuck off me and get the fuck out of my way.'

The paramedics pick themselves up and get ready to leave before turning to Natloz, one of them about to confront the ghost himself. Ted has something he needs the detective to hear. 'You're out of your mind, detective. Do as you please, but I will be reporting this.' They grab their gear and head back to the ambulance. They don't plan to sit around and be verbally abused by someone they just saved.

Petridis cannot believe what he has just witnessed. He has seen his partner get angry but this anger is on another level. Rage begins to run through his veins like a volcano about to explode.

There was a look in his eyes, like the eyes of a man possessed, red like Satan's fire. This is a side of Natloz no one has ever seen, not even his partner.

The detective gets his slow-moving body up off the ground and starts walking towards the helpless body they had been called to inspect. The victim was found on the grounds of the Carlton Cemetery.

Natloz looks around only to realise his partner is not following. 'Oi, are you coming?'

Petridis pulls out a cigarette from his jacket and lights it. He takes a massive drag, holding it in for a few seconds before releasing the dirty smoke into the air. He then proceeds to follow Natloz, as requested. The nicotine smoothly runs through his system, calming the stressed detective. Once he gets a break in this case, he'll speak to Natloz about his actions and what happened. Petridis is concerned about his partner, concerned for his friend.

They approach the body with care only to find something they were both dreading; the same cause of death. The body has been mutilated, a mirror image of the body found last night, only this dead body is that of an elderly gentleman. Until they hear otherwise, this murder is related to Sally Jenkins's murder.

'It looks as though he has gone out for an early morning walk or exercise. The clothing he is wearing screams it.'

Petridis nods at his partner, thinking the same thing. T-shirt, green in colour with a splash of bright red blood. Black running shorts with pockets, and sneakers. One shoe is missing but the other is still on the deceased. The task of finding the other missing sneaker begins. That shoe could hold clues that could help the detectives with the case.

Natloz lifts his nose up towards the sky, then begins sniffing the air like a K-9. A smell has attracted his senses to a scrubbed area in the park.

Petridis looks at him with cautious eyes. Wondering what he will do next. The unthinkable happens. Natloz bends down, lowering his head to the body and starts sniffing the dead man's legs. It's like looking at a cadaver dog in action. Smelling death and pointing to the direction it's coming from. Natloz brings himself back upright and focuses on the body in front of him before turning away and looking into the shrubs beyond the body.

Petridis calls over one of the officers who is closest to him. 'Who's in charge here?'

'That would be Sergeant Copeland, sir.'

'Go get Copeland for me.'

'Yes, sir.'

Copeland arrives to find the detectives hovering over the body, trying to work out what has happened here. Copeland begins first.

'I've attended dog attacks in the past but nothing like this. I've seen wounds caused by dogs, chunks of flesh ripped off the body but this, this is no dog. This is not the work of a human, either. Whatever happened here, detectives, the victim would have died a painful death.'

'I didn't ask for your opinion, sergeant,' Natloz says in an angry tone. 'If I require one from you, I'll ask. Who called it in? Who found the body?' If Natloz wasn't higher ranked then he would have heard an earful from Copeland.

'It was a uni student heading out for an early morning jog.' He looks at his note book for the name. 'Xiyu Zhang. She also goes by the name of Jenny. She found the body at 5:15 this morning. She called 000 immediately.'

'Were you the first one here?'

'No. One of the patrolling officers was here first. Boulder. Max Boulder, and his partner, Dempsey.'

'Can you call them over? We need to have a quick chat.'

'Sure.'

They both come over, ready to hand over what they know. Boulder is young, fresh out of the academy. Clean cut mama's boy who looks eager to please. Dempsey is a little older and wiser. He's been around for a bit and knows how this works. Carrying a few extra kilos around the bread basket. Possibly another who loves his mother's homemade meals.

'Sir, I'm Boulder. We arrived here first.'

'When you arrived, was there anyone else hanging around?'

'Yes, there was. Jenny's boyfriend was with her for moral support, you know, to comfort her. There were also two guys who walked by with their dog, they stopped to see what was happening. Lend a hand if required, so to speak.'

'Where are they now?'

'Not sure. We told them to stand over by the rubbish bin, to keep out of our way.' He points past Natloz and Petridis.

'Did you get their names?'

'Umm, no. We didn't think it was necessary. We didn't think they had anything to do with it seeing what the body looked like.'

'No? Are you fucking serious? Did they not teach you anything in the academy? The first thing you do is take down names. You know what a name is, don't you? Like the one your parents gave you at birth. Always take down names, details, times, et cetera, et cetera, et cetera. Fucking moron.'

Petridis steps in between and cuts over the insult. 'Okay, partner, ease off a bit. A little over the top, don't you think?' He does agree with one thing his partner said; they should have taken down names that they could then follow up on. But he doesn't agree with the way Natloz has spoken to the young constable – he is way out of line and bordering on abusive language. A reportable offence in anyone's book. In the past, he has seen Natloz address staff in a respectable manner. He is so good at it; a natural. He defuses heated arguments in a few words and takes order of a room with respect. But today is another story. Clearly, he's not having a good day.

Petridis needs to put out the flames before they get any bigger. 'Let's go and speak to the lady who found the body. See what she knows. Come on.'

Petridis escorts Natloz away from the heated verbal discussion. Boulder and Dempsey are left there to lick their wounds, feeling like Natloz has taken a huge chunk out of them, like the body that has been discovered in the park.

The morning sun begins to break through the already overcast sky. It looks as though it might start to rain. Melbourne is renowned for having all four seasons in one day; radical weather that can change in an instant. Unpredictable is a better word for it, no matter what the meteorologist tells you. It's so unpredictable that Melburnians tend to carry an extensive number of extra items in the boot of their car. Umbrellas, thongs, a T-shirt, long sleeve jumper, jacket, closed shoes – prepared for any kind of weather that might hit them at that time.

The detectives approach the witness and her boyfriend, hoping to get a bit more out of them.

'Ms Zhang?' Petridis is taking control of this one. His questions are a little more mellow and inviting.

'You can call me Jenny.'

'Sure, Jenny. Can you tell me what you know?'

Jenny takes a moment to recollect her thoughts before answering. She wants to get it right and not look like she is making things up. She wants to make sure she tells the detectives everything. 'I came out for a morning jog. I do this every morning except Sundays. Sundays is the day I rest and spend time with my boyfriend.'

'Do you remember what time that might have been?'

'It was 5:30. Same time every morning.'

'Are you sure about the time?'

'Yes, I'm sure. I stopped for a drink at the water fountain. The one near the roundabout. I checked my watch to see how long I had before I had to start getting home for uni. It was ten minutes after I left home.'

'Do you always go to uni on a Saturday?'

'Yes. It's quiet. Not that many other students there. I can get work done.'

Natloz was eager to open his mouth and enter this conversation. Petridis notices this and continues talking.

'Did you notice anyone else around you in the park? Anyone running or walking through?'

'No, nobody else around.'

'Did you hear anything, screams or any yelling?'

'No, I just found the body.'

'Jenny, what did you do when you noticed the body?'

'I rang my boyfriend, Tommy. He told me not to touch the body. There was no way I would even go near it, let alone touch it. Tommy came right away. We then called the police.'

'Why didn't you call the police first?'

'I don't know. I got scared. I've never seen a dead body before. I didn't know what to do. So I rang Tommy.'

Petridis writes everything down, word for word. He needs to have a few words to Tommy. Petridis looks over his shoulder to see where his partner is. He's surprised he hasn't jumped in unannounced. He notices Natloz staring at the body, hypnotized. Just staring at the body like it's some kind of freak show. What is he looking at? What could he possibly be thinking?

'Thank you, Jenny. I'd like to speak to Tommy now and then have you both come down to the station for more questioning and to make a formal report. This will help with further our investigation.'

'Yes, we can do that.'

Petridis walks over to Natloz and taps him on the shoulder. 'Hey buddy, are you okay?'

Natloz is startled and jumps out of his hypnotic state. His body jerks before he realises what has happened. He turns to Petridis with a look of despair and confusion. 'Where are we?'

'What?'

'*Where are we?*'

Natloz's heart is racing at an unbelievable speed. He doesn't recognise his surroundings or where he is. He looks baffled.

As does Petridis. They have spent the last two days together investigating two separate crimes at two different locations. How much does his partner remember from the past couple of days?

'You really don't know where we are?'

'No. What happened here? Who killed this guy?'

'Do you remember anything about why we're here? Or what happened to you earlier?'

'No. What happened to me?'

'You don't remember?'

'I said no!'

Something must have happened to Natloz after he had passed out. Something has triggered his brain to forget, like amnesia. Not recalling what happened to him and not remembering why they're there is a real concern. It's like his memory over the past seven hours has been erased.

Natloz moves away from the body and heads towards some bushes where there are two paths. The one to the left leads down to the mausoleums. The one to the right has sparked the interest of Natloz. Petridis is watching him the whole time, wondering what the hell his partner is up to.

'What is it, mate? Did you see something?'

Natloz doesn't respond as he continues walking over towards the bushes. He's in the zone, focused and in his own world. It's bordering on Freakishland. He calls out to the nearest constable, giving him a friendly wave to come over. Hand gestures always do the trick. The constable comes over.

'Put on some gloves,' Natloz says. 'I need you to fetch something from inside that bush.'

The young constable puts on some disposable gloves, enters the shrubs, and emerges holding something.

'What is it?' Petridis asks.

'It's a foot, a fucking foot,' says the constable. The constable drops the foot, turns, and vomits. A weak stomach when it comes to body parts that are not attached to the body.

'Take yourself a bit further away, constable. We don't want anything contaminated here.'

The constable gets about two metres away before letting out another loud grunt. Last night's dinner or this morning's breakfast cascades all over the manicured cemetery lawn. Bile and chunks spill out of his stomach.

'Can someone please check up on him?' Natloz says. 'We have one body to contend with. I don't need another.'

Petridis can't get his head around how Natloz knew where the foot was. How could he have seen it from that distance? 'How did you do that? How did you know the foot was in there?'

Natloz is staring at the foot like it's the Holy Grail. Looking at how it was severed, the loose pieces of flesh dangling like shredded papier-mâché. He tilts his head, which he does quite often. He knows by looking at it that it had been mauled off. Evidence shows it was done by an animal. Torn through the bone, through flesh, with jaws big enough to bite it clean off.

'This is freaking me out, mate. How did you know it was there?'

Natloz looks up from his zoned-out state and locks eyes with Petridis. What comes next throws Petridis.

'I smelt it,' he says.

CHAPTER 7

Willem Natloz was an only child. His mother, Sultana, was a Belarusian immigrant who had come to Australia in 1962 with a whole group of Europeans. She was fifteen years old. She made Adelaide her home for the first twelve years before moving to Melbourne in '74. She met Joshua while doing her daily commute to work on the tram along Lygon Street in Carlton. Joshua worked for Vito Butti, who owned the fruit shop on the corner of Lygon and Elgin Street, the busiest part of the strip. Vito was heavily involved with the Calabrian underworld crime syndicate. He was involved in things most people would only see on a big screen. Joshua tried to keep out of that side of the business, but there were days he couldn't.

Sultana and Joshua were married in the winter of '76. Willem was born not long after. Sultana was pregnant before the wedding, possibly the reason for tying the knot in a short time. Joy filled their hearts from the moment Willem was born.

Butti was one of the most ruthless mafia bosses the country had ever seen. He migrated from Italy in 1952 and caused an uproar in the small local community. Joshua ran errands for the mob boss to make that extra dollar for his young family. The errands became a lot more frequent after the wedding. Willem grew up knowing he didn't want to be like Butti and that Butti had a strong hold on his dad. Willem wanted to make something of himself, and hopefully one day make his parents proud.

Willem decided he wanted to be a detective and put an end to crime and sadistic men like Vito Butti. Willem had seen the trouble his dad would encounter. There were times after a hard day's work when his dad would come home and tell Willem to switch off the TV. He had a sickening feeling in his gut his son might see something on TV that would incriminate Butti, or more so himself.

When Willem started high school, he became an easy target for bullies. His unique dark skin colour and stick figure physique brought on taunts from all non-European kids, which was about ninety-five percent of the school. His family's history with mob violence involvement, which hadn't been a secret, had led to verbal and physical taunts. Destruction was inevitable and there wasn't much Willem could do about it.

For the first two years of school, Willem played along with the abuse and assaults until one day he stood up to the king of school bullies, Thomas Finch. He punched him in the face and broke his nose. It gained him the respect and gratitude of the other kids, including the other bullies who had picked on him, too. He had earned it the hard way.

Willem had become a straight-A student, shooting to the top of his class, earning himself a scholarship in criminology and an easy entry to the police academy, but most of all he gained the utmost respect from Thomas Finch. He had changed the attitude and dynamics of the school's history, making it a fun place to learn. He excelled in physics and law, making a name for himself with his friends but most importantly with his peers.

By the time Willem was ready to graduate, regret and neglect had kicked in. He had wished his mother was around to see her baby boy become a man. His parent's marriage had deteriorated rapidly when he was much younger and by the end of grade three, his parents divorced. He never saw his mother again.

His life was turned upside down. His parents were his heroes. He looked up to both of them in a different way, but more so his mum. He had fond memories of his mother saying, 'Life is not what it seems. Life is a hidden maze and you need to find your way through it.' Willem's parents got lost in the maze of life and had to exit from opposite ends.

His parents sold the family home and moved to different areas. Willem's mum moved to Sydney while his dad stayed in Melbourne and became heavily involved with the mafia. Willem continued to university never mentioning his parents and speaking of his dad, wanting so much to be the detective he aspired to become. Any mention of his dad and the involvement he had with the crime syndicate would dampen his chances. He studied day and night, even on the weekends, for his police entry exam. His friends would invite him out with them many times but he was determined to make his dream come true.

Then on one cold, dull, rainy evening while preparing his dinner, Willem heard a knock on his door. It was after 7:00pm, which was unusually odd for Willem to have a visitor. A dark cloud had come over him, and he felt fear inside him like he was going to receive bad news. Opening the door would change his life for ever.

Willem opened the front door. There were two police officers standing there with a look on their faces that said they were about to deliver bad news. 'Mr Natloz? Willem Natloz?'

'Yes?' Willem replied, shivering.

'Is your father Joshua Natloz who works down at the corner fruit shop for Mr Vito Butti?'

'Yes, that's right. Is everything okay? Is my dad okay?'

The officers looked at each other, then one turned back and asked if they could come in. Willem knew from that moment his life would take another turn. The officers confirmed what Willem had thought; his father had been killed in an execution-style murder. His body was discovered by locals at the back of the fruit shop. Butti and one of his lieutenants were also gunned down and had been slumped over a pallet of sacked potatoes.

This was not the news Willem ever wanted to hear. He sat speechless for what seemed like a lifetime. He wanted confirmation, proof that it was his dad who had been gunned down. But deep down inside something was telling him that all the proof he needed was in the policeman's words. His dad was dead.

That day changed Willem Natloz. His dad had chosen a life of crime, the complete opposite to what Willem wanted for himself.

That day, Detective Willem Natloz was born.

CHAPTER 8

It had been a long and tiring few days. Natloz walks through the front door of his two-storey townhouse and crashes on the couch without removing his shoes. His right hand tucks under his head while his left arm dangles down beside him, his fingers brushing the soft woollen threads of the carpet. He spends the next few minutes thinking, trying to put the pieces of the puzzle together – but it's missing a piece or two. His mind is not functioning like it would normally.

He takes out his phone from his pocket and searches the gallery of photos that were snapped earlier today. Some were odd, others confusing, but all meaningful to the murders. As he scrolls through the photos, he comes across one that catches his attention. This particular picture makes more sense looking at it the second time around.

The photo is of the bloody doormat from the apartment where Sally lived. It had been taken by Forensics for further tests, and he makes a mental note to follow up on the results of the blood to see who it belongs to. Both Oscar and the witness who was hiding behind a car when the attack on Sally occurred described the attacker as 'a thing'. What could it be?

On the corner of the mat there is another bloodstain barely visible in the photo that has an odd shape. Natloz enlarges the photo for better viewing. It is still a little difficult to make out. He sits upright, his bones making a geriatric cracking sound. The sound of age rattling in his ears, he stares at the phone, the missing puzzle pieces becoming a little clearer but not enough to make a judgement call. He tries to focus on the picture and nothing else. The photo is trying to tell him something. He can't sleep until this is dealt with. He needs to make a phone call. He needs help.

Natloz closes the gallery and rings Peter Kirby, the Forensics agent.

'Hello?' a tired voice on the other end says.

'Peter, it's Will Natloz. I need a favour.'

'Will, do you know what time it is? Can't it wait until later? We've been up all night.'

'No, mate, it can't. I need something done and sent to my phone.'

Peter tries to hide his annoyance. He was asleep and had been for only a short time. He gets mighty cranky when his sleep is broken, his voice not holding back from showing it. Natloz had noticed it but continues anyway; the urgency of this request is more important than Peter's sleep. Broken sleep doesn't sit well with many people, but that's something Natloz has never felt.

'Mate, what is it?' Peter's voice is a little quieter now. He knows the quicker he does this, the quicker he can get back to sleep. He's aware that Natloz only rings when there is something urgent. It's not that often, so he does what he asks. He must be onto something. Natloz sees things that others don't. He knows things that nobody else knows. Peter is willing to help him get what he needs.

'I need a photo enlarged and sent to me right away. There should be a photo you or Sandra might have taken at the apartment the other night, the Sally Jenkins murder.'

'What, you want that right now?'

'Yes, right now. Don't waste any time. I need it, fast as you can.'

'What, like the Gingerbread Man?'

'No time for jokes, mate.'

'Okay. Which photo are you wanting?'

'I need the photo of the mat. The one with all the blood beneath it.'

'Give me about fifteen minutes.'

'I'll give you ten.'

Peter hears the urgency in Natloz's voice. His patience is running thin. He better get cracking. 'Okay, Will. I'm on it. See ya.'

Peter drags his tired body out of bed, puts on his clothes, and prepares himself for a long night. Sleep will have to wait a little longer.

Natloz waits impatiently for a text to come in from Peter. He checks for the time on his watch but realises he's not wearing it. *Where's my watch?* It constantly lives on his wrist. He looks on the coffee table just in case he removed it before lying down on the couch, but it's not there. He gets to his feet and walks over to the bench in the kitchen. Nothing there either. *It's probably on the bedside table in my room. I'll check later.*

A sudden urgency to go to the toilet strikes him. Pressure is building up against his bladder. He has an opportunity to go now while waiting for Peter.

He hears the sound of a text come through. And again, and again. Shaking and zipping up, he rushes into the lounge room where his phone is resting on the coffee table. He unlocks the phone and sees three new messages. He knows who they're from. He must have fallen asleep between speaking to Peter and going to the toilet because it has only felt like five minutes.

Peter has sent three photos through. He opens the first one. It's from a standing position looking down at the mat. It's a little hard to make out the shape of the stain. The second photo is a little closer and from a slightly different angle, but it's still not making much sense. The third photo is the one he was waiting for the most: an extreme close-up of the mat, and in particular, the corner of the mat. And that's when Natloz sees it, that odd shape he noticed earlier. It's right there in front of him.

He quickly rings his partner. It goes straight to voicemail. He hangs up and tries again. Same thing, straight to voicemail.

'Fuck, fuck, fuck.'

He rings for the third time and this time he leaves a message.

'Pet, it's Nat. Call me back ASAP. I have something. It makes no fucking sense but I have something. I have a print and I'm curious on how this print got onto the mat. It's a clear fucking print, mate.'

As soon as he presses 'end call', his phone starts vibrating. Its Petridis.

'Hey buddy, what's up?' His voice is tired and croaky.

'Sorry for waking you, mate, but I have something. I found a print on one of the photos.'

There's a pause on the other end of the phone. Petridis has possibly fallen asleep again.

'Pet? Are you there?'

'Huh … yeah, mate. Have you slept at all? You should get some sleep. You weren't well at all last night.'

'I'm fine. Listen to me. Did you hear what I said? Get the fuck over to the office. I have something, and we need to follow up on it, now.'

'It's 4:00 on a Sunday morning, mate. Can't it wait?'

'Not this. This can't wait.'

'Did you say you found a print? Footprint or fingerprint?'

'Yes, it's a print, and no, not a footprint nor a fingerprint. I found a print … of a paw!'

CHAPTER 9

Natloz doesn't waste any time other than to change his shirt, which he's been wearing for a few days now. It ponged like he has just taken it out of the dirty washing basket after sitting there on the bottom of the pile for days. He knows it is going to be another long day. No time to make a coffee at home, he'll pick one up on the way. He jumps into his car and reverses out of his car spot. It's an old car, so no fancy technology crap like Bluetooth or hands-free. The radio stopped working a while ago and he hasn't had the time to fix it. He hardly listens to it anyway.

The office is about a thirty-minute drive from where Natloz lives, and at that time of the morning it should be a clear run. No need to rush. Peak-hour traffic doesn't kick in for a few hours yet.

He thinks about running the siren; that normally gets him where he wants to be a lot quicker. He does that quite often when he's in traffic – watching the cars part for the screaming siren, like Moses parting the Red Sea. There is no need to today. Traffic is light and the roads are clear. Petridis lives a little further away so Natloz is certain he will arrive before he does.

He hasn't stopped thinking about the picture. It was there the entire time, a clear print. But what could have put it there? Is someone trying to hide something? Do Annie, Sally and Oscar have a dog they didn't mention? All of these are great questions. Sharing this with his partner is also floating in his head. How will he react to this? How would anyone react to this discovery? Surprised? It was hard to fathom and process. The detective knows they are onto something. It has been proven in the past that if you don't find any leads within the first forty-eight hours then the case goes cold. You could lose all opportunity of solving the crime. Natloz knows the importance and doesn't want that to happen here.

He turns down Bourke Street and hits a gridlock. Overnight construction work in the main CBD area plus the last of the patrons leaving the clubs is slowing him down. Taxis and Ubers moving around the busy street. He should have known this but his mind is scrambling with what is going on; his processing ability has been halved. There is too much going on for his mind to have remembered the busy nightclub hours of the city.

The thought crosses his mind again – siren plus clear road equals a path through the works and traffic. He raises his hand towards the magic switch and flicks it on. The siren blares loud and attentive. Cars don't waste any time moving to one side to let him through. The portable blue light flashes bright on the dashboard. Flashing with a purpose.

Natloz arrives at the office in no time. Switching on the blue lights paid off. The office is still quiet. It has that ghost town feel. Sundays normally house skeleton staff, catching up on reports. Natloz waits impatiently for his partner, pacing the corridor like a caged animal wanting to be freed. His fingernails have been bitten down to the quick and on his middle finger he has drawn blood from the eponychium.

As the detective is about to place another finger in his mouth, Petridis comes strolling in. Clean shaven and a change of crisp clean clothes. His hair is perfectly slicked back with not a strand out of place. His aftershave lets out a fresh expensive scent, like Gucci or Armani.

'Always looking your best. No one gives a shit what you look like, mate. I meant it when I said it was urgent,' splutters an angry Natloz. It is a tone that could start a war.

'Maybe in your world, but not in mine, mate. I'm going to ignore that comment and pretend you didn't just say that.'

Petridis standing his ground makes Natloz realise he is out of line. Something that has been happening regularly of late. Something Natloz needs to speak to someone about.

'I'm sorry, mate. Not sure why I said that. I'm a little on edge and haven't been feeling a hundred percent.'

Petridis ignores that response and gets right into business, not letting his partner off that easy. He lets Natloz sit on his guilt for a while longer. 'You mentioned something about a print?'

Petridis follows Natloz to his desk, photos already spread out across it. Natloz had time to print them on A4 paper while waiting for Petridis.

The photo was so clear it was like looking at the mat itself there in person. The paw was imprinted in blood, clear as day, under the corner of the mat. From that angle the paw looked big. It must belong to a large beast of some sort. The thing that didn't make sense was that there were no other pawprints anywhere else on the mat or in and around the apartment. Not even at the park opposite the building where the body was found. If there were prints there, then someone had erased them from the picture, erased them from the apartment, erased them from the scene.

Someone is covering up their tracks and Natloz and Petridis want to know who. The only indication that it could be an animal was the mutilated bodies. That alone makes no sense at all. And they now have a pawprint made by a large animal of some description, and a faint size 10 ½ footprint that was located on the bottom steps leading up to the apartment. That print could belong to anyone in the building, including Oscar. A phone call to the lock-up will determine that. It will be like finding a needle in a haystack searching for the owner. Uniformed officers have been at the complex door knocking for the last two days. Nothing has come up yet. No tracks or sign of any other prints have been found.

They have a prime suspect in Oscar, who is currently being held for further questioning. He told them he had seen who had done it … Or what had done it. They decide to chat with Oscar once more.

They make their way to the car parked out the front. Petridis decides to drive. After yesterday's performance, it's best if Natloz rides as the passenger. He's not confident that Natloz won't have a repeat episode and pass out while behind the wheel, a risk Petridis is not willing to take. Life is too precious to be played with and put in the hands of someone like Natloz.

The drive to the holding cells is quick. Both detectives keep to themselves; you could hear a pin drop in the silence. The radio is switched off and the air dull. There's a stale smell of rotting food and body odour. The body odour is pouring off Natloz. He hasn't rested or slept in days. Petridis is amazed how his partner hasn't crashed yet. Not his car, but himself. How is he still awake and functioning? No sleep, no food, sitting on three coffees already this morning. Once again, the feeling of concern for his partner needs to be made a priority. Once this interview with Oscar is over, he will have a chat with his partner. He needs to see someone about his episodes. He needs help.

That will have to wait a little longer, though. First things first. Oscar.

Time seems to be moving quite fast today. They arrive at the holding cells and get right into business. The building is busy with people walking in and out, looking like they're on a mission from God, or Lucifer, whichever way you want to look at it. The time is 7:37. The chilly breeze outside had the heaters running hot in the building. People move robotically, going about their day with a sole purpose just to get through it. Repetitive motions that seem to be the same, day in day out. Some faces are tired and stressed, others senseless yet focused. A look showing they would rather be somewhere else than there on a Sunday. Hoping for it to be kind and gentle with some excitement, and not cruel and unkind. That has happened in the past.

The detectives walk up the front steps of the building with anticipation, through the double doors and into the foyer with security guards on either side. A scanning machine is separating them from the guards. Every officer that walks through those doors needs to surrender their weapon. Everything is placed in a tray and X-rayed. Nothing will get through without the sensors going off. Guns are given back once they leave. A policy that has been operating for years.

Petridis goes first. He places his gun, keys, wallet, phone, and a packet of gum into the tray. His cigarettes and lighter were left in the car. He walks through the scanner, slowly. All clear. Natloz has only his gun and phone with him. He puts them in a tray and walks through. The alarm goes off.

'Step back through, Detective Natloz,' says Jimmy, one of the guards who knows both detectives. Natloz does what he's told. He steps back, waits a few seconds and walks through the machine again. The alarm goes off again. This time Jimmy says to empty everything from his pockets, but he doesn't have anything else in his pockets. He turns them inside out to show Jimmy, who he knows from previous visits. He sees the same guard on duty every time he comes here.

'I'm sorry. Something is setting off the alarm. Are you sure you don't have anything else on you? Keys or a wallet?'

He checks once more. Nothing. He is waved to head through for a physical pat down by Jimmy. He is asked to stand on the red line with his arms and legs apart. The pat down comes back clear. Nothing else in his possession.

'You're right to go, detective,' says Jimmy.

A quick nod sees them part until the next time they meet. Hopefully the next time will be buzzer-free. This has never happened before and is strange for it to happen now.

Natloz feels a little faint. He tries to hide it from his partner. The last thing he wants right now is another lecture. He feels uneasy and thirsty. His heart rate is a little faster than normal. He must be dehydrated. He'll head to the cafeteria later on and buy himself a bottle of water.

Time is taking its own time; nothing moves any quicker than it should. It's amazing how things seem to go a lot slower than usual when you're in a hurry, like watching everything move in slow motion. The detectives need to get to Oscar pronto, find out what he really saw two nights ago. It is the only lead they have on this case. Two mutilated bodies and no clues. Is he the killer, or is he telling the truth? Only one way to find out. Both detectives are tired and deprived of sleep but at this moment, sleep is waiting.

Petridis presses the button and they wait by the elevator for the doors to open. Natloz checks his watch. 7:48am. It took them ten minutes to get through security. A waste of valuable precious time that they won't get back because of that damn faulty machine that kept buzzing for no apparent reason.

The doors open slowly. Natloz doesn't wait for them to fully open; he desperately pushes himself past others to get in first, Petridis right on his heels. Natloz pushes the button for the ninth floor, the floor for the holding cells. Security needs to be tight on that level. They reach the floor and exit the elevator. The air is different up there, a lot thinner, and you can tell because you become a little light-headed once you step out from the elevator. Not enough air passes through your lungs, which doesn't allow the blood to flow through to your heart, and the brain suffers the consequences. It makes you a little drowsy and faint. The mysteries of the ninth floor. WorkSafe would have a field day up there. Paranormal investigators would too.

They pass through the first set of metal doors. These doors are three inches thick and the glass is bulletproof. You never know when they might come in handy. A few seconds later they pass through a second set of metal doors. They're confronted by Officer Pitkowski standing behind a high wooden desk. The desk is shielded behind a metal cage. Like Fort Knox.

'We're here to see a prisoner by the name of Oscar Lopez.'

'Sign the register, please. Both of you.' Pitkowski is munching on a Snickers bar. By looking at him, it seems he's been around this place for a long time; part of the second-hand furniture on display. Not a tall man, but very broad. Shoulders like boulders. Fifties or early sixties, but not close enough to retire. No ring on his finger which could mean anything. A wrinkled forehead, scar under his left eye, a three-day growth, and thick glasses completes his unusual face. A face that has seen its fair number of losers walk through those doors. Petridis and Natloz not included.

Natloz signs the book first, followed by Petridis.

'The young lad is in the cell down the end on your left. He might still be asleep. He was talking to himself last night. Didn't make much sense. It sounded foreign or some shit like that. I couldn't work out what language he was speaking.'

'Did he say anything you did understand?' asked Petridis.

'I don't fucking know. I'm not a babysitter, nor am I a translator. He was mumbling something and I told him to shut the fuck up. So, he did.'

'Did you go over to see him? Make sure he was okay?' This time it was Natloz who asked the question.

'No. I didn't have to. Like I said, I told him to shut up and he did.'

'How certain are you he was talking to himself? Was there anyone else here with you?'

'I was by myself. I don't need anyone to hold my hand, detective. What could possibly go wrong in here?' He looks around the floor, showing the detectives the empty space. 'Did you notice the security when you came through? Superman would have a hard time getting in.'

'Did he have any visitors?'

'No, no one came to see him. He was all alone. Well, I think he was. Carter came later to relieve me for my break. Carter finished at 8:00 last night. Neither of us approached the prisoner.'

'So how the fuck do you know he wasn't speaking to anyone if neither yourself nor Carter got off your fat arses to have a look? Did you check up on him at all?'

'We did. Well, Carter did and he said he was asleep. Sleeping like a baby who had a bad dream and put himself back to sleep.'

Natloz had to control his temper. Frustration could easily cause things to get out of hand.

'Open these doors and take us to the cell,' says Petridis in a stern and demanding voice.

When they got to the cell that housed Oscar, they saw that he was lying on the metal bed that was attached to the wall. He has a thin blanket and an even thinner pillow. Oscar is facing the wall. Hard to tell from that angle whether he is asleep or not. There is no movement from him at all.

Natloz calls out his name. Nothing. He calls out again. Still nothing. Natloz's mind spills over with horrified thoughts. He knows something is wrong. 'Open the door, now.'

Pitkowski fumbles with his keys, struggling to find the right one that opens the cell door. Out of fear and frustration the officer drops the keys. He bends over and picks them up. Half of the eaten Snickers sticks out of his back pocket. He tries once more and finds the right key this time.

Both detectives rush in. Petridis puts his hand on Oscar's shoulder, gives him a slight nudge. Oscar feels cold and stiff. Not the way a living body should feel. Natloz reaches down and turns Oscar over. They can't believe their eyes.

Oscar's eyes are missing. Taken out of their sockets. Empty holes in his head where his eyes used to be. The sheets are covered in blood.

'What the fuck?' says Pitkowski, taking a few steps back. 'His fucking eyes are missing. Someone has taken his eyes!'

They weren't expecting to find Oscar dead in his cell with his eyes missing. It was an understatement when Pitkowski said Oscar must have had a nightmare. Someone has come into the cell, removed Oscar's eyes, and then vanished into thin air. Someone didn't want him to talk about what he had witnessed. Someone has killed him to protect the truth.

Natloz notices Oscar's hands are clenched into fists, bloody. There are no wounds or cuts on the hands. They are certain that the blood on the body belongs to Oscar. There are no weapons in the cell. Maybe he has used his hands to protect himself, hence the blood. But from what?

This 'foreign talk' Pitkowski was talking about was probably Oscar calling for help in Spanish; calling someone because he was being attacked and was in pain. As Natloz looks closer at the clenched fists, he notices there is something inside one of the palms. Oscar is holding something. Petridis pulls the fingers open. Rigor mortis has settled in which gives the detectives an indication that the man has been dead for at least two to six hours.

The sound of breaking bones echo through the cell. Petridis has forced the hand open. He quickly drops the hand and takes a step back and lets out an emotional cry. 'WHAT THE FUCK IS THAT?'

Stuck to the inner palm of Oscar's hand is the answer.

In his palm lay his missing eyes.

CHAPTER 10

It was a long night, both detectives feeling the pressure that has crept in to their bodies. Not much more the detectives can do at the moment but wait for the post-mortem examination. The Perth police have been informed of the death, and they have the almost impossible task now of notifying the family and loved ones of their loss. News no parent wants to receive.

Natloz hitches a ride home with Petridis. Silence fills the air as neither has much to say. It will take time to sink in. The unfortunate death from their number one suspect has put a damper on this case. Back to square one.

The car pulls up at the front of Natloz's place. They acknowledge each other with a simple nod of heads, like two best friends parting for the day. A standard code meaning 'Catch you later', or somewhere along those lines. Petridis drives off and turns the corner. Within seconds, he and the vehicle are out of sight.

Natloz turns and faces his place with dead eyes. He starts walking slowly towards it. His eyes are bloodshot and his legs all wobbly, not responding to the message sent through from his brain. He knows for the next several hours his bed will become his best friend. He has been awake for over thirty hours. This will be a perfect time to transform into a vampire, minus the blood. Close the lid of the coffin and not wake up until sundown.

Natloz reaches the front porch. Someone has left a bag at his doorstep. In it there is a container with food and a note.

Hi Will,

I thought you might get hungry at some point seeing you haven't been home for a few days. I hope you're well. Eat up, it's your favourite.

Love Cindy xx

A tired, half-hearted smile and a sniff of the food was all he could muster. He and Cindy have been friends since graduating from uni together. She had married his best friend, Spencer. Their posse of friends had always thought he and Cindy would and should have ended up together. They were a better match. That didn't happen though. Friendship got in the way of relationship; both scared a relationship might have ruined it for them. It was safer this way.

She has three kids with Spencer. It wasn't long after the third child was born that she realised what her friends had been telling her about him all along had been true. A cheating, lying, manipulating ass. In the end, she ended up leaving with the kids and made sure there was no way he could have contacted her. She moved in with her mother for a brief stint before she got back on her feet and was now running her own business working from home. She is surrounded by friends and family who love her dearly. Natloz is one of those friends and will always be there for her. Intervention orders were made out to keep Spencer away. It worked. Cindy considers Natloz as her closest friend. Hints of them getting together are still in the making. But for now, friends is all they both want.

Natloz takes his keys out of his pocket, unlocks the door, and heads straight to the kitchen. He places the food on the bench and opens the bag to see what Cindy has made him. She was right. His favourite; lasagne, and it was still warm. He must have just missed her.

Even with the delicious aroma of the Bolognese, he couldn't bring himself to eat it right then. His energy is running on empty. Like a car running out of fuel halfway up a hill. He can feel himself starting to roll on a backwards slope. And with that thought, he makes his way to his bedroom and crash lands face first onto his bed.

Petridis is driving home from what seems to have been the longest day he has ever had. Thoughts rush through his head like electricity through a power line. There are a lot of loose ends that need tying up. None of it makes any sense. One thing is for certain; Natloz is not well. He noticed some unfamiliar behaviour that he has never seen before, and it has him thinking. Natloz has issues he needs to sort out, but most importantly, he has a secret he hasn't shared with Petridis yet.

You should tell your partner everything about you. EVERYTHING, he thinks to himself. It was a conversation they had when they were first partnered. A very important rule. Probably the most important of rules as partners.

He arrives at his apartment block in St Kilda. His unit is not that far from Natloz's, but still, when you're tired a twenty minute ride can seem like a lifetime. He parks his car in the underground carpark that is provided for the tenants. It's a modern building in a very posh area of Melbourne. It's where all the yuppies hang out. Flash cars, flash clothes, and flashy people walking around believing their own crap don't stink. Petridis inherited a large sum of cash when his parents were tragically killed in a boating accident when he was young. Petridis was left an orphan and placed in the care of his uncle and aunty. He moved to Greece when he was ten years old and spent seven years there until he was at a legal age to return back to Australia. He moved in with his godfather, Demetrios, for the next three years of his life.

Petridis became a policeman for similar reasons to Natloz. In this case, he had some doubts about his parents' boating accident. The doubts grew stronger, the doubts turned real. There was something more to that story that cannot be shared right now, but the truth is, it wasn't an accident. Tragic and sad, but that is another story to tell at another time.

Petridis parks his car in his designated spot and jumps out. He locks the car and the sound of central locking echoes through the carpark. He is the only one there. It being dark and cold and with low visibility makes this scene look scary, like a horror flick. The scene is set for a possible disaster that could happen at any time. The detective feels like someone is about to jump out from behind the cars and attack him. He gets that feeling every time he parks down there. He needs to speak to the other occupants and raise awareness with body corporate. They definitely need more lighting down there.

He makes his way to the elevator. He presses the button and waits for it to come down to the basement. The building has seven levels and the basement – eight if you count the rooftop pool. It's a new building with the slowest elevator he has ever encountered. Petridis lives on the sixth floor. The apartments on the sixth floor are a lot more spacious with large rooms. Three bedrooms to be precise. He couldn't afford the penthouse suites on the seventh floor – three suites make up that floor.

He hops into the lift and the door closes behind him. There's no elevator music, which only makes the cables sound louder. Not many people love elevator music anyway. There is a bright light in the small claustrophobic space that gives off an interrogating feel.

It takes almost a minute to reach the sixth floor thanks to an unusual and unscheduled stop on the second floor. No one entered the lift when it stopped. Matter of fact, there was nobody in sight on the floor anyway. It's unusual for elevators to stop unexpectedly without the button being pressed for that desired floor. This hadn't happened before to Petridis in the two years he's lived there. It's a place he has grown to love and call home. The lift reaches the sixth floor. It's quiet and peaceful, with the lights in the hallway a little more dull and gentler on the eyes. A nice warm comfortable welcome.

He walks towards his apartment door. The room number is sixty-seven, but the door is missing the seven. It has been missing for the past six months and needs replacing. Something he needs to get around to do. NASA is more likely to put another man on the moon before his door sees the number seven replaced. He removes his keys from his jacket pocket and puts them into the lock, turns the key, and unlocks his haven, his palace, the most comforting place on earth.

As he enters, he senses a presence. Not in the room, but outside his apartment. He steps back outside into the hallway. There are a further two apartments on that floor. He knows both occupants but none he could say he would spend more than half a day with. It's a simple 'Hi' and 'Bye' and the occasional 'How are you?' He knows them by first name basis and what they do for a living, but nothing more.

The detective looks down the corridor. Nothing in sight. He keeps still and quiet, just in case he hears anything. Nothing. Not a sound, not even a creak. He stops and stares at the dark grey carpet that looks like it belongs in an office. They could have done better with the design. The elevator pings. He waits to see who gets out. The door opens. He waits. No one comes out. The doors close and it moves to another floor. Weird.

He heads back into his apartment, placing the keys down in a bowl that's housed on top of an entrance table. He enters the kitchen and heads for the fridge. He has a dry throat and needs to quench his thirst. He feels a little dehydrated. Opening the fridge door, he grabs a bottle of water, takes the lid off, and drinks about three quarters of the bottle.

He wipes his caterpillar of a moustache with his sleeve and heads to the lounge room window which overlooks a park. It's dark, with only the light of a lamp post. How did it get dark so quick? Has he taken longer than he realised? Where has the day gone? Not much went on after finding Oscar dead in his cell. A stop for petrol and cigarettes was all he did. The day seems to have gotten away from him. Tiredness has slowed him down and sped up the day.

He's still able to make out anyone walking past. He questions whether he should go across the road for a quick cigarette before he turns in for the day. He doesn't smoke in his apartment and the other occupants don't like it when people smoke in the parking area. It had been decided it was best for everyone to smoke away from the building. Body corporate making that unanimous decision. Tiredness gets the better of that thought. He decides to stay put.

As the detective gazes at the lamp post, a large figure to the left of the park bench moves. It is a quick movement, blurry and unnoticeable to anyone who hadn't been paying attention – but the detective knew there was something there. It's now hiding in the shrubs and staring up at the detective. Petridis can see its bright beady eyes, glowing like a lighthouse. They lock eyes for a split second before it turns and runs off through the still of the night, into the park under the cold bright stars.

The detective is left with questions that need answering. With no time to waste, he grabs his phone, runs out of the apartment forgetting to lock the door and heads to the lift, hoping it doesn't take long to arrive. He presses the button but the door doesn't open. The lift is stationed at the basement level. Someone must have used it not long ago. The wait is going to annoy him. He needs to get down to the basement and out of the building as fast as he can. He decides against the lift.

He decides to use the fire escape. Six floors of stairs take him almost a minute to get down, the same amount of time coming up with the elevator. He exits the building and runs across the street, not watching for cars as he crosses. He stops at the park bench, reaches for his gun, and unlocks the safety latch. The thought of calling for back-up eludes his trained mind, deciding to go at it alone for now. He needs to be sure within himself there is something there before he makes that call. He enters the park with his gun drawn and pointing directly in front of him, chest height.

It's not long before he gets to the running track. He walks in stealth mode when he suddenly stumbles on something large. That something is a body. There are now three bodies and counting. The thought of it being Oscar is wiped clean as he's no longer with us; he is just as dead as this guy at Petridis's feet. Another sleepless night is brewing.

He makes the call to dispatch and then sends his partner a message.

We have another body.

CHAPTER 11

Flashing lights, police and forensic personnel around the body at the park, paramedics waiting for their cue. Déjà vu and bad memories. Somewhere a life is just beginning, while here another life has ended.

Police tape flaps around in the slight breeze, reminding people that it's there. Birds in the trees chirp out a death song, the words only they know. There are reporters held back, trying to get close to the body but still too far to snap pictures. A dark cloud has surrounded the area of the body. The police are not letting anyone in or out of the park. People have gathered at the perimeter, watching from a distance. It's not hard for them to guess what has happened. Their minds are entertained at someone else's expense. A sick thought, but true. Curiosity has channelled its way through their minds, curious to whom this lifeless body belongs.

Word gets around fast. Chief Inspector Moore from Homicide has made an appearance. Jerry Moore is a veteran in the police force with an old school, bat crazy attitude. He's a tall Irishman who towers over most of the division. His colleagues all look up to him, no pun intended. He's slightly balding with a coarse beard, clothes fashioned after ancient TV shows like *Kojak* or *Dirty Harry*. A cop show from yesteryear.

Moore hops out of his car and steps under the police banner. You know when Moore's around – the next suburb would be able to hear the arrival. He's vocally enthusiastic. 'What do we have here? Who is running the show?'

'Me, sir,' says a young officer.

'Okay, don't just fucking stare at me, talk. What do we have?'

'Male, early thirties, local guy with an extensive rap sheet. No ID on him but we know who he is. Known on the streets as "Jabber". He's from Richmond. About $20 and a handful of loose change in his wallet and pocket. Looks like he was walking home from somewhere. We'll ask around. I don't think it was a robbery. Nothing missing besides …' He can't bring the right words to his lips.

'Spit it out, son. Besides what?'

He composes himself and finishes the sentence. 'Besides pieces of flesh from his torso, sir.'

Moore wishes he didn't get him to finish.

'There is something else, sir. Something that we found on the body.'

'What is it?'

'Dog hair.'

'What?'

'Dog hair. It's all over his clothing.'

'Okay, dog hair! What kind of dog hair? Long, short, thick? You need to give me more than that, son. Also, what the fuck is dog hair doing on him?'

'Not sure yet, sir.'

'So, what you're saying is that he was killed, brutally, by someone who possibly had a dog with him, who then let the dog rub itself all over the body? Or second scenario, the dog has killed this man in a vicious attack and fled the scene of the crime through the park? So, what we're looking for is a dog. Is that what we have here. Does that sound right to you, constable? Crazy, don't you think?'

'Actually, sir, there is something else.'

'What more could there possibly be?'

'He is missing part of his face.'

'Part of his face?'

'Yes, sir.'

'Which part and how much of it?'

'Well, sir, it—'

'Is Natloz and Petridis here?' Moore interrupts.

'Not sure, sir.'

'What do you know? Actually, don't answer that. Someone get me Petridis and Natloz. Where the fuck are they?'

Inspector Moore is in a foul mood. He's probably been woken up from a deep sleep or he might have been out drinking with mates. He could also have been having some one-on-one time with Mrs Moore. Sexy time. Nobody ever wants to be taken away from that.

✝

Petridis is standing under the lamp post near the seat. He's staring directly up to his apartment. His eyes are glued to his building. He wanted to stand in the same position he saw that figure, that same person he saw run into the park.

His phone beeps. It's a text from an unknown number. He opens it.

> **I need to chat with you. Detective Natloz is not answering his phone. He's not responding to my texts. I need to talk with you ASAP. Please call me,**
>
> **It's Annie Carter**

Petridis hasn't spoken to her in a few days, not since Sally's body was found. He wonders what she wants. She might have information to share about the death of Sally. Or maybe she has something to share about Oscar. Both equally possible. He feels the urgency behind the message. She sounds very distressed and troubled over it.

I'll call her once I'm done here. A thought crosses his mind. Something Annie just mentioned – where is Natloz? He'd messaged him over an hour ago. It's not like Natloz to not answer his phone or not reply to a text. His phone is usually glued to his hand. This is out of character; something must be up.

He decides to ring his partner before responding to Annie. He has his number on speed dial. He can hear the ring tone and waits for a response. The call rings out.

'Hi, you've contacted Detective Natloz from the Homicide Division. I can't take your call right now but please leave a brief message and a contact number for me to get back to you, thank you.'

He sends his partner another message, hoping he gets a response this time. He then tries Annie, but that rings out, too. He wants to see if she's been in contact with Natloz.

He hears a commotion in the distance; Moore yelling like he always does. He's like a pit bull let loose amongst chickens. This guy has no filter.

'Talk to me, what do we have here?' He's making his way towards Petridis. The look on his face is deadly, like a volcano just about to erupt, or dynamite with a short fuse, or the Berlin Wall about to be pulled down.

'Are you all fucking deaf?' Moore's arms are spread in an interesting stance, wanting answers but going the wrong way about it.

Petridis moves slowly closer to Moore, each step he takes with ease, trying to steer the vessel into the narrow harbour. The vessel in Moore's head is about to pop.

'Sir, I can shed some light on what might have happened. I live across the road and made the call. I found the body and I'll tell you what I saw.'

Petridis explains how the evening unravelled, leaving out the bit about not being able to contact his partner. He didn't lie to the inspector; he just didn't tell him the entire truth. 'A team has been deployed through the gardens to look for clues and any suspicious activity.'

'Good. Keep me informed with the progress. Where is the body?'

'Right over here.'

Moore looks over his shoulder. 'And someone get me a coffee, today.'

Petridis begins putting everything in perspective. Firstly, the body found in the park. Part of the face ripped off and the clothes covered with dog hair. Natloz not responding to texts or phone calls. And Annie, the young lady whose friend was brutally murdered has sent a text sounding concerned. What does she have to say?

First things first, he needs to get in touch with Natloz.

CHAPTER 12

The first bit of light has just emerged from the dark skyline. A new day waking up from a night many would love to forget. Melbourne is experiencing some uncommon behaviour of late. The city has swept in something inhumane; something unearthly is happening to this normal but sometimes chaotic town.

Petridis wakes up to the sun peeking in through his bedroom window. His shift should have started over two hours ago. Too tired to get changed into his PJs, Petridis had fallen asleep in his jeans on the couch.

He reaches over to his phone which is sitting on the table. He taps the buttons but nothing happens; his phone is dead. He had forgotten to charge it last night. He needs to charge his phone to see if Natloz or Annie have tried calling or texting him. He hadn't heard back from either of them. Petridis looked through his bedroom door at the digital clock beside his bed and worked out he had only three hours of sleep. He spent most of the night with Moore across the road dealing with the body that was discovered.

He connects his phone to the charger in his bedroom. By the time he showers, his phone should have charged enough to get going. He turns on the water in his shower. After fifteen seconds, the room has steamed up. Petridis stands in front of his mirror, naked, staring at himself while the water overheats. He hops into the shower and lets the water run all over his body. His head is positioned downwards, staring at the water running down his legs to his toes. The water is hot, burning but sustainable. He closes his eyes and tries to picture himself elsewhere. Somewhere other than Melbourne.

He hasn't seen his work partner in over twenty-four hours, and he hasn't seen his life partner in over a month. Lenny is on holidays in Greece visiting his brother. Being gay in the police force was once frowned upon but nowadays, besides a small group of his colleagues, homosexuals are more welcomed in this society. Petridis and Lenny have been together for six years.

Petridis comes out of the bathroom with a towel wrapped around his waist. He has a slender, solid build. Years of working out in the gym clearly show on his muscular frame. His chiselled features and sexy moustache complete this attractive physical specimen.

He picks up his phone, hits the power button, and sees there is enough battery life. He waits for it to turn on fully before he is able to retrieve any texts. But when it is, there's no messages or missed calls. He stares at the phone for a little longer, just in case the messages were delayed coming through. Nope, nothing. He scrolls through his contacts and finds Natloz. There must have been a software update on his phone overnight because the speed dial contacts are no longer there.

He rings, hoping to get through. That thought is short-lived. The phone rings without being picked up. He tries again. Once more, no response. He decides to drive to his partner's house on his way to the Forensics headquarters in Richmond. He might be taking it easy for the day. But he would have called. He always called when he wasn't coming in to work.

It's dark down at the building parking area. Petridis searches for his keys. Not in his jeans pocket. He checks in the pockets of his jacket. Nothing there either. He feels something scrunched. A piece of paper. He pulls it out. It's a note.

Keys are in the wheel arch.

He checks all the arches and finds his keys sitting on the rear left tyre. Who put the keys there? Who wrote the note? Someone must have had his keys. He remembered he had them with him when he came back home. He used them to unlock the front door. Or did he? A thought halts him.

When he came back in from the busy evening his door of the apartment was open. Thinking back now, he can't remember taking his keys with him. There was an urgency to get across the street. That thing he saw. He didn't want it to escape. He makes a mental note to check his apartment but for now he needs to get to Natloz. Something doesn't feel right.

He clicks the button to unlock his car. He loves the central locking aspect of new cars. Petridis thinks it's the best automobile invention of his time. He remembers back when he was younger. The thought takes him back to the day he passed his driving test. He'd had lessons in an old Falcon. The year was 1992. His instructor was Greek; his grandparents' recommendation, of course. Everything had to be Greek.

Back then, central locking wasn't even an idea. The cars had buttons. If you had passengers, you had to lean over the front seat and lift the button that unlocked the door to let them in. A prehistoric contraption. The evolution of the automobile has changed over the years. Nowadays, cars can park themselves at the push of a button. Give it time and they will drive themselves. Punch in your destination, sit back, and sleep for the rest of the journey. Crazy but possible.

Petridis swipes the pass and the roller door lifts up. It should take him no more than twenty minutes to get to Natloz's house in Carlton which is on the outskirts of the CBD. Drive around the city instead of through. It's almost 10:00am and the sun is picture-perfect, the beams full of life and no sign of rain to dampen the mood.

Petridis pulls up in the front of his house. Natloz's car is out front. How did he get his car home? He had left it at the station yesterday. He must have had someone pick it up and drop it off at his apartment.

Petridis looks in it. The car keys are in the ignition. Why would Natloz leave the keys there? Did he forget them? Hard to know what is going on in his partner's head. He notices something in the back seat – a dirty grey towel with what looks to be grease or paint on it. He can't quite make out what it is. He'll come back to that later. He pulls on the handle of the car. It's locked.

He walks up the stairs to the front door. Natloz has a spare key in a secret hiding spot only he and Petridis know about, but the key isn't there. Nothing seems to be out of the ordinary. Doormat in place, front security door untouched. No sign of any intruder to surprise him. The door handle is locked. He tries ringing the doorbell. He can't hear the *ding dong* sound the doorbell normally makes. He knocks on the security door. After a few attempts to no avail, he knocks harder. This time he places his ear up to the door to see if he can hear anything inside. Doesn't seem like anyone is at home.

He makes his way to the end of the street. There is a laneway behind the house. The garage backs into the lane. There is also a back door that leads into his yard. The lane door is unlocked. It has always been that way. Natloz leaves it unlocked so his neighbours can drop in to water the garden when he's away.

Petridis walks through the gate and makes it to the rear door of the house. He tries the handle, and it's unlocked. This door is always locked, so it's unusual. Reacting as a police officer would, Petridis unclips his gun from the holster and holds it down beside his leg, ready to use in case he needs to. This could turn out to be a hostile situation if he's not careful. He's put himself in a dangerous position without back-up, again. He really doesn't want to have to shoot someone unexpectedly or accidentally. He enters the house cautiously. His ears sting with silence.

'Will? It's me, Spiro.'

Not a sound inside. He walks through the laundry and enters the kitchen. A couple of empty coffee mugs in the sink. The coffee machine is cold. Hasn't been used at all this morning. The bench is clean. An envelope addressed to Natloz from Telstra sits unopened on the bench. He approaches the lounge room. Television is off, half-eaten packet of Smith's salt and vinegar chips on the coffee table. Bread crumbs from what was once a sandwich sits on a plate on the couch. A glass of water filled to the top. Stains on the carpet leading out to the hallway. He can't make them out. They look identical to the stains on the grey towel in the back seat of Natloz's car.

'Police! If there is anyone in here, make yourself known now. Come out slowly with your hands where I can see them.'

He could hear a pin drop as he passes the spare room. Petridis looks inside. It looks like a dumping ground, a graveyard for unworn clothes and items that don't belong anywhere. It's a small room with a tiny window. A stale and damp smell comes from the mouldy walls. There's a hole in the top right corner of the cornice. He pushes the door open to have a better look. No one is inside. He moves further down the corridor. The next room, the largest room in the house is the front bedroom. That's Natloz's room.

The door is slightly open. There is a foul smell that trickles up his nose. The odour is creeping out from the open door. It smells like death. Or at least death has something to do with it.

'Will? Are you in there? It's Spiro. Will ... say something.'

He hears a moan. It sounds like someone is in trouble. Petridis raises his gun and aims it chest height. He holds his breath, stands firmly with both feet on the ground, arches his back and lifts his right leg up. With brute force he kicks the door wide open.

Still holding his breath, his eyes take a while to adjust to the dark. When they do, he notices the figure lying on the bed. He can't believe his eyes.

It's Natloz. Lying in a pool of blood, moaning. It's a blood bath.

CHAPTER 13

It's busy as normal at The Royal Melbourne Hospital. It's Monday, just an ordinary day following an unusual evening. Hospital staff pace the corridors doing their usual morning routines. Announcements made frequently over the PA and mechanical beeps and noises fill the air around the ward.

Natloz was rushed in that morning with unexplained puncture wounds to his entire body. He's been in the operating theatre for over five hours now, doctors trying to repair the injuries he had sustained. His body resembled a sieve. There's been no word on his condition, or how he would have sustained his injuries. Police are working frantically back at his house, trying to work out what happened. Blood had covered the carpets leading to the bedroom, the hallway, and parts of the lounge room. The majority of it was inside the four walls of his bedroom. The rest of the house was clean. Forensics had taken samples from every area in the house that had blood, including the grey towel from the car.

Petridis sees a coffee vending machine down the end of the corridor. Coffee from those machines taste like dishwater, but right now he would drink whatever came his way. He has coffee and a cigarette on his mind. He places two dollars into the machine and hits *Latte*. He considers something stronger but there isn't a pub in the hospital. This will do.

He senses someone watching him. He turns his head to the right and notices a woman at the end of the corridor, half hidden. Her eyes are fixated on Petridis. She looks creepy, like Jason Voorhees does as he sizes up his next victim. Petridis looks down at his cup, steam rising from it, and when he looks back in that direction, the creepy mystery woman is gone. The end of the corridor is empty but for an unused wheelchair.

He takes his coffee and heads towards the waiting room. Finding a seat, he takes a sip of his coffee. It's so hot he burns his lips and the inside of his mouth. He has forgotten to add sugar. Being a sweet tooth, Petridis normally has two teaspoons of sugar in his coffee and three in his tea. Tea is something he rarely drinks, which is why he compensates for the taste with the sweet sugar.

He makes a call to Forensics.

'Good morning, Dr Langer speaking.'

'Sandra, it's Detective Petridis, how are you?'

'Detective Petridis, to what do I owe this pleasure?'

'I'm ringing about the hair found on our victim last night. Anything come back on that? And what about the blood found in Detective Natloz's room? Do you have anything on that or is it too soon?'

'Yes and no.'

'What does that mean?'

'I have something on the unusual fur but nothing yet on the blood from Detective Natloz's bedroom. Too soon to make out anything yet, and it's been a busy morning. I should have that out to you by mid-afternoon.'

Petridis pauses for a second. He's not sure if he heard right. Unusual fur?

'Detective? Are you there?'

Nothing but silence, like a little boy too frightened to answer his mother when he's done something wrong. 'Did you say unusual fur?'

'Yes, I believe I did say that. That is what the test has come back with. And we're not talking dog fur, detective. We're talking something more predatorial. Something like a wolf.'

'You have me confused, Dr Langer. I don't think I'm following what you're saying.'

'The fur we collected from the victim's clothes is like that of a wolf, but it's not necessarily a wolf. Whatever it is, it's definitely not native to this continent.'

'Thank you, doc … I'll, um … get back to you. Once you have anything on the splatter at Natloz's house, please let me know right away.'

'Well, I'm here all day and doesn't seem like I'll be leaving anytime soon, so yes, I'll call you as soon as I get anything.'

The phone line goes dead. Probably not the right word to use at this point.

CHAPTER 14

After a lengthy time on the operating table, Natloz is out and resting in the ICU. He still hasn't woken from the operation. The main thing is that he's out of immediate danger, but not in the clear from any infections. A team of respected doctors are keeping a close eye on him. The hospital staff will have to be there when Natloz wakes up. Their guesstimate is within twenty-four to forty-eight hours.

The surgeon enters the room where Petridis is waiting. The detective has fallen asleep on the comfy recliner. It beats a plastic chair any day. His jacket is balled up against the wall and his head rests on the jacket. He wakes with a gentle tap on his shoulder. He opens his eyes and sees the doctor's face up close to his.

Petridis abruptly gets to his feet. 'Doc, how is—?'

'He's fine. Stable for now. We need to keep an eye on him. He is still sedated. We won't know for sure how successful the operation was for some time. He will need twenty-four hour supervision until he wakes up. He lost a lot of blood from multiple stab wounds and lacerations all over his body. He is one lucky man, detective. Someone from up above is keeping an eye on him. I did find something else, though. Something that we need to look into further.'

'What is it?'

'We found traces of two different blood groups, most likely from two different people. One of the blood groups is current, the other much older, my guess from a few weeks back. It is outdated and should have been discarded. Either way, this had to have belonged to someone and we need to find out who. I don't want to alarm you, but this other group … the older one, well, let's just say it's unique and unusual. Matter of fact, I've never come across anything like it before. We have sent a sample to Forensics and they should work out the results we are after. Once that is done and we have a DNA result, we'll pass it over so you can do your work, see if it matches anyone in the NCIDD system. This next bit I'm going to tell you is not going to sit well with you, and it's a little hard for me to explain the reasons behind it.'

'Just spit it out.'

'Detective Natloz is under police guard. There is a possibility he might have hurt someone severely, or worse. We are phoning around other hospitals to see if anyone has been admitted with similar injuries. We'll keep you posted.'

'Detective Natloz hasn't killed anyone, if that's what you're saying. You've got it wrong. No fucking way would he kill anyone unless it was self-defence.'

Petridis thinks back to the previous night when he wasn't able to get in contact with Natloz. Best not to mention that.

Taken aback by the response, Dr Ludwig now faces the task of keeping Natloz away from others, especially the media. They would have a field day if this information was leaked. He will inform all staff to keep tight-lipped.

'Like I said, Detective Natloz will be under police guard and supervision until we have a better understanding of what has happened, and who this blood belongs to. I'm sorry, but that is protocol.'

Petridis watches him leave. An announcement comes over the PA.

'Telephone call for Detective Petridis, call for Detective Petridis. Please make your way to ICU Station 2.'

Petridis heads over to the nurses station. He rests his elbows on the counter and tells the nurse that he is Petridis. She hands him the phone and presses the flashing key.

'Hello, Detective Petridis speaking.'

'Meet me at the café on the ground floor in ten minutes. Don't be late.'

The phone goes quiet. A dead tone rings in his ear. He drops the phone and bolts towards the lift, stumbling over a bag of dirty laundry that was left on the floor. He reaches the lift but before he has a chance to press the down button, a small child hits up. The kid looks up and gives Petridis a dirty smile.

You little shit, thinks Petridis. He would love to give this kid a piece of his mind, but decides against it – he's the adult here. He heads for the stairs. The stairs are narrow and steep – he's fit but his fitness is still tested. Petridis takes two steps at a time, trying to make up the time he lost with the elevator. The look on the kid's face pops into his head once more. Damn kid. He jumps the last three steps in one leap. The café is ahead of him, but it's closed. A sign on the door says:

UNDER NEW MANAGEMENT
RE-OPENING SEPTEMBER 2ND
PLEASE USE OUR OTHER CAFÉ
LOCATED ON LEVEL 2
SORRY FOR THE INCONVENIENCE

'Are you serious? Fuck!' Petridis couldn't believe his luck. The first thing that pops into his head is that the caller is playing him and pushing his patience. He decides to head up there anyway. It might not be a hoax. He heads back to the lift and hits up. The light above the lift says it's coming from level 10. More lost time.

He has to decide to either wait for the lift or walk up the two flights of stairs. He chooses the stairs.

He runs up the first flight and notices someone entering the stairs via the side door on level 1. A young couple of hospital staff in green uniforms, nurses or orderlies. He speeds past them, his shoulder brushing up against the other guy. They exchange looks. One foul, the other doesn't give a shit.

'Police business.' yells Petridis as he continues up the stairs. He reaches the second level and barges through the door, looks both ways, and notices the café to his left. It's a small café with a handful of tables and chairs. A woman is sitting on her own, the only person in there besides the two elderly ladies working behind the counter. He approaches her with caution. He doesn't know who she is. He has never seen this woman before.

'Did you have me paged? Was that you on the phone?'

'Detective Petridis, it's me … Annie.'

She's in disguise.

CHAPTER 15

Annie and Petridis sit at a table at the furthest corner of the café. One of the workers behind the counter is on a call with a friend, planning a day out on the bowling greens. The look on her face shows her excitement.

Annie has transformed herself into someone completely different. She has done a great job with her appearance, but who is she trying to elude?

'I tried calling you last night after I received your text,' Petridis says. 'The phone rang out. What happened to you? Are you okay?'

'I'm doing fine, I think.'

'You look like you haven't slept in days.'

'I haven't. I'm … I'm tired and scared that someone might be after me, too. Someone killed Sally, and then they killed Oscar. I don't know what is happening.'

'We're looking into the murder. No one has come forward with any information yet. The media is doing their part. It's all over the papers and TV. Someone will come forward with the information we're seeking. Where have you been?'

'I've been staying at a friend's house. I haven't been out in days. I'm so afraid.'

'Have you eaten?'

'Yes … I think I have … yes, I have eaten. I'm not thinking straight. I can't stop thinking about Sally and Oscar. That person said he saw something not human attack Sally. What was it? Do you know? Have you spoken to Sally's parents? They would be so devastated.'

'The police departments in their hometowns were informed about the deaths. Both families have been notified.'

Breaking the news to the family was hard. Sally's mum still lives in Broome. Her dad lives in Fremantle. Both had been notified. Oscar's parents in Perth took it pretty badly. His brother is flying in from Singapore. He's been living there for the last year.

'Is there anything you can tell me that might help with the investigation? Have you heard from anyone or has anyone approached you?'

'No, no one has spoken to me. I haven't been out. My friend is overseas. She has let me use her house.'

'It is really important, think hard. You might have heard something about the death?'

'I haven't heard a thing. Who would do something like this?'

'I don't know. There are sick people out there. How did you know where to find me?'

'I was there.'

'Where?'

'At Detective Natloz's house.'

What was she doing at Natloz's house? Did she have something to do with the attack?

'Did you—?'

'No, it wasn't me,' she interrupts. 'I promise. It wasn't.'

'What did you see? Was someone there?'

Annie stares at the detective, her eyes focused on his chest. She doesn't move a muscle as she thinks about what she had seen. The events from the other night are hazy. She will try her best to remember every detail she can, not leaving anything out.

'I watched as the detective parked his car. He got out but was staggering. He was unstable on his feet, like he was drunk or something.'

'That's bizarre because I dropped him off at home. Did he have anything in his hands? Was he holding anything?'

'I don't think he was holding anything. His hands were free because he had to hold onto the car to steady himself. At one point I thought he was going to fall over.'

'Where were you standing at this point?'

'I was across the road. There is a wide nature strip in between the two roads.'

'What happened then?'

'As he came up to the gutter, he stumbled over it and had to sit down. He had his head between his legs and his hands up to his face. I thought he was praying or something like that. Possibly even crying.'

'Did he see you at all?'

'No. I doubt it. I just stood there watching him from across the road. There was a large tree blocking his view. I could see him but he couldn't see me. At one point, I honestly thought he was going to pass out, you know, like I honestly thought he was drunk.'

'Then what happened?'

'He eventually got back to his feet. He went to his front gate and leant over to his right. He crouched down a bit and I think he threw up in the flowers. That's what It looked like from where I was standing.'

'At any point did anyone approach him or did he use his phone?'

'The phone rang twice but he didn't answer it. I don't think he realised that his phone had been ringing. He looked like he was in a trance, hypnotised. He got to the front door. This is where it got strange. He knocked on his own front door like he was the visitor and waiting for someone to answer it.'

'Did anyone answer the door?'

'No, he waited there for a bit and then left.'

'Where did he go?'

'I followed him around to the back of the house. There is a laneway there. He walked down it.'

'Did you follow him down there?'

'No. It was dark and I got scared. I didn't know what was down there, so I didn't go. I don't know what happened after that. What do you think happened to him?'

'Not sure. I found him in his room. He had stab wounds all over his body. We're looking into it now.'

'That's terrible. I found out from one of the triage nurses that he's doing okay. Will he live?'

'Yes, I believe he will. Where are you going to go now? Are you still at your friend's place? I suggest you give me the address in case I need to check up on you.'

Annie writes down the address where she is staying. It's not far from where Natloz lives. They say their goodbyes before Annie gets up and walks out of the café. She heads towards the lift. Petridis is about to order another coffee to take with him when his phone buzzes.

'Detective Petridis, it's Dr Ludwig. You need to come now. Your partner has just opened his eyes. He's awake.'

CHAPTER 16

Natloz has been placed in a room of his own. Uniformed police guard the door to make sure no one unauthorised enters. Nobody yet knows whether Natloz is a victim or a suspect. Just by looking at him, you would think he's definitely the victim but looks can be deceiving.

'Knock-knock, buddy.'

Natloz gives him a painful smile. His arms, legs, and torso are heavily bandaged. It seems as though Natloz is in some discomfort. It brings a tear to Petridis's eye – flashbacks of what went down flood his mind. 'How are you feeling? Sorry, wrong question.'

'Like shit. Like I've been hit by a runaway bus.' He lets out a cry of pain.

Sorrow builds up inside Petridis. 'It's okay, mate, no need to talk. Just rest.'

'No … I need to talk. I need to explain what happened.'

'Do you remember anything that happened last night?'

'I remember stopping for food and eating it. I remember the drive home, but I … I don't remember if I was driving … I don't know what happened after that. I have a mental blank. To be honest, I don't think I was in my car. Someone else was driving. That part is still a blur.'

'It's okay. Take your time, mate. Do you remember getting into the house?'

'Um, not sure. I need to …'

Natloz takes a moment to try and remember. Nothing comes to him. His memory is blocked with a haze, a cloud, a wall of forgetfulness. He fights with his inner self to remember. Frustration and anger build up.

'I'm on your side, buddy. No matter what the fuckers at the station think, I'm on your side. You're my partner. I believe you.'

Natloz turns his head away from Petridis and stares out the window. It's a gloomy day. Rain lightly falling. The world continues outside without him. People do what they normally do during the day. Some good, some bad. Part of him is glad he's inside and not out there. But, then again, his day is not any better inside. He tries to remember what else happened that night. His memory has been washed away by the rain.

'I want to remember, Spiro, I really do. It's like … it's like something inside my head doesn't want me to remember. I'm feeling lost. What happened, Spiro? What happened to me? What have I done?'

Petridis takes a seat on the chair beside Natloz. He explains the horrors that had unfolded. How Natloz was found in his house covered in blood, stabbed multiple times, deep wounds and traces of two other blood types on him.

The world is caving in on Natloz. Everything he had worked for is coming down in a heap. Everything he stood for, the badge, the honour, everything is now in jeopardy. The thought of having killed others in the process is making him sick. Maybe he should vomit out all the monstrous bile that has built inside him. Maybe the truth might come out, too.

Petridis puts his hand on Natloz's shoulder. A gesture of care. Petridis knows him well enough to know how he's feeling. Not knowing what has transpired is eating Natloz up.

There's a commotion outside the door. The door is closed but whatever is happening out there, it's loud and argumentative. Petridis quickly stands up and makes his way over there. Before he has a chance to reach the door, it swings open with tremendous force. Chief Inspector Moore with his six-foot-five frame comes barging through, a sense of authority like he owns the place.

'Detective Petridis, I thought I'd find you here. How is Detective Natloz doing?'

'Ask him yourself, sir.'

Moore gives Petridis a sideways look. His eyes squint and his left eyebrow raises. 'Well, Detective Natloz, how are you feeling?'

There is a long pause. Natloz is trying to muster up the energy to respond, fixated more on what is happening outside the window than inside. He would rather be anywhere else than there in hospital. He would rather be asking the questions than being asked them.

'I asked you a question, detective. Don't ignore me.'

'Ease up, chief,' says an annoyed Petridis. 'He's just woken up. Go easy on him for Christ's sake. Have a heart.'

Moore looks at Petridis. Getting to the position of Chief Inspector wasn't an easy haul, and being nice wasn't how he did it. He turns back to Natloz. 'You have some fundamental issues here, detective. Do you know the situation you're in? The superficial accusations against you? The odds are stacked against you Natloz. Do you have anything to say?'

Natloz slowly turns his head and looks at Moore. His eyes are shot red. A look of despair and acknowledgment. 'I've been told what has happened. My question to you is, do you think I did it? Any of it? Do you believe I am capable of willingly hurting another human being?'

'It's not up to me to make a decision like that, son. It's not going to make a difference what I think. These are strong accusations.

I'm here to tell you that once you are cleared, you need to take some time off. Go away for a month or two. Disappear from the city. Recover and clear your mind. This won't get any easier. You need to deal with it.'

'I need to know, sir.'

'Know what?'

'Do you think I am capable of doing this?'

The question sits there like tightly packed frozen peas. It could only mean one thing. A stare down between the two.

'Capable? Yes. Do I think you would do it? No. Either way, you have my and the entire division's support. Now get yourself better. That's an order.'

Moore leaves. Elvis has left the building. That is the exact presence Moore has in the force.

Tears begin to form in Natloz's eyes. Moore is on his side. The inspector has ordered him to take some time off once he is up to it, and Natloz will take up that offer. He needs a break from all this. If he doesn't, he might end up in the same plot with his dad.

Petridis goes to close the door and notices the uniformed officer who was sitting outside the room has collected his stuff and vanished. He closes the door and walks back to his partner. His thoughts are interrupted once again, this time by a knock at the door. A yellow A4 envelope is slipped under it. It slides across the floor and comes to rest at the size eleven boot of Petridis. There is something written on the front.

Detective

Natloz tells him to open it. 'What is it?'

'Photos.'

'Photos of what?'

The world stops for a brief moment. 'Of you leaving the park across from my apartment on the night of the murder.'

CHAPTER 17

Natloz was discharged from hospital four weeks later. It's going to take a while for him to fully recover from his injuries. Medication is packed neatly into a brown paper bag, given to him along with a get-well card signed by all the kitchen staff who looked after him, meal-wise.

His mind is still blank from that evening. He knows his job is dangerous and it comes with all sorts of issues, but who would go to that extent to kill him? It's a question for another time. He's reluctantly agreed to take a two-week vacation, as instructed. He has also decided not to tell anyone where he is going, including his partner. He's hoping he'll understand why.

An Uber drops him off at his house. Canning Street is a little quiet for that time of the day. His place is a stone's throw away from Lygon Street, one of the busiest strips of Italian eateries. Over the years, other cultural eateries have opened up there but Lygon Street will always be known as Little Italy.

Natloz walks up to his front door and dread sinks in. What if things are still as they were on the night of the attack? What if he remembers what happened, and it puts a damper on his time off?

He unlocks the door. Before he steps in, he takes a few moments to collect his thoughts. Four weeks ago, he was lying in a pool of blood on his bed. That room is located just inside the front door. He's not sure he can cope if the room hasn't changed. The thoughts are short-lived. He bites the bullet and enters the house.

His eyes automatically move towards his bedroom. Most of the items have been removed. Sheets, pillows, doona, and rug. He rifles through his drawers for clothes, grabs a handful of items and accessories, and shoves them into a backpack. Then he locks the house back up and writes a note for his neighbours, telling them he will be gone and for them to keep an eye on his place. He drops it in their letterbox.

He thinks about his own parents. What if his parents were here? How hard would it have been as a parent to be told that your son has been hurt and is fighting for his life? That there is a possibility he won't make it? That would be their worst nightmare, to hear those dreadful words from the doctor. *'We did everything we could to save him, but … Our hearts and prayers go out to you and your family.'* He tries not to think about it. Unfortunately, those thoughts can't be deleted and will remain with him until further notice.

He walks to the back of his house via the laneway, presses the button on the remote, and watches the garage door slowly make its way up, revealing his prized possession. A '65 Shelby GT Mustang is sitting there, ready to be released into the wild. He hops in and places the keys in the ignition. The beast comes to life with a huge roar, the entire garage vibrating with excitement. He reverses it carefully, making sure he doesn't hit anything. The narrow laneway doesn't give the car much room. His other car, the old one he uses everyday has been taken in by forensics to see what more they can find.

Before he puts it into drive, he connects his phone to Bluetooth and opens up his Spotify app. He scrolls through until he finds what he is looking for; an eighties playlist he loves listening to. He hits shuffle and right off the bat, the song *Summer of '69* by Bryan Adams comes on. The volume is cranked up and the windows wound down. It is a beautiful morning. The air is fresh and road clear.

Natloz heads towards the freeway, aiming for Geelong. His home for the next two weeks is going to be Apollo Bay.

The drive to Apollo Bay usually takes just under three hours, but today he's going to take his time and get there whenever. After a quick stop at a chemist for additional painkillers, he is back in the car and on his way. He decides to take the scenic route along the coast. It will take a little longer, but the drive will keep him calm and relaxed.

The wind is blowing through the car like an air conditioner turned up to full. The smell of the ocean takes the detective back to when he was a kid. His godparents had a holiday house in Portarlington, a little beach town about half an hour past Geelong. He has fond memories of his time there.

This one time when he was about eight years old, before his godparents had bought the house, they had a caravan that was stationed in the Fairhaven Caravan Park. It was about three blocks from the beach. Young Natloz had named that part of beach 'The Cove'. Mud steps were carved out of the large rock that led down to the water. It was always packed, overpopulated with families. Kids ran around like headless chooks. They screamed and played in the water, splashing and making a racket. Natloz's favourite game that he played with his cousins was 'Classic Catches'. They would get in a circle and throw a tennis ball out wide to where you were standing. The object of the game was to see who could do the best dive catching the ball. The prize was bragging rights, which was something Will loved doing the most. Those were the days.

One night in the caravan, around 2:00am, Will woke up screaming in pain. He was holding his abdomen, feeling like it was about to explode. Not knowing what was wrong, his godmother suggested to wait it out until the morning. If the pain was still there, they would take him to the hospital. She gave him tea to ease the pain, but nothing helped young Will.

At 4:15am, Will's godfather made the decision to take him to the hospital. The closest one was in Geelong. He drove the car up the Emergency ramp and stopped right in front of the doors. Medical personnel came out to assess the situation. At that time of the morning there was no way to phone the hospital in advance to let them know they were coming. The caravan park office was closed and mobile phones had not been invented yet. Will was rushed to surgery within minutes. The outcome was appendicitis. If Will's godparents had waited until morning, his appendix would have ruptured and Will would have died.

Close calls have followed Natloz his entire life. He's had a few too many to mention. The last one had been four weeks ago. That memory has taken over all the others and has pushed its way to the front, leaving the others way behind. But … how can he remember things from his childhood yet nothing from just weeks back?

Natloz reaches Apollo Bay with lots of daylight still left. It's just after 3:00pm. He pulls up at an IGA supermarket. He needs to stock up on some things. He hops out of the car and gets the whiff of salty seaweed air. Glancing over to the beach across the road from the supermarket, he sees a whole bunch of kids playing beach cricket. He hears one boy yell, 'My turn, my turn!'

A group of guys gather around his car, admiring the beauty. Natloz lets them look as he enters the store to pick up some supplies for the next couple of weeks, and most importantly, some beer. Dinner tonight will be fish 'n' chips. He's been told that

Theo's makes the best fish 'n' chips along the coast. There is one other place in Torquay that comes close, but apparently Theo's wins hands down.

He leaves the store and heads up the hill towards the house he has booked through Airbnb. It's a little one-bedroom shack that stands alone amongst some units. He drives up the long driveway and parks his car right in front. The units have their own carport attached to them. He gets out and stands there admiring the view. The shack is so far up the hill it overlooks miles and miles of ocean. If you head south by boat, you would come across King Island, Tasmania a little further out. A larger boat is needed to get out that far. And if you were a thrill seeker, you can go a little further than that and hit Antarctica. How's that for an adventure? But for now, Natloz is staying put in Apollo Bay. Rest and recover.

He unlocks the front door and walks into the musty shack. The air is subtle and stale, like it hasn't been used in a while. Natloz walks around the place and opens the windows to let some air in. There is no back door; a poorly designed shack with only one entry and exit. No fire escapes. He expected more for the overly priced, yet underachieving hut. The photos of the place made it look bigger. It will have to do. Beggars can't be choosers.

He heads back out to the car and brings in his bag and groceries. It's still quite early for dinner so he twists the top off a beer and sits outside on the balcony to drink it. The view is breathtaking. If you listen carefully, you can hear the waves crashing onto the shore. He closes his eyes and for a moment he fades away into childhood memories. Soft visions appear before him, which make him smile.

He remembers the envelope he received at the hospital, photos secretly taken of him at the park. He's brought them out with him and places them next to him. He takes a long swig of his beer and puts the bottle down. He opens the envelope and pulls out the photos. As he stares at the first photo, his phone starts ringing. He jumps at the sound. The volume was set on high. A private number.

'Hello, Detective Natloz speaking.'

The line stays quiet for a while. A sweet female voice cracks the silence. Soft, but sounding scared.

'Detective … it's Annie. Annie Carter. Not sure if you remember me?'

He has to think for a brief moment to wade through his hazy and clogged memories. Then it comes to him. 'I do remember you. How can I help?'

'I need to see you.'

'I'm on vacation. Ordered to take time and rest. It will have to wait.'

'It can't wait. I need to see you.'

'What's so important that can't wait?'

'It was me, detective. I was the one who slipped the photos under the door in the hospital.'

CHAPTER 18

It wasn't long after their conversation that Natloz received a text from Petridis.

Hey buddy,

Hope all is well. Rest up, you're going to need it. Lots of work piling up on your desk ha-ha. I hear the fish are jumping out of water this time of the year. Catch a live one.

Here if you need me.

Later

By fish, Petridis is referring to women; there are lots of single mums that go to Apollo Bay this time of the year. Petridis had a fair idea where Natloz was heading but wasn't certain of it.

Natloz had decided to give Annie the address and allow her to come up. He is curious as to what she has to tell him. She's catching a Greyhound bus from the depot up to Apollo Bay. She needs to talk with him about the photos. *What was he doing in the park that evening?* He could probably ask her the same thing.

Annie recalls Petridis asking her if she had noticed anything unusual about Natloz's behaviour that night she saw him, but

Annie had left out the detail about seeing Natloz in the park; the same park where that body was discovered. She doesn't know that Petridis lives across from there.

Four bottles of beer had piled up next to the envelope. At the rate Natloz is drinking, he will surely end up with enough bottles to play tenpin bowling.

He can see a red car slowly approaching the shack. The plates read 'ANNEEE'. You don't need to be a brain surgeon to work out who it is. But to his surprise it wasn't her; funnily enough, it's the lady who has rented the unit next door to Natloz. He finds out she and her boyfriend are staying there for the weekend. Some coincidence having the same name. Luckily Natloz is not a brain surgeon.

Annie pulls up not long after in an Uber. She booked one from the town centre once she got off the bus. It pulls up a little further down the driveway. She opens the door and gets out. The driver remains in the car. Prepaid rides are the way to go these days. As soon as her door closes, the driver sparks up a cigarette. Highly illegal for Uber drivers to be smoking in their vehicle. Natloz is tired and can't be bothered saying anything to him. He's trying to keep a low profile and not make it known he's a detective on rest leave. The driver opens his window and the cigarette smoke escapes like a signal that's heading to the town over the hill.

Annie looks like she hasn't slept in days. She was wearing a black Puma jumper and grey tracksuit pants, and Converse sneakers with different coloured ankle-high socks. One pink and one yellow. She closes the door and walks around the back to the boot. The boot is already open when she gets there, the latch released from inside the car by the driver. She grabs her bag and closes the boot. The car vanishes down the slope, waiting for his next call-out.

Along with her bag, she is also carrying a 10-pack of pear-flavoured Somersby cider. She's planning for a longer visit than expected. She walks up the stairs and sits down next to Natloz. She places the ciders next to her and gives him a half-hearted hug that surprises him. His instincts tell him to hug her back, so he opens his arms and gives Annie a hug in return, whilst trying not to hurt his healing wounds.

'I'm scared,' Annie says abruptly. 'I came to the hospital needing to see you. I waited until the officer moved away from protecting your room and I slipped the envelope under the door. I think someone might be after me.'

'Why would they be after you?'

'I don't know. I can't think of anyone who would want to hurt me, but they hurt Sally and Oscar. I haven't done anything to anyone. I don't know why they would be after me, but I'm so scared.'

Natloz doesn't know what to say. They sit there infused in the fear. The silence lasts longer than it should – Natloz can see the use-by date on it. It expired about fifteen seconds ago.

'I don't think they're after you, Annie. I think it was a random attack on Sally. We still don't know for sure anyone had anything to do with Oscar's death.'

'But how did Oscar die then?'

'Oscar's death is a mystery to us. I don't have an answer for you yet.'

He does know that there was no evidence in or around the cell to indicate Oscar was murdered. The DNA on Oscar's body, including his hands, is his own. The investigation is leaning towards Oscar taking his own life. Natloz is not going to share that news with Annie yet.

They both sit there staring out at the serene ocean. It is past 6:00 in the evening. His stomach is growling and he knows it's time to eat. Time to order some food. He looks at her bag.

'My guess is you're planning to stay the night? Do you have anywhere to stay?'

'Well, no. I had planned to stay, but hadn't booked anything.'

'I'll give you the bed. I'm happy to sleep on the couch. The company will be good for both of us.'

'That won't be too much of a problem?'

'Yes' would be the real answer to that question, but Natloz wasn't going to mention what he thought. Sometimes it's best not to repeat one's thoughts, especially out loud.

'It'll be fine. We'll have to call your Uber driver back to take us into town for food. I can't afford to have a DUI on top of whatever else they're planning on throwing at me.'

They both chuckle. Annie books the Uber.

Theo's is busy. They order food and a numbered docket is handed over to Annie by Theo himself, a good-looking Greek immigrant with a slight accent. Dark black hair slicked back like a rocker from the sixties. No sign of greying yet; he must have youthful genes running through his veins. For someone of his age, he looks bloody fantastic. Theo's daughter, Chrisoula, and his son, Vasilios work there in the evenings on weekends. Uni and their social life take up most of the week in Geelong. Weekends are usually reserved for family and helping out in the shop.

Annie and Natloz wait for their order to be made. They sit at a little table just outside the shop. Theo told them it would take about fifteen minutes – enough time to start the discussion about the photos and why Natloz was at the park.

'Why did you follow me?' he asks.

'I had rung you so many times but you hadn't picked up. I sent you multiple texts, too. It seemed to me you were avoiding my calls or like you didn't want to talk to me. My friends were killed and I wanted answers. I was scared and I knew the police could help me. I knew you could help me.'

The detective kept quiet. Listening, but not listening. He felt he was caught in two different worlds. One he lived in, and the one he floated to and from – the one he never remembers anything about. He's not sure which one he is in right now.

'You're safe now. Can you tell me what you were doing out at the park that night spying on me?'

'I wasn't spying on you. It was a coincidence – I was walking to a friend's house when I saw you walk out of the park. You didn't seem yourself. You looked lost. Like you were someone else.'

He thinks about how he would look if he were someone else. Probably better than how he's looking now. A smile trickles onto his face. Annie doesn't notice.

'Then what did I do?'

'You stopped at the corner. You had your arm out calling a cab.'

'Did one come?'

'Yes, but not right away. I called out to you but you mustn't have heard me. I called out twice. A cab eventually pulled up, and you hopped in and it drove off.'

'So, you followed me?'

'Yes. I had to find a cab but there weren't any around. I tried an app and luckily there was a cab just dropping someone off up ahead. If that hadn't happened, I would surely have lost you.'

'How did the driver catch up so fast?'

'It's Melbourne. Pay the driver a little more and they'll get you there faster. They don't drive slowly when you dangle cash in front of them. I had offered to throw him an extra twenty if he caught up to the cab you were in, and then he was driving like he was on *The Amazing Race*. Sorry to mention this to a detective, but he didn't follow the road rules like he should have.'

They both smile at that.

'The cab you were in dropped you off at your house. I didn't know that at the time. You got out of the cab, unlocked your car and put something in the back seat. Locked it again and went about your unusual business. You began acting weird in front of your house. You knocked on your door like you were expecting someone to come out. When no one did, you walked around the back of the house down the laneway before disappearing. I waited about ten minutes, then left.'

'So, my car was already at my house? I don't use cabs, I drive everywhere. Are you sure it was me? Come to think of it, my partner dropped me off that day. The photos, were they taken with your phone?'

'No. I carry my digital camera everywhere I go. And yes, your car was already there. I am 100% sure it was you. The photos won't lie.'

Natloz thinks about what Annie has just said and not much is making any sense to him.

'Did you see me do anything … like … kill anyone?' Natloz continues.

'No. I feel like you could never hurt an innocent person.'

They look at each other briefly before turning their attention to the beach once more. Theo's voice calls from inside the shop. 'Number 24.'

Natloz gets up from his seat and makes his way inside to get the food while Annie waits outside. A group of teens have gathered outside the shop and are yelling abuse to another group across the road. The argument escalates, things heating up pretty quickly. Natloz hadn't noticed the commotion right away. It was loud in the shop and his mind was elsewhere.

The teens from across the road start to cross over. It looks like trouble is brewing. Turf war that is about to end badly for one group. There is going to be trouble and Annie is stationed right in the middle of it. The most intelligent teen phrase is used – 'Fuck you!' The argument escalates to a rumble. Weapons are produced. Bats and chains, and even a knife.

Someone runs into the store. 'Call the cops, Theo!'

Natloz looks out the window and sees Annie in harm's way. From that moment on, everything moves in slow motion. He can't move quick enough. His own injuries prevent him. Annie falls to the ground. The metallic smell of blood fills the air along with thunderous punching sounds. The two groups panic when they see Natloz and a few other customers running out. Theo is dialling the police.

Annie is on the ground, hurt. She isn't moving.

CHAPTER 19

Annie opens her eyes. Natloz is sleeping on the chair next to her. He has his feet up on the edge of the bed. He looked as comfortable as a weightlifter in a hundred-meter backstroke final.

Looking at Natloz, Annie realises she has grown fond of him as a father figure. Her dad is thousands of miles away, and Natloz reminds her of him.

Natloz feels Annie move, and it wakes him. He looks at her happily. 'How you doing, kid?'

'I'm okay. Did you sleep here the entire night?'

He looks down at his clothes before answering. 'Yeah, looks that way. Someone needed to keep an eye on you, seeing as you don't have any family here. I feel a little stiff though. I might be walking like a crab until my bones and muscles loosen up.'

Annie smiles, and puts her hand on her head. There's a bandage covering most of it. 'What happened?'

'One of the teens came running across the road swinging a chain. It hit you across the side of your head. You hit the pavement quite hard. You stopped breathing. Quite a frightening situation. The gang of teens came back and confessed to the local police.'

Annie asks, 'Did you get the chips at least?'

Natloz points at the small table beside her bed where cold, unopened fish 'n' chips sit.

'Never got to find out if all the hype was true or not. There's always next time.'

Soon Annie dozes off again, but Natloz is awake and wants a coffee. He goes in search of a caffeine hit.

Later, the discharge papers come through and he pushes Annie in a wheelchair to his waiting chariot. He opens the door and helps Annie in. They drive back to the shack and spend the rest of the holidays relaxing. Annie has to recover before they are able to drive back to Melbourne. Natloz has almost fully recovered from his injuries and he is eager to get back to work. There are quite a few more bad guys to catch, and murders to solve.

The drive back isn't as exciting as his drive up. They drive in silence listening to music Annie has chosen. Natloz had compromised his eighties tunes for music he couldn't understand. He peered over and noticed Annie smiling. That was worth the compromise.

Petridis had updated Natloz that morning. Everything had been quiet in Melbourne over the last two weeks – not a single murder that was related to the ones Natloz and Petridis were investigating. No animal attacks, no beast sightings, nothing. It's like the crime spree had taken a vacation. That seems a little odd considering four bodies had surfaced within three days. It doesn't make any sense.

After dropping Annie off at her friend's house, Natloz drives himself to the office. He pulls up at the station and parks his car in the spot marked with his name. He walks through the main doors and into a cheering office. It was like running through the banner on Grand Final Day. Natloz is overwhelmed with the response from his colleagues.

'Good to have you back,' says a voice from the back of the room.

Petridis greets him with a hug, which he finds a little embarrassing – two blokes hugging is never something he'd do. The hug and cheek kissing is a Greek thing Petridis grew up doing with men and women, though he keeps the kisses hidden for later. He doesn't want to further embarrass Natloz – his cheeks are already rosy red.

'Aw, you blushing mate?' Petridis says with a smile.

'Real men hug,' yells out Constable Lyon. The whole crew starts laughing.

Petridis feels his phone buzz in his pocket. It's Dr Langer. 'Detective Petridis. I tried calling Detective Natloz. His phone is not connecting or it might be switched off. I have something to show you both.'

'He was on leave, but he's just returned back to work today. Great timing. What is it?'

'I don't want to discuss it over the phone. Can you both come down here now?'

'Sure. Give us half an hour.'

Petridis makes his way over to Natloz. He interrupts the little mothers club meeting.

'Sorry, mums. Police business.'

'What is it?' Natloz asks.

'Langer just called. She's got something she wants to show us.'

'Perfect timing' says Natloz.

'That's what I said.'

The detectives grab their stuff and head out the door. The Forensics building is a short drive from the station.

'How was your time away?'

'Relaxing.'

'Just relaxing?'

'Just relaxing.'

'Hmm.'

They drove the rest of the way exchanging small talk about things not related to their work. They arrive at the lab in less than twelve minutes and park underneath the building in the area for authorised vehicles only. A pass on the windscreen lets the car in. They park in the closest spot to the elevator, and hop out.

'So, what did you get up to?'

'Not much. I wanted to try Theo's in Apollo Bay but didn't get around to it. Things just popped up. Worth the drive up there just for the chips they say. Hung out and relaxed.'

'You've said relaxed three times. How relaxing was it?'

'Very.'

Petridis gives Will a stupid look.

'Okay. What do you want to know? Annie came up. It was unexpected. She came up to talk to me about the photos.'

The lift opens. A couple of uniformed officers walk out. Natloz and Petridis take their place inside the lift. At this point, elevator music would have been ideal to break the monotony. He's quite sure that the discussion about Annie coming to Apollo Bay will continue at a later stage. The lift door opens up and they step out and get straight into police business mode. The conversation about the relaxing time off Natloz had ends there. Dr Langer's office is at the end of the corridor. The last room on the left, to be precise.

The detectives get to her office, and notice through the window that Peter Kirby is with her. They knock. Dr Langer waves them in.

'That was quick,' she says.

'We had just arrived at the office when you rang. What's up?'

'You remember Peter, don't you? He's one of the leading analysts here, and also my right-hand man.'

'Good morning, detectives. Nice to see you both again.'

'Yes, yes it is,' says Natloz.

Petridis confirms with a nod. Sometimes a simple nod is all is needed.

'I'm quite sure you know why you are both here.'

'The fur?'

'Yes. At first we thought it was from a dog. But when we studied it closer, we found it belonged to something more than just a dog. We found two different types of fur as you're well aware of. One was long and stiff, outer fur called guard hairs. The second was more like an undercoat, soft fur that grows thick during winter. Seeing that we are coming to the end of winter, it makes sense that it's falling out.'

'Okay, so what you're saying is that this fur we found on the victim is animal fur, but not necessarily from a dog,' Petridis asks. 'But something like a dog, right?' You've already told us that.

'Yes I have and I can confirm It's not from a dog.'

'Okay. So what's it from?' asks Natloz.

'A wolf.'

CHAPTER 20

The bodies of Sally and Oscar were finally released to their respective families. They had ample time to prepare funeral arrangements. Both bodies were flown back to Perth.

Annie had received a copy of the obituary from Sally's family. She had met Sally's mum, Raechelle, and her aunty, Merri, when they had made the trip to Melbourne to visit Sally last August. They had come to celebrate the wonderful year Sally had had. That had been the only time that year Sally had seen her family.

They'd gone as a group, including Oscar, to Phillip Island to watch the penguin parade. It was cold and wet, perfect for the little fairy penguins. The evening wasn't any better weather-wise. They had dinner that night in Cowes. Nothing fancy – Pino's Trattoria. Pizza and pasta, everybody's favourite. Annie watched Sally and her mum interact, laughing and crying. It was sad because Annie could relate to them missing each other. She watched them enjoy their time together like it was the last night on earth. That made her realise how much she missed her family back home. Mum, Dad, and her siblings. Annie missed them all equally. The heartache of living abroad.

Natloz decided to make the trip over to Perth with Annie after she had asked him to, mainly to keep an eye on her. He felt the need to attend for moral support, and also for her safety. Plus, it would be a good opportunity to get to know who her friends were. That could help in the investigation. You never know what that could lead to. Protect the only living survivor of the three from a potential serial killer. Annie could possibly be the next target.

The service for Sally is held at Mareena Purslowe Funeral Home in South Fremantle. The chapel holds approximately ninety guests indoors while a further few hundred remain outside. Speakers were placed outside for the guests who couldn't fit in the room. It's nineteen degrees, the average temperature for that time of the year. The sun is out and the crows have gathered by the dozen. A norm for funerals.

The service is conducted by the family's parish priest, Father Jordan. He has known the family for over twenty years. Father Jordan had watched Sally grow from a young girl to a loveable teen. The ceremony is so beautifully organised that it runs smoothly. There are lots of people crying and cuddling. Sally's old school friends and teachers all turned up. A large projector screen provides an abundance of happy memories in a slideshow, Sally's life the way her friends and family remember it. There are photos from when she was a baby right through to her teens and adulthood. Annie had provided the family with many photos from their time together in Melbourne, many of which pictured Sally and Oscar together, sharing laughter and fun. Father Jordan also spoke about Oscar and his tragic death.

Oscar's funeral will be held tomorrow at a different location. His family have done it that way so people who have travelled from interstate have the opportunity to attend both funerals.

The final speech is conducted by Sally's father, Brian. He broke down and cried while sharing with the others the words he had written down on paper, the love he had for his daughter and the short amount of time they had together, and a trip to Singapore that was meant to happen next year. His little baby taken from him before her time. His dreams shattered and a life not worth living for now. May she rest in peace.

Sally's final resting place is Karrakatta Cemetery in Perth. It opened for burials in the late 1800s. The most famous resident there is Australian actor Heath Ledger. The grounds are well manicured with flowers and shrubs, bringing brightness to this beautiful haven. The bright foliage covers the cemetery plots from end to end.

People gather around the casket before it is lowered into that dreadful hole in the ground that goes six feet down. A place we all end up when our expiration date comes.

Father Jordan finishes with a soft, 'Amen.' The family come through first, all with a handful of dirt that they sprinkle over the casket; their final goodbyes. It takes over twenty-five minutes before the final person gives their condolences to the family and drops soil into the ground.

Natloz and Annie walk slowly back to their rental car and drive back to the motel in silence. The only noise comes from the engine and the passing cars.

'Can we please stop to buy some wine?' she asks, breaking the silence.

He nods. 'Are you hungry?'

'I guess I can eat something. I shouldn't drink on an empty stomach.'

'I'll find a place close to the motel.'

There was a little Chinese place a block away from where they were staying. They order their food and take it back to the motel. They eat in Natloz's room, then Annie retires to her room. She lays on her bed thinking of all the good times she and Sally had together, and how she has to do this all over again tomorrow for Oscar.

Annie glances over to the clock radio. Two minutes past nine. She's tired, but it's too early to fall asleep. She wonders what the detective is up to. Whether he was awake, watching tv, or if he was chatting to someone. Maybe a wife or girlfriend? Annie hadn't noticed any rings on his finger. Maybe Petridis? Maybe she should go over and see how he's doing. Knock on the door and say … what? What lame excuse can Annie use to not make her look or sound silly?

Annie turns over, closes her eyes, and goes to sleep with a smile on her face.

†

The funeral for Oscar is lowkey. Close friends and family, invite only. Natloz patrols the area on foot, keeping an eye out for anything that could be coming for Annie. But there's nothing out of the ordinary here.

The service is completed in half the time of Sally's. A friend of the family who is a funeral celebrant conducted the service, short and sweet. Sadness fills the air. Sobs that can be heard and seen from where Natloz is standing. Nothing in this world can muffle the sound of grief.

Soon Natloz and Annie are on a red-eye flight back to Melbourne. The flight will take just under four hours. With the time difference, the plane won't get in until 5:40am. Annie sleeps the entire way. She is tired and needs rest. Natloz, on the other hand, wants to study the photos. He knows he has a lot of catching up to do. He spreads the photos out in front of him, using Annie's meal tray, too. He looks at every photo with extreme caution, just in case he's missed something. What is he not seeing?

And there it is. He can't believe his eyes. He brings the print closer to him, just in case his eyes are playing tricks. But no, this is no trick. In one of the photos, something is sticking out of his back-right pocket. From the angle of how the photo was taken, a blur made it unnoticeable at first, but looking at it again with a clear mind, he can see it a lot clearer.

Sticking out of his back pocket was a human body part.

CHAPTER 21

I t is a long walk to the baggage carousel – the aircraft was given the furthest gate. On top of that, they had to wait for a long time for Annie's bag, which extended their unwanted stay at the airport. Natloz only had carry-on.

They said their goodbyes then went their separate ways. Annie ordered an Uber to take her home. Natloz had his car in the short-term carpark. He rings Petridis from the car.

'Hey, buddy. How was it?'

'Sally's ceremony was nice. Both were really sad.'

'I bet. Nice of you to tag along.'

'I'm glad I went. Listen, I have something I need to talk to you about. Are you in the office?'

'Not yet. I'm still at home. I should be leaving in about twenty minutes. What's up?'

'Something in the photos I need to show you.'

'Okay. I'll leave soon. See you in a bit.'

'Do you have the coroner's report on the vics?'

'It should be on my desk with all the other crap. Why?'

'I'll tell you when I get there.'

Something is not adding up. The missed evidence in the photo is disturbing – the hand that is sticking out of Natloz's pocket. How does he explain himself when the evidence is in the photo?

Natloz is trying to remember whether he had picked anything up that night, but the problem he has is that he still can't remember anything about that night.

His phone vibrates. A text has come through from Chief Inspector Moore.

> **I need to see you as soon as possible.**
> **I'll be in my office. Don't take all day**
> **to get here.**

Natloz has a fair hunch he knows what Moore wants to see him about. Petridis has already told him that Moore was there at the park that night asking about him. The accusations against him plus him missing from the crime scene will come back and bite Natloz in the arse. It has been over six weeks since that brutal discovery in the park opposite Petridis's unit, with no leads besides the photo. The dilemma they have is that the photo clearly shows Natloz in the park that night, the same night he was found in his bedroom covered in blood. Inspector Moore must think both attacks are linked. Natloz had been attacked and seriously injured in his own home by someone, or was he? He also had possibly two other people's DNA on him. He needs to find some answers and find them fast. He's their suspect and witness all rolled in to one.

The photo doesn't lie. How many other people have copies of these photos? Did Annie share these photos with anyone other than Natloz? He should have asked that when they were in Apollo Bay. Natloz hopes she's the only person who has them. What does Petridis think of all this? Is he with or against him?

Natloz and Petridis haven't discussed the evening at the park, nor have they spoken about the photos. What does Moore know about that night? Some things are not adding up to Natloz. The one thing he remembers waking up from after surgery in his room was the foul aftertaste in his mouth. What if he did hurt others that night? He would never have known it even happened.

Who does the hand belong to? The question is, is the person the hand belongs to alive and breathing or, buried somewhere only Natloz knows but can't remember? If they are alive, where are they? And where is the hand now? The police searched his house, but what if it's in some undetected hiding spot? But then again, what if they did find it? What if that's why Moore wants to see him? All these questions with not much head space to hold all the answers. He yells from the top of his lungs the only word that comes to mind first. 'Fuuuuuuuuck'.

Natloz arrives at HQ and parks right in front. Every time he visits Moore, he seems to be lucky enough to find a spot out front. Petridis arrives a few minutes later.

'You look like shit, mate,' Petridis says as he approaches.

'It's a result of being an insomniac, living on no sleep. Does it show?'

'Sure does. You look like one of those bodies lying on the metal table in the morgue.' They both laugh as they walk up the twelve steps of the city building and through the main doors. They remove their belongings before walking through the metal detectors.

'Good morning,' says one of the security guys.

'Morning,' says Petridis.

This guard is new. He looks familiar, but Natloz can't pinpoint where he's seen him before. They walk through, collect their belongings from the other end, and proceed to the lifts.

Moore's office is the biggest in the building. They knock on the door.

'Come in.'

They look at one another before opening the door and walk in.

'Sir, you wanted to see me' Natloz says.

'Yes. Come in. Shut the door behind you.'

Moore has his head down, reading something on a sheet in front of him. Petridis looks over to his partner and mimes, 'WTF?'

Natloz shrugs.

'I won't be long,' says Moore.

It's been a while since Natloz was in this office. A bookshelf covers the entire right wall, five levels with books covering the entire shelves. They are in alphabetical order, and there are enough books to warrant a library card. Natloz smiles at his thought. Behind Moore is a large window overlooking Albert Park Lake. On Moore's desk is a photo of him and his lovely wife. Natloz spares a thought for her, being married to that grumpy old fart. But then again, she could be just as bad. Possibly a female version of Moore, a grumpy old lady. Natloz hides his smile with his hand.

There is also an empty mug, a stained ring of what was once coffee around the very top. Either the mug hasn't been washed properly or it's left there to remind whoever is making him a coffee when to stop pouring. Quite gross. The colourful mug has the words 'Awesome Dad'. That thought makes Natloz's face scrunch up. Hard to believe that the ogre in front of him has produced kids.

Moore looks over at Petridis and then to Natloz. He stares at Natloz for a little longer. Then he pushes the papers to one side, removes his glasses, and holds them in one hand by the frame. The words that Moore speaks next are not the words Natloz wanted to hear.

'I wanted you to know that we've had a call from the morgue, detectives. They are reporting a theft, and I want you two to check it out. A corpse is missing a hand.'

Natloz stands abruptly and staggers a few steps back. His heart beats faster than a ceremonial drum.

'Are you okay, detective?' asks Moore. 'You look like you've seen a headless ghost.'

A dark cloud moves over him. He thinks of the photo and the body part that's sticking out from his pocket. That body part in the photo is a hand and it belongs to someone in the morgue. They will be spending the rest of the day searching for a hand.

CHAPTER 22

Vision of the photo flashes across his mind. Dangling there like a negative in a dark room. Could it be the same hand that was in his possession?

Natloz's eyes are fixated on the movement of Moore's mouth, but the words are muted. Then sound comes flowing back like someone had suddenly unmuted the button and the volume is turned up to high. Natloz has an idea.

'Sir, you need to be pretty sick to steal a hand from a morgue. Maybe this sick bastard has something to do with the bodies that are popping up around town. I think Petridis and I should go and check it out.'

If there was anyway of Natloz finding this hand or who had taken it from the corpse then this was a perfect plan to make that happen.

Petridis looks over to Natloz, staring and not sure what just came out of his partner's mouth. Petridis is just as confused as Moore. Or is he?

'I think that's a brilliant idea. I want you guys to get out there and find me that fucking hand and return it to its rightful owner. Then I want you to track down that thieving son of a bitch and hand him what he deserves. We know that hand would not just get up and walk out on its fingertips like the hand from *The Addams Family*. Don't come back until you have something. Now, go.'

Satisfied with what Moore has just told them, Natloz puts both hands on the desk. 'Sir, the hand we are looking for – is it a male or female hand? It might make it easier if we knew the gender.'

'Natloz. The hand belongs to a woman. What difference does it make what gender the hand belongs to? It's a fucking hand and you need to find it. They don't just pop up everywhere. Did you want the make and model, too?'

You're a fucking smartarse, thinks Natloz.

'Unless it belonged to Frankenstein, which I'm certain it doesn't, I can't give you any more clues. Come back with some answers, detectives.'

Both Natloz and Petridis leave without another word spoken.

'Did you notice something odd about the chief?' Petridis asks.

'Like what?'

'That was the least amount of swearing he has ever used in a sentence.'

They both leave the building with a good laugh but Natloz has something more on his mind than a few swear words.

After arriving home from the airport and unpacking her bag, Annie washed her funeral clothes and decided to have a quick shower before tackling anything else. She undressed and walked into the bathroom. The room quickly steams up; the water is piping hot. She glances in the mirror as she walks past, then pauses. Her reflection fades away behind the steam on the glass. Like she no longer exists, put away in some secret chamber only to reappear when commanded.

She rubs her hand over the steamy mirror from left to right. At that moment she sees someone standing behind her. She screams, the only reaction her body could muster. But when she turns around, she sees that there is no one there. Her mind is playing games with her. She opens the shower door and lets the water run over her body. The temperature is turning her skin red. Any hotter and she would definitely have some degree of burns.

The evening is welcomed with the decision to have a quiet night in. UberEATS and Netflix sit at the top of the agenda. What to order is a decision Annie finds hard to make. She missed out on fish 'n' chips last week, but still couldn't convince herself to order it. A glass or three of wine will definitely help her make up her mind.

She relaxes on the couch after deciding to order Thai for tea. There's a nice little family-run restaurant in Fairfield called Narai Classic Thai. She has eaten there many times before, mostly with Sally. The thought saddens her; it was one of their favourite restaurants. The other was Dainty Sichuan in South Yarra. Tonight, Annie will eat Pad Thai with chicken, some fried rice, and satay beef. She knows she won't finish it all; her eyes are bigger than her stomach. Then she'll have a few glasses of wine in memory of Sally.

Annie chooses to watch *Pearl Harbor* on Netflix. She's watched it before with both Sally and Oscar. She loves the heartfelt love scenes in it. And that the soldier comes back from the dead and is reunited with his love. Wouldn't it be great if this was all a movie? Sally and Oscar would return home after a night out. Both in one piece, smiling. Wouldn't that be nice? Then the thoughts fade away into thin air like they never existed in the first place.

After scoffing down the food without chewing, Annie is now in a relaxed, comfortable mood, lying on the couch with a glass of wine in one hand and a box of tissues sitting next to her for easy access. This movie has caused some unexpected tears in the past.

She takes a sip of her wine when she hears a knock at the door. She jolts, almost spilling the wine. *Who could that be?* She looks at her phone to see what time it is. 9:23pm. She doesn't have any friends who visit at that time. She puts the glass down and walks into the kitchen. She opens a drawer and retrieves a knife. Fear runs through her body when she sees her reflection on the silver blade. What if it's the killer knocking on her door? What if he's here to kill her?

She makes her way over to the door slowly, dragging her heels, in two minds about opening the door. She stands a few metres away, knife in her right hand ready to strike. She sees the door handle move. They're trying to get in! They want to kill her!

Annie is ready, holding the knife now with both hands. Whoever walks through that door will walk straight into the knife. She waits for a sound. It goes quiet. She opens her mouth to try and speak. Her mouth is dry. No words, only fear.

'Who ... who is it?' she whispers. 'Who's there? Please ... who is it?'

Then a calm and reassuring voice on the other side of the door responds. 'Annie, it's Detective Natloz. It's Will.'

She puts the knife down and closes her eyes for a brief moment. Her knight in shining armour has arrived. The fear disappears into thin air. No one is killing anyone tonight.

CHAPTER 23

The media has been in a frenzy over the stories that have been shared with the nation. Some true, others made up. Most false accusations. Over the last few weeks they have had just that, exaggerated stories. No suspects to mention, no witness to follow up on. They did have one suspect who ended up a victim himself, now six feet underground. They do have plenty of victims to count. Bodies keep piling up in the city morgue.

Head of Editing for the major paper is Steven Cervetto. He took over the throne from his dad, Steven Snr. Steven Cervetto Snr died three years ago. Hit and run just outside the building. Drunk driver, they said. He died outside the building he owned, surrounded by complete strangers. His head injuries were so prolific they had trouble identifying his face. If it wasn't for Mr Cervetto's identification in his wallet, he probably would have ended up as a John Doe, sitting on the racks for some time until someone reported him missing. The driver of the car handed himself in after a few days. The heat and guilt got too much for him. He is serving a lengthy sentence. And so, he should.

Stories have been coming in thick and fast from sources unknown. The public wants to get involved with made-up murder stories. Most, if not all, of the information coming through is false or taken from a fairy-tale. The paper has heard it all before.

Some stories suggest a pack of dogs could have done this, Rottweilers sitting top of the list; or an international serial killer. Stories the paper are more than happy to publish, just to make a sale. Stories like these will make the public panic. Humans are gullible by nature. They believe everything that is written in newspapers. If it's printed, then it must be true.

After spending the previous day in search of a hand, Petridis stops at his regular café for a caffeine hit and his morning paper. A perfect way to start a day, adding a cigarette to complete that trio. Latte with two sugars. The lady behind him orders a soy latte. Petridis doesn't like anything soy.

He takes a seat outside as he waits for his coffee so he can secretly light up. A fag and coffee for breakfast has always been his treat. He unfolds the paper and reads the headline.

FULL MOON MURDERS - WHEN WILL IT END?

BODIES OF VICTIMS KEEP TURNING UP UNEXPECTEDLY,
ONE AFTER THE OTHER, AND THE POLICE STILL HAVE
NO CLUE WHO IS BEHIND IT ALL.

Headlines like this make the cops look incompetent and lazy, something that doesn't sit well with Petridis. Frustration floods him. He takes out his phone and rings Natloz. He picks up on the second ring. His voice sounds a little rough, like he had a long and eventful night.

'Will, where are you?'

'I'm just getting into my car. I'm still at home. What's up?'

'Have you read the papers this morning? These fucking idiots are making the public panic. Someone needs to shut these guys up. I'll meet you at the office.'

'Who are we talking about?'

'The journos.'

The phone drops out and the conversation is over just like that, without warning.

Natloz just lied to his partner. He was only just getting out of bed – off the couch, actually. He stayed the night at Annie's for security. She told him she had felt scared and worried someone was out to kill her. Danger lurks across the city and Annie is too close to it. Having a cop in the house made her feel safe, and she was able to get a full night's sleep. Natloz, on the other hand, spent the night on a very uncomfortable couch. He woke up with stiffness all over his body. He almost required a walking frame to get himself to the toilet.

Natloz arrives at his desk to find the pile of files on his desk has grown a few inches. Any higher and it will topple over. He should spend a few days sorting that out. A huge sigh to begin what looks like a long day. He brings his computer to life. Wires stick out of it like it's on life support. The computers in the office are so out of date, you would think they arrived on Noah's Ark. Prehistoric.

The computer asks for a password. He has to think about that. Mental blank. He's forgotten the password. He looks in the top draw of his desk and removes a little black notepad. He flicks through the pages until he comes to the page he wants. The password: Tobyobe78.

How could he forget that? Toby Obe was his beloved stray cat that ended up being a pet back when he was a teen in '78. He was glad he wrote it down. Age does something to your mind, and to your body.

Petridis walks in and drops a newspaper on the desk. The noise makes a few heads look over.

'Look at this shit! I mean, what the fuck are these journos doing? Are they trying to make our job harder? We should let Moore know so he can have a word to them.'

Natloz takes the paper and flicks over to pages three and four. He reads silently, pulling a face with everything that sounds remotely crazy. Most of the things mentioned haven't happened. It's like they know the future and are advertising it. Prewarning the public.

'None of this has happened,' Natloz says. 'Where did they get their information from?'

Petridis stands there with a dumb look on his face. The same question rolling around his own head. Natloz almost says something but decides not to. He smiles before putting his head back down to read on.

'ONE WITNESS REPORTED SEEING A "CREATURE, MONSTER-LIKE" FIGURE. POLICE ARE KEEPING A TIGHT LID ON ANY INFORMATION, BUT WE HERE BELIEVE THE PUBLIC HAVE A RIGHT TO KNOW WHAT WE ARE DEALING WITH. "WE NEED PROTECTION FROM THIS BEAST," WRITES THE EDITOR. "WE WANT ANSWERS."'

The editor of the paper knows more than the police have told them. The witnesses who have come forward with information have been kept under wraps, under police protection. They know better than to speak to the media. Someone in the department is talking to the press. Natloz wants to know who, and there is one way to find out.

'We need to visit the newspaper,' Natloz says.

Natloz and Petridis were about to leave when Detective Pollard yells out. 'Natloz, phone call. Some lady asking for you.'

'Who is it?'

'Not sure. She might be ringing to ask you out.'

The group on the table behind Pollard break out in laughter. Petridis gives Natloz a smile. He makes his way back to the desk, but before Pollard transfers the call over, he places the phone on his chest so the caller doesn't hear him. 'She sounds hot, mate. This could be your lucky day.'

Natloz lowers his voice. 'Piss off, you idiot.'

There's a stand-off, the other not wanting to back down. Natloz finally has to break the stare, to talk with whoever is on the other end of the line. He clears his throat before he speaks.

'Good morning, Detective Natloz speaking.'

'Detective, it's Annie. Sorry to bother you, but I tried calling your mobile. It seems to be switched off.'

He takes his phone out of his pocket. It's off. He had forgotten to charge it last night. Once again, another forgetful moment. Sleeping away from home doesn't help the situation. Pressure is beginning to build up and it's starting to show.

'Sorry about that. I was just on my way out of the office just as you had called. Are you okay?'

'I'm fine. You left abruptly this morning without saying bye. I thought I might have said something to upset you.'

He has forgotten where he was last night. He's racking his brain to remember but can't. frustration builds up like Lego that at any moment could topple over like Jenga. He must have been with Annie because she mentioned that he left without saying goodbye. He vaguely remembers the night. He remembers waking up on the couch in the morning, but not the conversation they might have had. Natloz thinks long and hard about the night before but can't seem to piece it together.

'Sorry … I had to be somewhere,' was the only thing he could come up with. A little white lie to get him through this conversation until he can remember the night before and what happened.

'Okay, but I need to see you. Someone saw what happened that night.'

CHAPTER 24

Where there's a witness there's a story – true or not – the story will go on regardless. Annie had found out some juicy information that someone has seen something and potentially might speak to the media. The story is already in motion and words will be shared about the murders. The memory loss that Natloz has been experiencing is causing him to fret and stress. Worried something that has been said or seen might involve him. His whereabouts and possible involvement in some of these heinous crimes are still unaccounted for or explained. Disturbing photos have shown Natloz in uncharacteristic situations, ones he can't remember, which makes things a little hard to deal with.

The sound of distant sirens fills his ears. Unfamiliar drums begin to beat. He fears it's a distant call for his head on a chopping board. Has the story he is dreading to hear been leaked to the press already? The same authorities he swears by are now coming for him? Maybe they have discovered another body that will link this chain of horrid events? His mind races to the worst possible thoughts and makes him sweat. The foul taste in his mouth, the secretly taken photos, the attempt on his life, the memory loss. All of these are beginning to play a huge part in his head, thoughts only he could work out if only he can remember.

He waits a minute, then thinks, *What story? There is no story.*

Natloz types the address Annie has given him into the GPS. It's a restaurant on Rathdowne Street in Carlton called La Porchetta.

Natloz pulls up and finds a parking spot two shops down. He switches his car off and sits there for a few minutes, scouting to see if anyone of interest is around. All clear - no beady eyes on him. He is about to get out of the car when he notices a man walking towards him with a dog. He is tall with broad shoulders, short crewcut hairstyle with salt and pepper strands; a look George Clooney made fashionable. He also has a three-day growth that shadows a sunken chin. Any facial hair would have done the job. Crater scars show the aftermath of a pimply teenage past.

Carlton is the capitol of crime syndicates here in Victoria, the mafia headquarters. If anyone knows what that looks like it's Natloz. Bad memories of his father creep in. He stops it there.

Maybe this guy is a hired gun, sent to take out Natloz. In all honesty, he's probably just out for a leisurely stroll with man's best friend, the dog. A Turner and Hooch afternoon along this busy part of town. Either way, Natloz is ready for the worst-case scenario. He unclips the button on his service revolver and withdraws it from the holster. Innocent-Until-Proven-Guilty Guy with his dog walks past the car without even looking in Natloz's direction. Natloz follows the man with his eyes, noticing the dog stop at the next tree along the nature strip for a quick wee. Marking his territory for the next dog to sniff who's boss.

A thought pops into the detective's head and he begins to think out of the box – the dog having a piss made him think of something that could be useful to this investigation. What if the murder spots have some significant meaning to the perpetrator? Natloz knows this could be a long shot, but then again, it could be the breakthrough he was looking for. Some of the evidence found so far has shown that it could be some kind of animal. Animals urinate. Dogs urinate on trees and walls. Fur was found at the scenes. It could be worth a shot. Human or animal, they have nothing to lose. Before ringing his partner, he has business to attend to. He needs to go in and meet with Annie. She has something to share with Natloz. Someone has seen something and he wants to know what.

It was a quiet morning compared to usual here in La Porchetta. A few people have occupied the large venue, with takeaway coffees being busy. The chef isn't having to out-do himself yet with breaky. 'Latte with one sugar' is thrown around the room by the young barista with red dreads and earrings.

There is no sign of Annie yet. Natloz glances at his watch to check in case he is late, but he's right on time. He takes a seat opposite the counter to keep a watchful eye out for when Annie arrives. Person after person enters, orders their coffee or food, and leaves. It's like watching a merry-go-round in action.

He looks at his watch again. Twenty minutes has elapsed since the last time he checked. Something must have happened. Annie is very punctual and he believes she is never late. But if she were, she would have texted him or rang. He checks his phone to see if it is still on. No text.

The time is 11:17am, thirty-two minutes after rendezvous time. Finishing his coffee, he stands up, leaves a five dollar note on the table, and walks out. He looks both ways, hesitating before he makes a move for his car. Getting his keys out, he slides it into the lock and opens the car door. The alarm starts screaming at him. *For fuck's sake!* he thinks. *Of course, I have a car alarm.* He needed to unlock the car with his remote to deactivate the alarm. How could he have forgotten? His car is from the sixties but it's equipped with all the modern gadgets. The alarm switches off with the click of the button. He hops in and puts his phone on charge, turns the key, and the engine begins to rev. 350-horse power with uncontrollable grunt.

He searches for Annie's number on his phone, then taps the call button. It goes straight to voicemail. Annie has such a sweet and calming voice that could probably get her into trouble one day.

You know the drill. Name and number, followed by a brief message. Bye.

Short and to the point. What more do you want from a voicemail message?

He leaves a message; his even shorter and to the point.

'Annie, it's Natloz. Call me.'

He disconnects and dials Petridis. It rings three times before it disconnects. Easier to text.

Spiro, I'll meet you in the office in twenty minutes. I might have something.

When will this break come? Natloz can smell something brewing in the air.

CHAPTER 25

Nightfall approaches fast as Natloz and Petridis began finalising some new theories. A long day means it's going be an even longer night. This will continue well into the evening. No set times are ever published on a detective's roster; payroll hate it. They start and finish their shift whenever they feel it is appropriate. They never go by time or how many hours they have worked. In line with most detectives, a fifteen-hour day is normal to them. The question is, what is normal these days?

'Looks like another full moon tonight, mate Let's hope nothing happens out there. We could be dealing with a werewolf,' says Petridis, smiling and laughing at the same time.

Natloz locks eyes with Petridis, like a scud missile locked in on a target, ready to destroy.

'Mate, are you okay?' Petridis asks.

A pause, then a confused look from Natloz. Like time stood still, even though the minutes kept ticking over. Something out of *The Twilight Zone*. Natloz snaps out of what he was in with a jolt, like electricity just ran through his body.

Petridis is noticing more and more of these little lapses. It's another side of his partner he can't put a finger on. Some time ago Natloz had collapsed while on duty. Struggling to come to terms with it all, Petridis feels like his partner hasn't fully recovered from it. Ever since that day, Natloz hasn't been himself. Besides the attack on him, there's something different about him. Petridis needs to keep a close eye on him.

Natloz and Petridis are now standing in front of their murder wall where they have placed and pinned all photos, documents, ideas, and theories. It shows the structure of the crimes and everyone involved, key points, and destinations that are the main focal points. Every investigation their department handles has one of these murder walls in place. It helps them solve crimes.

The sky is growing darker by the minute. The clock on the wall shows 6:43pm. The rumbling sound coming from Petridis's stomach indicates that he needs to eat. Tonight, his gut is craving pizza. The words are said aloud as he thinks them. 'I'm starving, mate,' he says.

'Again? You ate two hours ago. Your buttons are getting a little tight around the bread basket.'

'Fuck off. I just have large stomach bones. You just can't handle the fact that my muscle is real, and yours is something you find attached to rocks in the ocean.'

They both crack up laughing, but the thought of food has made Natloz's stomach turn like an expecting mother with morning sickness.

'I'm going to get something to eat. You want anything? I'll bring it back with me.'

Petridis gives Natloz his best puppy dog eyes. They don't seem to work. Natloz is feeling something he hasn't felt before. The thought of food is making him want to throw-up. He knows if he takes Petridis up on that offer, they would have certainly had a major disaster on their hands. 'Clean up on aisle five' would have been heard by all.

Natloz decides to not take the chance and declines. Petridis decides to go without him. Pizza first, work later. He departs.

Natloz gets up from his desk, still feeling nauseas. He hurries towards the toilets. Bile fills his mouth and is about to spill out from the sides. He reaches the male toilets and uses his foot to push the door open. He runs towards the first cubicle. Locked. He can smell someone in there creating an infamous number two. Five cubicles left to check, but he heads for the furthest one when he sees the door is already open. As he walks in, vomit projectiles from his mouth like a scene from *The Exorcist*. The smell quickly rises to his nose, overpowering even the dreadful stench from the first cubicle. This new smell brings a new meaning to the word putrid.

Sweat runs down his cheeks. His shirt sticks to his chest, armpits wet. He needs to get out of there, out for some fresh air. He leaves the bathroom and turns towards the lift. He doesn't have to wait long before the doors open. Three people walk out, all staring at him like he's the Elephant Man. He pushes past them, knocking into Pat Short; another detective in the unit. He's been there for less than twelve months but has already had a few run-ins with some staff, Natloz being one of them.

One time, Petridis had walked past Short's desk and accidently bumped into the corner. Coffee spilled and Short lost it. He became a wild dog, barking at Petridis like he was stealing his food. A scuffle broke out and Short was asked to take some time off to sort out his issues. A transfer would have been better. Nothing more came of it. Ten months on and he is still there. He's mellowed out since then, though, put into place by Moore. The Chief Inspector was bark *and* bite that day. Short walked out of Moore's office with his tail between his legs and his ears red raw from the yelling.

Short looks back and is about to say something when the lift doors shut. Natloz presses the ground floor button. It lights up bright red, the light filling his eyes. As the doors open onto the ground floor, he runs out like he's in the hundred-metre dash for gold. People hurry to move out of this freight train's way.

The coolness of the air outside smacks Natloz square in the face, hard enough to make his eyes water. Not waiting around to recover, he turns and runs off towards the park. His body is feeling a change that he hasn't felt before, his heart racing faster than a cheetah's. Strides longer than a racehorse. Something unexplainable is happening to him, and fear is setting in. Natloz enters the park and vanishes into the night like a comet shooting through the sky.

CHAPTER 26

Detective Short is sitting at his desk, working on a case that is dragging on longer than he wanted. He has his earbuds in, playing music that only he would relate to, blocking out everything else around him. A salad roll sits on a plate cut in half. Two bites taken from one half, lettuce crumbs around it. Why is it always the lettuce that falls out of a sandwich more than any other filling?

Short has been a detective for three years, less than twelve months in this division. A clean-cut country boy who moved up from uniform officer to detective after a few years. It's where he wants to be. The first in his family to be in law enforcement, which makes his mum and dad really proud. He matches his surname in height and haircut. Handsome to many, pretty boy to others. He's there to do a job and he's good at it. He has two older sisters who run the family business, a horse stable in Woori Yallock, which is in between Seville and Yellingbo in the Yarra Ranges. Amanda and Belinda run the horse-riding classes and equestrian training. Both his sisters are ranked fairly high in the equestrian world.

His dad, Bruce, is a breeder of champion trotters. Many of the horses Bruce has trained have had big wins. A perfect family business that has been running for over thirty-five years. His mum, Carole, is the brains behind the whole organisation. She is also the bookkeeper and the family caretaker.

The case Short is working on is an underworld murder from 2004. New evidence has been brought forward from two key witnesses, and Short was given the case. Short has worked most of his career on his own when he was running a small online horse-trading business he started. It wasn't successful, even though he had the surname to back it. The last time he worked with a partner was when he was a uniformed officer out in the North Carlton station three years ago.

Short feels a tap on his shoulder. He turns to see Jenny, the detective assisting him with the key witness. She is a tall woman, just on six-foot-two. Solid build with a sleeve of tattoos covering her entire left arm. She is built like an army tank. Her clothes fit perfectly snug around her physique, curving around her bulging biceps. Her hair is long, tied into a plaited ponytail. She spends equally as much time on her hair as she does in the gym. Her face is quite attractive, not at all like most body builders. Both men and women's appearance can change with heavy steroid abuse. Jenny on the other hand doesn't take steroids. She is as natural and pure as the Great Barrier Reef.

She says something, but the music is turned up so loud that not even a marching band could penetrate the sound coming from the buds. Short removes the buds and gives Jenny a half-arsed smile. There's a look on his shmuck face that she would love to knock off. She could easily use Short like a stress ball, squeeze the life out of him to calm herself down.

'Sorry, just a little busy here. What's up?'

Jenny is annoyed with his response which open up the floodgates to bad memories. Memories of her ex-husband fill her mind. Jenny's ex was abusive and violent towards her. Bradley was a general in the Australian Defence Force based out of Sydney. He was asked to make the transfer after he and Jenny separated. The kids ended up living with Jenny. They see their dad for a week around Christmas. Not the most exciting time for the boys. There are discussions currently going on between Jenny and Brad to change the time the boys visit him. The decision was made by the boys themselves. They want to spend that time with their mother.

'If you speak to me in that tone again, I'll punch you in the throat. Got that, turd?'

'Woah, settle there. Didn't mean to get under your skin. Fuck.'

'Just saying. Show some respect.'

'Right-o. What's up?'

'The boss wants to see you. Pronto. And if you speak to me again like that, you'll have more than just me going at you. Do you understand?'

Short knows when he's defeated and acknowledges Jenny and how she feels.

'Hey, sorry about that. Didn't mean to disrespect. Thanks for the message.'

Jenny turns on her heel and walks off without saying another word. A satisfied smile creeps over her face. She's proud of how she handled the situation. Long confident strides make the light shine upon her from every angle. No one in the office dares to mess with Jenny. Period.

Short closes the lid of his laptop and makes his way to the boss's office. He stops in front of the office door and pauses before clenching his hand into a fist and knocks .

'Come in,' Moore says in a voice so harsh it seems Short is about to be blasted for something he has said or done. Something that has happened in the past that has scared Short. Whatever it is, news travels faster than lightning around here. *Okay, Pat. Relax, deep breath. Relax. Walk in and stay calm.*

He walks into a smoky room. The air is filled with a sweet smell mixed with a pong of sweat. It is numerous sticks of incense, not tobacco smoke as Short originally thought. He looks around like it's his first visit to a museum. There are scuff marks on parts of the walls that look like they have been made by shoes with dark soles or things that had been thrown around the room. Two chairs in the room are placed up against the wall to the right. Moore has people in his office all the time, from the police commissioner himself up to the Premier of Victoria, many have sat opposite Moore discussing ways on how they can better improve the State. Clean up the streets and rid the rubbish, or something along those lines.

'You wanted to see me, sir?'

'Yes, yes. Sit down.' He doesn't look at Short, focused on his laptop in front of him. 'Don't just stand there like a stunned mullet, grab a fucking chair.'

Short grabs the nearest chair and sits directly in front of the firing squad. He waits with anticipation, like a pupil in the principal's office waiting for his punishment.

Moore is now typing something on his laptop. He lets Short wait a little longer in silence. Short looks over at the bookshelf. He notices photos of Moore and his family. He looks happy, opposite to how he's sounding now. The wait is killing him. The anticipation and suspense are making this time go even slower. Moore finishes his work on the laptop and places it to one side, shuffles some papers in front of him, and retrieves a printed email that came through earlier that morning. The same email he's probably read over and over again before Short walked in. 'I have some news I need to share with you, Short.'

He drops the sheet of paper back down and leans back into his ergonomic chair, folding his arms across his chest. 'You heard about Detective Natloz?'

'Yes, sir. He's been missing for a week?'

'Well, missing in a sense that he has gone away somewhere, and hasn't bothered to tell anyone. After all I have done for him and reassuring him that I have his back he goes and does this. Fucking idiot, if you ask me. But then again, no one is asking me, are they, Short? Let's hope he's okay and not in any trouble. I'm having mixed feelings about this, Short. He's listed as a missing person. He can stay missing for all I care. You didn't hear that from me?

'Anyway, we need someone to assist Petridis until we work out where the fuck Natloz is. I have asked around the office, asked for someone from this office to step up. Not sure why but most in this office mentioned your name. Personally, I don't know why but I'm going to give you an opportunity. Do you even know who Petridis is, Short?'

Short takes a moment to let this news sink in. This is what he has worked so hard for. He has been waiting for his opportunity to join the elite team in the office. Everything he has done, everything he has compromised, every sweat and tear his body has produced has finally paid off. Now he just needs to prove himself. All shit aside, he is fucking stoked.

'I do, sir. I also knew Natloz. Sir, why me? Did they tell you why they said me?'

'No, they didn't. They asked for you and I have no fucking idea why. A big mistake, if I have a say. Rookie in the elite division is a big mistake to begin with, leading a major case is fucking insane. I will be going against my better judgement so don't let me down Short. Anyway, get your shit together and go and see Petridis in his office. He's using the spare one until we work out more room for work stations.'

Short isn't sure whether he should stand and leave or wait for further instructions. Quietness stills the air like he was guarding a cemetery. Short gets to his feet and looks towards the door. *Should I go or should I stay?* The chief looks up and notices Short is still there.

'Didn't I make myself clear, Short, or are you hard of hearing? Leave my fucking office and go see Petridis.'

Short almost jumped out of his skin like he was a jack-in-a-box and turns like a ballerina. He has his orders to march and doesn't look back.

'Wait – take this with you. Petridis might not believe the news, like I still can't believe what I've done. Fucking bureaucrats and their fucked-up ideas have this state in turmoil. Don't fuck this up, Short.'

Short walks back to the chief's desk, collects the sheet of paper, and leaves without a word. A sheet explaining what Moore has decided with pairing up Petridis and Short. He now has the task of convincing Petridis that he is the perfect replacement for his missing partner. Giant shoes to fill. Short knows it's not a permanent position, but the thought of the opportunity alone is overwhelming. He cannot let the reputation of Detective Natloz cloud his judgment. Doing that could be costly. He needs to have a clear mind when making important decisions.

Short approaches the tiny office that Petridis shared with Natloz. The plaque of 'Det. Willem Natloz' is still displayed on the wooden door.

The door is closed, minimal ventilation circulating in the room. Short feels hot air coming from under the door, which must make it an uncomfortable environment. The thought of not knowing what he might walk into is like confronting the abyss. His right hand rises to face level, preparing himself to knock. He follows through with a rap on the door and waits for a response. Nothing.

Maybe he didn't hear it? Maybe he's not in the office? Could he be out? Questions that will shortly be answered. He waits for what seems like a lot longer than it really is. He knocks again. This time he can hear a muffled noise coming from inside.

He opens the door and walks in to the abyss.

'Get out' are the words catapulted towards Short. Not wanting to overstep his mark, Short turns and walks out, shuts the door and stands there stunned.

What the fuck just happened? Arrogant prick. He has confronted many pricks in his short career as a cop (no pun intended) but today he isn't taking any crap. If there was one thing he took from the confrontation with Jenny it was not to take shit from a fellow detective. Short turns around and pushes the door open with his elbow. It swings open with authority. Petridis lifts his head and is about to say something when Short stops him mid-breath.

'You need to get used to the fact that I'm your new partner, whether you like it or not. Whether it's long term or short, these are the facts.'

Fire breathing from his nose, he stomps towards the desk, ready to attack like Godzilla terrorising and threatening to topple Tokyo.

'You already know me, detective, but I'll introduce myself anyway. My name is Pat Short, Detective Pat Short, and I'm your new partner until further notice. Here is the note from Inspector Moore. I'm going to get my stuff from my old desk, then we can sit down and talk about where we go from here.'

Short walks out with his head held high and slams the door behind him.

Thank you, Jenny, he thinks. He owes this one to her.

CHAPTER 27

A husky voice echoes across the room. No PA needed for Chief Inspector Jerry Moore. His lungs are full of hot air, enough to raise a hot air balloon. Growing up, Short's mum had always mentioned to be well aware of the slow flowing river and not the fast, ravaging stream. Moore's yelling and screaming was intimidating, but not scary. It hadn't been long since the *mariage de convenance* of Petridis and Short, and Moore was onto them with their first assignment together, or more so, continuing the existing one with a new outlook.

'Petridis, Short – my office, *now*.' He prolongs the word 'now'.

Petridis gets out of his chair first, looks over to Short, and tells him to keep up. They leave their office and thunder across the carpet to the boss's domain, like a herd of wildebeests crossing the Serengeti. Petridis is the alpha beast. Before Petridis can grab the handle to the partly closed door, it opens with quickness that startles Short, almost making him topple over backwards. The chief is standing there with a stern look of concern.

'I have a body that has just turned up at the gardens of the MCG. Get onto it now. And you two better learn how to work together as a team.'

Petridis takes the sheet out of the chief's hand and turns towards the lift, Short trailing behind like a kid trying to keep up with his dad. The elevator pings open, they both hop in, and it closes shut. Two mummies in the same sarcophagus. The lift heads to the basement where the carpark is located, buried underground. It pings open and they both sprint to the car.

'You drive,' says Petridis, throwing Short the keys. Short catches them with one hand and unlocks the car. They enter and the doors close behind them. One feeling the other's vibe, not happy about being paired together. The department has recently invested in getting new vehicles, this precinct being the first. There are five new cars. Moore received the most luxurious one out of the lot. It pays to be chief.

The detectives leave the underground carpark, lights flashing on the dashboard, clearing the messy path in front of them as they make their way to the MCG. Luckily there's no footy on, otherwise the grounds would have been packed with people contaminating and destroying possible evidence. It takes them seven minutes to get there. Traffic makes way for the screaming car with flashing lights. They drive in silence, both knowing it won't stay that way for long.

Marked and unmarked vehicles have flocked to the scene. Police tape already surrounding the area of the crime like streamers set up for a party. Spectators are lined up close by, trying to work out what's happened, held back by junior officers and tape.

The detectives flash their credentials to be let through, Petridis as the senior leading the way. Two uniformed officers hover over the body, three more keeping some bystanders at bay, and one on the phone, probably to a loved one, letting them know she will be home late. A large team of police and paramedics make up the death squad.

A young officer approaches Petridis and Short with eager eyes. He wants to get the words right and not sound like an idiot. His name badge reads L. Thomas. A young constable in ranks.

'Constable Liam Thomas,' he says to the detectives.

'What do we have here, constable?' asks Short as Petridis gives him a dirty look. Short turns his head to shelter the look.

'Caucasian male, aged between eighteen to twenty-four, about 178cm tall with a slim build. Fully-clothed with the back of his jumper ripped to shreds, right through to his skin.' He pauses to make sure the detectives have caught every word he has just said before he continues. His voice a little quieter and crackly. 'It looks like whatever did this wasn't messing around and knew what they were doing. Pretty gruesome, I'd say.'

Petridis glances over to the slumped body against the tree, noodling over some possible scenarios. 'Thank you, Thomas. You can head over and give the others a hand.'

The young constable nods and leaves, making his way over to his colleagues to join them in what they are doing. Petridis moves closer to the body, looking in both directions and then glancing around the back of the tree. His vision is beyond the taped area. Nothing in sight besides trees. He turns back to the body. Without looking away, he speaks to Short. 'What do you think happened here, Short? What do you make of all this?'

Short moves closer and brushes past Petridis. He knows Petridis is testing Short's knowledge on the crime. Short crouches down and places one hand on the ground, staring at the corpse, trying to work out some possibilities. He gets up and turns to face Petridis.

'It seems like he was attacked by a madman, a psychopathic maniac, and got carved up bad enough to kill him. Most likely the choice of weapon to be a meat cleaver or something similar. Drug deal possibly gone wrong, or alcohol-infused robbery that will make the headlines tomorrow. Very similar to the other murders.'

Petridis breaks out with a smile. Short has gone with the obvious here and not really thought about the scene. This differentiates detective from rookie cop. Short is a rookie cop. He needs to earn his rank before Petridis can classify him as a detective, even though Short has been one for three years. Petridis needs subtitles to help him understand Short.

'Nice try, little man but wrong.' The words stick like flies to shit. 'If you take a look around the other side of the tree you will find he was attacked further away from here and dragged himself to this tree. A surprise attack by the look of it. This poor fella didn't see it coming. Looking at the injuries sustained – he must have been in extreme pain before closing his eyes and resting for good. He leaned up against the tree and bled out. This is not done by any sort of weapon, Short. He was attacked by something, not someone. The slashes on his back look evenly spaced. The attacker wouldn't have had that much time to perfect it. Screams would have had the neighbours out of their homes. Whatever did this, something must have surprised it, which made it panic and flee in that direction.' Petridis pointing towards the foot bridge at Jolimont Station. 'Do you know what that means, Short?'

'I think I do.'

'What does it mean, Short? Enlighten me with your answer.'

'There is a witness who has seen something. The witness must have chased him over the bridge because that is the closest escape route to the train station heading the opposite way away from the city, and there are bits of the victim's shirt dangling on the rails. One of these bystanders must be the witness.'

'Too fucking right there is. Well done, Short.'

A positive start to this new superhero duo.

CHAPTER 28

Detective Short pulls into his driveway. He purchased this house with his sisters who come out and stay there from time to time when they're not working or have something on in town. He parks behind Belinda's car. It was strange to see; she is never there at that time, especially on a Monday.

Short sits in his car for a moment before he hops out and walks to the front door. Everything is quiet, way too quiet for his liking. He peeps through the front window. The lights are off and everything is dark, no sound coming from inside. He takes his keys out and looks for the house key. A thought crosses over him, a thought he has been trained to deal with. He puts the keys back into his pocket to stop them rattling in his hands, steps off the front porch, and makes his way to the side gate. It's locked, which he already knew. He also knows that if he jumps over the gate it will make too much noise, alerting anyone inside. He needs to avoid doing that. If anything is going on in the house, they will definitely hear him. His sister might be in danger. He takes his jacket off and places it on the plant pot, covering the large geranium known as Big Red, now in hiding from the bright light of the moon.

He puts his left foot into the gap of the door and lifts himself up, and cocks his right leg over the top, followed by the left leg.

He hangs there for a few seconds just in case he has made a noise that might alert the intruders, if there are any. Then he lets himself down gently and plants both feet securely on the ground. He is over the side gate and turns to face the darkness leading to the backyard. He draws his revolver, a registered Glock-22 with the Victorian Police Force. To be safe, he points it towards the ground with the safety latch still locked as he makes his way towards the back.

On his way he passes the window of Belinda's room. The blinds are open but the room is dark. He can't see anything besides the light of her digital clock radio that has the exact time flashing brightly. 19:32pm. He turns and continues further down the path, coming to a standstill in front of Amanda's room. No different to Belinda's room, dark without any lights on except the bedroom door is ajar and he can see the dimmed faint light coming from the hallway. Whoever is in there must have just switched it on because he couldn't see any lights when he peeped in through the front door. He stares at the door hoping to see something. Nothing.

Before he continues walking, he sees two figures walk past the door, one of them he was certain was a male. He couldn't quite make out for certain but he thought he might have seen them carrying something. Regardless, there is someone inside the house, people who don't belong there. He also knows it can't be his sister and her friends because Belinda and Amanda have a deal with Short that if either were going to bring friends over, they would need to let the other siblings know, a warning for them not to interrupt one another. It came down to respecting each other's privacy.

He checks his phone to make sure there are no last-minute texts from his sisters, especially from Belinda, seeing that her car was in the driveway. Nothing. He sends both of them a text asking. He waits a minute with no response. He pockets his phone and continues. He moves quicker towards the back, reaching the steps of the pergola in no time. He takes his first step up before he comes to a halt. They had installed security lights that switch on with movement. If he takes another step, the lights would definitely switch on.

He has two options. One, retreat and go back to the front door, which would mean having to jump the side gate again, possibly making a racket, and putting his sister in extreme danger. Two, he could continue walking up the steps and risk the security sensor lights switching on and possibly alerting the intruders inside. That could be a risky move and might put his sister in some danger, but might not be the safest option at this point. There is a third option: call Petridis or the cops and have some back-up before going in. The smartest option.

He doesn't have time to think about either option any longer; his legs move before he has time to think and proceeds towards the back door. One step at a time, he waits for the lights to come on but something strange happens. The lights don't switch on. With every step, his mind repeats that the lights will switch on, the lights will turn on, the lights will switch on. But they don't.

He reaches the back door and puts his hand on the door handle to see if it's unlocked. Stupid thought – of course it's locked. He reaches into his pocket for the keys but they aren't there. He had put them in his jacket pocket, which is resting on the plant pot on the other side of the gate. *Well done, dummy*, he thought. *How am I going to get in now?*

Then a figure walks towards him from inside the house. He noticed the shadow from the window. He quickly hides behind the barbeque that is to the right of the door. He bobs down and stays out of sight. The back door opens slightly, and a short man puts a hand out and flicks a cigarette that is still lit onto the lawn.

A quick thought enters his head to jump the man, but a thought like that might backfire and get him into trouble. The man closes the door and walks back towards the kitchen. Short didn't have a clear view of the guy, so the opportunity went begging from the start. With any luck, he might come back out. Short waits for a minute and decides the man isn't coming back.

But then Short notices that the man has forgotten to lock the door. Luck is finally coming his way. A simple mistake by this man has given Short that opening he needed to save his sister. He moves away from the barbeque, puts his hand on the door handle, and this time the handle turns and the door opens. He is inside the house. Before he goes any further, he checks his phone for messages. Clear. He proceeds with his plan.

He can hear whispers coming from the lounge room, low voices. He can't make out what they are saying. His Glock-22 is still drawn. He makes his way through the laundry into the kitchen, and stops behind the door leading into the lounge room. His heart begins to race so fast it almost pops out of his chest. He takes a deep breath, holds it in, and barges through the door into the lounge room. He rolls through the door and lands on one knee, pointing the gun and yelling, 'POLICE!'

Screams startle Short in return. The lights switch on and before his eyes can adjust to the brightness, he hears Belinda say, 'Don't shoot! Put the gun down, Pat.'

Short notices there is a room full of people.

'…surprise.'

It's Short's birthday today and his sisters have organised a surprise party. His parents have come down from the country, and his friends are all there, too. There is a birthday banner across the archway, streamers hanging from the walls and balloons dangling from the ceiling. You would think they have prepared for a kid's party. The only thing missing is a jumping castle.

The figures he saw from the window were his mates, Trevor and Roger. The hand that came through the back door and flicked the cigarette was his dad. It wasn't a cigarette though; it was a sparkler. They had tested one to make sure it didn't smoke up the lounge room.

A smile is conjured up on Short's scared face, colour returning back to normal and before anyone gets shot, his Glock is returned to its spot in the holster. Enough excitement for one night.

'Let's have cake!'

CHAPTER 29

As the final guests leave the house, including his sisters who have a huge day scheduled at the farm, Short sits down on his ever-comfy two-seater sofa, removes his shoes, and grabs his bottle of light beer before sinking into the cushions. He sits there with his eyes half open, staring into space. Actually, he looks at a tiny space on the wall opposite where he is seated. He tilts his head to the right slightly and squints. There's a spot on the wall that he hasn't noticed before. It's red in colour, but not as dark as blood. Like a mark made with a texta. Almost a perfect circle.

He takes a swig of his beer and places the bottle down on the table, glass on glass. The table was full of plates and bowls with the remains of nuts and crackers. He gets to his feet and stands there, his eyes still focused on that one spot. He walks around the table and makes his way to the wall. He's about a metre away when he notices that the spot is not just a spot, but actually a word.

BOO

At first, he thinks it is a practical joke played by one of his friends. But he knows too well that they would never stoop that low to write on his walls. He takes out his phone to snap a photo when his phone begins to buzz. Someone is ringing him. It's a private number. He answers the call.

'Detective Short, Melbourne Homicide, how can I help?'

The person on the other end remains silent. Short can hear slight breathing from the other end, but nothing else.

'Hello? Not a joke, mate. I can trace this call, you know.'

Then the line goes dead. But before the caller hung up, Short heard a motorbike revving in the background. He takes the phone away from his ear and stares back at the screen. At that same moment he hears a motorbike revving outside his place. The caller is outside his house!

He draws his gun and kills the lights inside the lounge room. Darkness fills the room with fear. He can feel it run through his veins, an adrenaline rush he needs to confront the biker. He makes his way to the front door and looks through the peephole. It's too dark to see anything. He needs to think fast. Should he go outside and face his fear, the confrontation, head-on, or call for back-up and hope he hasn't wasted an opportunity that might go begging?

It didn't take him long to decide. Like earlier on, he's going at it alone. He would never want Petridis to think any less of him, of his courage, knowing he was too scared to walk out and approach the bike guy.

He releases the safety on his Glock, the second time tonight, and reaches for the door handle. He turns the knob slowly. The door opens with a creak he has never noticed until now. It's quiet enough that whoever is out there won't know he is coming. He steps outside his front door, gun pointed chest height, moving stealthily towards the nature strip. He looks first to his right. Nothing. He looks to his left and notices a figure turning the corner. No bike in sight.

'Hey … hey, you!'

Short runs towards the end of the street. When he reaches the end and takes a look around the corner, there is nobody there. He takes a few more paces before he hears the alarm to his house go off. He turns around and quickly races back to his house. Usain Bolt would have had a tough time keeping up. He makes it to his front gate and notices the front door is closed. He could have sworn he had left it open when he walked out. Someone has closed the door, and that same someone could be inside his house.

His heart begins beating faster than normal, picking up speed with every beat. He can't hear anything over it. Fear building rapidly which is congesting his chest. His fear level is shooting through the roof. It feels like someone has placed headphones over the entire situation, vision there but noise blocked out. Heartbeat thundering. He opens the front door. The same creaking noise happens, only this time it's in sync with his heart. *Creak ba-boom, creak ba-boom, creak ba-boom.* The creak eventually stops once he closes the door but his heart is still pounding, getting faster and louder.

Ba-boom, ba-boom, ba-boom, ba-boom.

He takes a step inside.

Ba-boom, ba-boom, ba-boom.

The room is dark, he remembers switching off the lights when the call went dead.

Ba-boom, ba-boom, ba-boom.

He walks through to the kitchen.

Ba-boom, ba-boom, ba-boom.

He sees someone at the end of the room, standing under the archway. The light from the stove clock is too dim to see details, he can only see the outline of a figure.

'Freeze! Play it smart, mate. I have a gun pointing right at you and I'm not afraid to use it.'

The person says nothing. They just stand there, watching and ignoring what he has just told him.

'Make yourself known. Who are you?'

Still nothing. Eyes and gun still locked on the figure. He reaches over with his left hand, rubbing blindly on the wall, searching for the light switch. After a few seconds of feeling around, he finds the switch. He flicks it on and—

Nothing. What he saw was an indoor plant that was given to him by his parents, a housewarming gift. His heartbeat slowly decreases and returns to almost normal. Fear remaining on alert. With his gun still drawn, Short checks out the entire house, room by room, cupboard by cupboard. Nothing pops up that is out of the ordinary. Everything seems to be in place. He walks back to the front door, takes another quick walk outside, scouring the area once more before he heads back inside and locks the door. He puts his gun back into the holster and takes a walk out to the side of the house and laneway before making his way back inside. He remembers his jacket, the one he left on the plant. He would have left it for the morning but he has his keys in the pocket. He makes his way over to Big Red and retrieves the jacket. Then he locks the house securely.

He has a few things he wants to do before bed. He starts by grabbing a wet cloth and rubs the writing off the wall. He'll ask his mates about it tomorrow, see if anyone knows anything about it. After a quick shower, he gets into his pyjamas and checks the doors and windows are all locked, again, before hopping into bed for the night. He can never be too sure. It's been a weird kind of night. He sits there staring at the ceiling for a bit, lying there like a soldier before rolling over and closing his eyes.

Then out from the darkness in the corner of his room, a dark figure emerges.

Someone is in his bedroom.

CHAPTER 30

Petridis is never on time and this morning was no different. He opened the door to his office and Short was nowhere to be seen. Petridis had imagined him sitting at his desk catching up on work but no, he wasn't there. Short is always punctual; matter of fact, he is always premature, at his desk at least thirty minutes before he is meant to be. Working closely with a colleague, even though it has been a short time, you begin to learn most of the little things about them that make them tick, make them who they are.

Petridis takes off his jacket and places it over his chair, then takes out his phone and scrolls through his contacts until he finds Detective Short's name. He has his number saved under the name 'Dipshit'. He rings and it goes straight to voicemail.

'Hi, you've reached Detective Short. I can't answer your call right this minute but if you leave a brief message with your name and number, I should get back to you shortly. If it's an emergency, please dial 000. Thank you.'

Petridis walks out his office and looks around to the other desks, just in case Short is chatting with someone. Only a handful of heads seated at their desks. 'Has anyone seen or heard from Short?' All heads are immersed in their work or ignoring Petridis. 'Anyone?' he says a little louder.

One head pops up from the partitioned cubicle. It's Constable Annwen Kirby, no relation to Peter Kirby from Forensics. She and Short transferred over to this office from the Carlton Precinct around the same time. They became close friends without benefits. Annwen is engaged to Short's mate, Chad.

'He was home last night, sir. His sisters had organised a surprise birthday party for him. Myself and a few of the others were there. He's probably just slept in. We left a little early. Not sure what time it ended.'

'Okay. Any idea why I wasn't informed about this?'

'We didn't think you would have come, to be honest. You know, coz you and Short don't really get along and all.'

Petridis couldn't care less about it and is not too bothered he wasn't invited. Out of principle, he should have been invited. He brushes it off with his hand, gesturing he didn't care. 'Anyway, I was busy last night,' says Petridis, a lie. The truth is that Petridis had nothing on at all. He spent last night alone on the couch with his remote. Sad but true.

Petridis decides to drive over to Short's house to make sure that everything is okay. He grabs his jacket and leaves, mentioning in passing that he's going out but no one really notices.

The drive takes about twenty-seven minutes with morning peak hour traffic. Trams are the cause of this delay on St Kilda Road. They can be a bitch sometimes, especially in the mornings with commuters still half-asleep; eyes popping out of their heads and not watching the cars when they hop off the tram, like a deer heading directly towards headlights.

The neighbourhood seems quiet. Not much activity at that time of the morning. School mums returning home from drop-off and elderly residents watering their gardens. Petridis walks up to Short's front gate, opens it, and reaches the front door. It's locked, but there nothing suspicious at that point. He rings the doorbell and rests his ear on the cold wood. It sends a shiver down his neck. No sounds coming from inside, no movement inside the house. He takes out his phone and rings Short again. No surprise there, the same voice message. He rings the doorbell once again. This time he thinks he hears movement, like someone is running inside the house. Petridis starts banging on the door with authority.

'Short! Short, it's Petridis, open up!"

Everything has gone quite again. Petridis moves around to the side gate. He tries to open it but it's locked. He peeks through the gap. He has a clear view of the path leading to the backyard. He grabs the top of the gate and lifts himself up and over. He makes it look so easy. Petridis makes it to the backyard, looks to the left, and notices the rear door is ajar. He reaches for his gun only to find that spot empty. He has left it in the car. He doesn't go back for it. Petridis enters the house only with his bare hands and confidence.

His path leads him into the laundry. That's where he notices a rag in the basin with what looks like blood all over it. Blood is also smeared on the taps that have dripped down the basin. There is a trail of blood droplets leading out into the next room.

Petridis takes out his phone and calls through to report it and ask for back-up. This doesn't look good, and he can't wait for the back-up to arrive. He continues forward through the house. Petridis now makes his way to the next room, the kitchen. Looks around the corner. If anyone is there, they would equally be as surprised. From experience, if you find the back door ajar, it could mean one of two things: either the perp is still inside, or he has escaped. There is a third reason, which will be highly unlikely in this situation – that Short has forgotten to close it. For those who know Short, that would never be an option. Petridis strongly believes his intuition, something of a gut feeling that hasn't failed him yet.

Smashed glass is all over the floor. Blood on the broken pieces. A chair turned upside-down like it had been thrown over. Two top cupboard doors open and the top cutlery draw open, too. A bloodied knife sitting on the floor near the overturned chair.

Petridis enters the lounge room. Evidence of a struggle and fragments of what could have been a party. Crushed chips and nuts on the floor. A couple of pillows along with other crap scattered all over the room. They could be used as evidence if this is a crime scene. Petridis notices no blood on any items in the lounge room. The struggle could have started in there then escalated into the kitchen, but where is Short? Whose body is he going to find? Petridis hopes it's not Short's.

He heads towards the hallway and front door. The door is locked from the inside with the key still in the lock. Petridis tries the handle, definitely locked. He looks back up the hallway at the three doors that run along the left side of the wall. He makes his way to the furthest of the three, which for some reason feels like the obvious danger room. The door is closed.

He knocks and whispers. 'Pat?'

He puts his hand on the handle and turns it anti-clockwise. The door opens. Petridis looks over his shoulder before he pushes the door open. The room is dark, almost pitch black. The blinds are drawn shut. An empty bare bed fills the room with somewhat emptiness. A free-standing wardrobe up against the opposite wall takes up almost the entire area. The doors are open with its contents hanging neatly on the hangers. Female clothes dangle there in a colour co-ordinated fashion, most likely belonging to one of the sisters. The room is tidy with nothing much going on in it.

Petridis leaves that room and makes his way to the next one. The door to this room is also shut. He places his right ear up against the door and his left hand on the handle. He listens first, nothing. He's about to turn the knob when he hears a noise coming from the first room, the room closest to the front door. He takes his hand off the handle and walks quietly down the hallway. This must be the main bedroom. Petridis has a vision; Short lying there in a pool of his own blood, dead. A scene he has seen before with Natloz. This job tends to give you morbid thoughts. Petridis tries to shake those thoughts out of his head with no success.

The handle turns in and the door opens in one motion.

He notices a limp body lying on the bed, motionless. It's Short.

Petridis walks over to the body, looking over his right shoulder at the door just in case. Short is lying face down in his pyjamas, his pillows thrown to one side. Petridis reaches out and checks for a pulse under his jaw. He can't feel anything. He tries again. He thinks he feels a pulse. Short makes a noise, the same noise Petridis had heard earlier. He walks over to the blinds and flings them open to get a clearer look. As his eyes adjust to the light, Short rolls over, mumbling something under his breath and then covers his eyes with the sheet.

'What are you doing? The light, it's so bright, it's blinding me,' says Short in a croaky voice.

Nothing dead about him.

CHAPTER 31

Short spent the next thirty minutes explaining what went on in the house the night before, and why the inside of the place looked like a crime scene.

He had been woken up in the middle of the night by a noise that was coming from one of the rooms. He explained the incident he had with the phone call, and chasing someone down the street that turned out to be nothing. When he got out of bed, he'd walked out into the hallway and into the next bedroom down the hall where the noise had come from. He looked inside but there was nothing there. He checked the doors and windows, front and back, and they were all locked.

He'd felt thirsty and opened the cupboard to grab himself a drinking glass. As he opened the cupboard, a knife fell out and landed on his hand. He showed Petridis where the knife had stabbed into him. There was a white gauze wrapped around his left hand. The knife must have hit a vein, causing his injury to bleed so much that it poured all over the tiled floor making it look like a crime had been committed. He'd patched himself up and said to himself he would clean up the blood in the morning. He'd felt so woozy and nauseated that he almost passed out.

He'd eventually gotten himself the glass of water, became dizzier in the process, and dropped the glass, shattering it all over the floor. So now there was blood *and* glass all over the floor. This all seemed surreal, like a horror show that you would pay to watch, but it all fell into place with Petridis's journey through the house.

Petridis tried hiding his feelings, not letting on that he was worried about the safety of Short. He found it hard to say the word 'partner' because his real partner is still missing, presumably dead. A feeling he can't shake off.

The sun is quite bright this morning, and the light coming through the window takes Short a few minutes to adjust to.

'What's that on your neck?' Petridis asks. 'It looks like a needle mark. Are you using?'

Short stares at Petridis stupidly, having no idea what Petridis is talking about. Short raises his hand to feel his neck. The pressure from his fingers on the spot makes him squint and moan with pain. He gets out of bed and stumbles, losing balance and falls straight back down onto the bed.

'Woah take it easy there, buddy. Are you okay?'

Short tries getting himself back up, this time a little slower. He manages to get to his feet, waiting a few seconds before moving towards the bathroom. Short has to support himself by holding onto the bedside table, then manoeuvring his body against the wall. He looks at his neck in the mirror. A pinprick mark that has bruised and become lumpy.

'I don't remember … I don't remember how I got this. It wasn't there last night.'

'What do you remember?'

'Besides the incident with the phone call and bikie, I remember everyone leaving. My sisters went home because of work. I checked the doors and windows were locked and I went to sleep.'

Short leaves the bathroom abruptly, walks down the hall, and stops in front of the wall in the lounge room. Petridis follows him.

'What is it, Short? What do you see? You're kinda freaking me out here.'

'I remembered something else. Something that was on this wall. There was a word written on there, but I can't remember what it said.'

'You can't remember?' A thought pops into his head, seeing the similarities to what Natloz was experiencing. He begins to feel nervous and hopes Short doesn't pass out.

'No … wait … I remember. I remember what was on the wall. I remember the word.'

'What was it?'

'Boo.' Short collapses to the ground and passes out. The stress of what went down the previous night has caught up with him. Luckily for him, Petridis is right there to help. Another partner passes out in front of him.

†

Short wakes feeling dazed and confused. He is in a bed and has wires and cables attached to his chest. He looks around the room and notices everything is white. He feels like he has died and gone to that place people go to when they leave this round planet called Earth.

Colour begins to appear, his vision finally correcting itself. Everything in the room coming to life once again. His head aches like someone had bashed it with a brick. The penny drops and he realises where he is. He's lying in bed in a hospital.

He can hear people making a racket outside his room. The voices sound very familiar to his ears. The door springs open and a gang of thugs barge through the door. Actually, it is Short's family. They are just as loud as thugs, breaking and entering in the nicest possible way. His mum comes over to his bed and gives him a huge hug and one of those sloppy granny kisses.

'How you feeling, son?' says his dad, not showing any emotions. Deep down he would be worried for his son. He's one of those Aussie blokes who has a hard shell but is soft as butter on the inside. A bit like a hermit crab. Probably more like a marshmallow.

'I'm fine, Dad. Just a little tired.'

'My boy,' says Carole with tears in her eyes. 'A mum never stops worrying for her children. You had us all worried. And they wouldn't let us see you right away. I can never understand these hospitals.'

Amanda sees an opening and cuts in over her mother. 'How you feeling, Pat?'

Belinda is at the back on her phone, chatting to her boyfriend about their cancelled dinner plans for that evening, paying the least attention to her brother who she calls 'Squirt'.

Pat looks past them, seeing if he could spot Petridis. For a brief moment he thought his partner might have been there. A glimmer of hope vanishes just as quick as it had popped into his head.

'Who are you looking for?' his dad asks, noticing the expression on Short's face turn to sadness.

'Hey? Um ... no one.'

As Short's family gathers closer around the bed, the door swings open, making everyone turn and look in that direction. A tall European man dressed elegantly with his detective's badge neatly on display around his belt, right beside the police-registered Glock on his hip, securely nestled in its holster. It is Detective Spiro Petridis.

'How you doing, Short? Sorry to interrupt the family gathering of the Brady Bunch but I needed to check up on my partner, see if he needs anything. From the look of things, I can see that he's doing well and is taken care of.'

A smile creeps onto Short's face. That grand entrance and listening to Petridis mention the word 'partner' has made his day. To have Petridis there says a lot about the man he is. Things are already feeling better.

'Thanks for coming to see me. I'm not really sure what happened to me last night. I - I was not feeling the best.'

Petridis gives Short a confused stare, like he didn't hear him right.

'Last night? Mate, you've been here for three days.'

CHAPTER 32

Short spends the next three days in hospital, a total of six, having all the necessary tests done that is required to clear him for returning to work. He waits outside the hospital entrance for Petridis to pick him up. He digs into his bag and grabs his phone, wanting to check if there is a text or missed call. Clear from both. He looks at his watch. 10:10. Petridis was meant to be there at 10:00. But all he can do is wait.

A car pulls up at the front, a little black Ford Fiesta with a thin rear spare tyre instead of its normal tyre making the car look awkward. The window scrolls down and a soft voice calls out.

'Are you Pat? Pat Short?'

The voice belongs to a beautiful Middle-Eastern woman with high structured cheek bones and long brown hair tied up in a double bun. A pair of stylish black glasses completes her magazine-cover face. She seems young, but is clearly old enough to drive. No P-plates displayed.

'Yes, I'm Pat. Do I know you?'

'No, sweetie, you don't. But Spiro sent me here to pick you up. He didn't want to wake up early on his day off.'

Early? It's past ten in the morning, and he's calling that early?

'Um, yes, we don't want him to lose any beauty sleep, do we?'

The girl laughs like it is the funniest joke she has ever heard. It doesn't take much to make people laugh these days.

'You're so funny. That's what I said to Spiro earlier about his beauty sleep. He never mentioned how funny you are,' and she laughed again, this time even harder.

Short smiles, opens the back door, and places his sports bag in the back seat. There is a mat covering the entire back seat, which is occupied by a German Shepard. The dog and Short eye each other before closing the door. He hops into the passenger side and shuts the door.

'I'm Pat,' he says, holding out his hand to shake hers. 'Nice dog.' The dog watches them converse.

'I know your name. Remember, I called out to you?'

Short feels so stupid and silly that his face begins to turn red, blushing a bright burgundy, like a baby's face when pushing out a turd.

'I'm Leila, a friend of Spiro's,' she continues. 'That's Arthur in the back. Say hi, Arthur.' She looks at the back like she is waiting for the dog to respond. 'We're both happy to meet you, Patrick,' she says as if the dog is responding.

'Likewise, and it's just Pat,' is all he could muster. Not much of a ladies' man. He might need to get some tips from Petridis on how to chat and communicate with women, or men, and now dog.

'Are you dropping me off at home?'

'If you want me to, sweetie. You tell me where you want to be dropped off.'

'Home would be great, thank you.'

The entire journey to his house is spent with Leila talking and Short listening. A few questions from him, but nothing too strenuous, just enough to keep the conversation going and his interest known. It dies before it can even begin. Arthur is bored with the lack of conversation towards him. He falls asleep with his head resting on Short's sports bag.

Short is dropped off at home. He thanks Leila for the lift and before he can say bye to Arthur, she speeds off down the road, turning the corner almost on two wheels. Short takes a few steps before realising he had forgotten his sports bag in the backseat of Leila's car. He feels his pockets of his jeans. Phone in one and keys in the other. Wallet in the back.

He'll ring Petridis in a bit to thank him for organising the ride, and ask him to let Leila know he forgot his bag in her car. She might notice it there and come back before she gets to where she's going.

The phone starts ringing, He reaches for it and takes it out of his pocket. Petridis's name pops up on the screen. He swipes the bar and answers the call. Before Short has the chance to say anything, Petridis cuts in sounding really annoyed.

'Hey, where are you? I'm waiting outside the hospital.'

Short brings the phone down to eye level to see the time on his phone. If that were true then Petridis is forty-five minutes late. Not only is he late, but he has forgotten he had sent someone to pick him up.

'Are you being serious with me, or are you pulling my leg? I've already been picked up. You sent that young lady to pick me up because you wanted to sleep in on your day off.'

'What young lady, Short? Are you having a wet dream?'

'I'm standing outside my house. The girl, Leila, she picked me up. She had her dog Arthur with her and said you had sent her. I'm confused.'

The line goes quiet for a long time.

'Petridis? Are you still there? Did you send her or not?'

The line was still quiet. Then a laugh brings relief to Short's face and oxygen to his lungs.

'Yes, mate, just fucking with you.' He can hear Petridis puffing on a cigarette and then exhaling. 'Shower and get yourself ready. I'm picking you up in thirty minutes. A body has turned up that we need to investigate. Chop-chop, Short.'

The phone goes dead and Short makes his way inside to get ready. These bodies won't stop pilling up unless the killer, or killers, are caught.

CHAPTER 33

Petridis and Short make the fifty-eight minute drive from Melbourne to Geelong with anticipation. Traffic is light on the freeway with roadworks on the West Gate Bridge taking a chunk of that drive time.

The drive is spent in silence, with Short needing all the rest time to recover. He asks a handful of questions and Petridis throws short responses back at him. Moore hadn't mentioned too much to Petridis, only that the M.O and injuries behind the attack were the same. The victim didn't see it coming.

They arrive at the scene of the crime, the area taped and cordoned off, officers scattered around the perimeter doing what they're trained to do. They pull up next to a bunch of marked police cars, a few cops standing around laughing at something that was said by one of them, most likely the clown out of the lot.

Petridis and Short hop out of their car and pass the young group of rookies. They stop and straighten themselves up before one of them addresses the detectives, unaware that Petridis is about to bite.

'The chief is just—'

'No need to let me know anything, officer …' Petridis squints to read the badge. 'Smith. Continue your very exciting conversation. It seems to me that what you guys are gasbagging about is more important than the lifeless body covered with a sheet up there. Pity he can't join in the conversation. Show some fucking respect.'

Petridis and Short leave the group and proceed towards the body. The posse of officers look at each other with amazement. Smith mumbles some verbal diarrhea before turning to be amongst his followers again. Luckily, Petridis hadn't heard what was said.

The body was spotted by a local retired lawyer while walking his dog – aptly called Judge – along the foreshore beach in Geelong. Eastern Beach is normally packed with holiday-goers during the summer period. People from all over Victoria flock to this part of Geelong for the clear water, cafes and restaurants, vibrant atmosphere, and secure waters caged in to keep large predators out.

By looking at the way the sheet is positioned over the body Petridis believes this attack could be the worst out of the lot. It looks a lot worse the closer they got.

A young constable lifts the police tape to let the detectives through. There are multiple sheets covering items on the ground, possibly body parts. This attack looks as though it's been done by a savage gang.

Petridis and Short approach the officer in charge. 'Detectives Petridis and Short from Melbourne,' Petridis says. 'What can you tell me about it?'

'Not sure why they sent you guys. Out of your jurisdiction don't you think, detective? We've got this, boys. You can drive yourselves back and let us do our job.'

Petridis cracks a little smile, Short standing there next to him feeling a little uncomfortable, not sure which way to turn. There's a stare down between the two seniors. A battle of two superiors. Then a voice comes over the top of both of them like a speaker in a shopping mall. This voice is more superior than both put together.

'Back off, Corbett, this one is for the boys from Melbourne.'

Corbett looks over to his left and notices Chief Inspector Moore making his way towards them like Hulk Hogan.

'But, chief …'

'Don't 'but chief' me, Corbett. This is something the team in Melbourne have been working on for a while now. You boys need to step down. You want to help? Then stay and help. If not, then turn around and make yourself scarce. My report will go in regardless. Up to you how you want it to sound.'

'That's not fair.'

'Nothing to do with it being fair or not, Corbett. Now rack off. There is work to be done.'

Corbett keeps his angry glare for a few moments before turning around and walking off with his tail tucked between his legs. He knows when to step down from a battle he can't win. Defeated and dishonoured. The only consolation prize to this is that no one was around to witness the demeaning comments that came his way. The chief will get his one day.

'All yours, boys,' says Moore. 'I want a report on my desk before the day ends. Got it?'

'Got it, chief.'

The chief exits the scene and marches towards his new car, courtesy of the department. A strut that Elvis would be proud of. He came to Geelong to make sure there was no misunderstanding. It could have been an all-out war if he wasn't there. The distance wasn't a problem, he has a new car to play with.

The Geelong foreshore resembles a movie scene from *A Nightmare On Elm Street*. Actors, props, cameramen and a director. The body playing an Oscar-winning performance. Dead set winner. The murder is gruesome and disturbing, the scene violently aggressive and repugnant; all things Petridis is all too familiar with. The scene is just like the killings, the murders, the body count in Melbourne. Mutilation, torture, and brutality are amongst some of Petridis's thoughts. It felt like the killer was trying to make a statement with his victims. Tell a story so to speak. They have all been killed the same way. Serial killer status written all over it. Only time will tell whether his theory is correct.

Petridis and Short approach a couple of plain-clothed officers and begin the task of asking questions. 'Who can tell me what happened here?' Petridis asks.

The three officers look at each other, not sure which one should respond first. There is always one with an attitude, one who likes to show off in front of mates and tries to be king dick, the cream of the crop. Petridis tackled guys like that in high school: bullies, smartarses, dropkicks. So many names for these dipshits that any new word for them is likely to be a compliment. The old school words stick like glue. Petridis thought about asking them to answer but thought better of it and backed off, waiting for them to take control instead of him always initiating responses. Some things are better left untouched. This is one of them.

One of the Geelong detectives sees Petridis and takes charge, explaining everything they know to Petridis and Short. Short takes notes with his pen and paper, Petridis takes mental notes with his ears. Petridis leaves the Geelong detectives to Short while he goes to speak with the witness. Over the other side of the carpark, the witness sits with his dog and a few officers. A cup of coffee in one hand, the other holding the lead.

'Hello, I'm Detective Petridis from Melbourne Homicide Squad. What's your name?'

The man looks dazed. 'I was surprised to find something down here you know. I always wondered what it would be like if I found one, you know.'

'Well, now you do.'

'You bet I do. Sorry, my name is Gerald. Gerald Homes. I've lived out here my entire life, but never thought I'd find something like this. Never.'

'Tell me how you came across the body.'

'It was Judge actually, my dog. He found the body. Well … body parts. The smell is pretty bad. My guess is that they have been here for a while.'

After dealing with so many witnesses you get to understand the picture people try to paint. Understand what they are trying to say. They say if you've seen one dead body then you've seen enough. It's never easy coming to the scene of a fatality, especially coming to a scene like this one in particular.

At some point during this train of thought, Petridis must have said or given the witness an indication that he was done talking, that Gerald was free to go. The witness had a lot to say but nothing of any use. Petridis tells one of the officers to escort Gerald and his dog down to the station for further questioning. See if they can get anything useful out of him. Petridis would just love to quantum leap right out of here to another year. One a little more peaceful.

Something catches Petridis's eye on the edge of the path that begins not far from where Short is standing. The sunlight makes this object shine so bright it is like a flashlight trying to get his attention. It worked. He makes his way over to it without making it obvious to anyone else. It's a phone. The screen is cracked and there's a smear of blood on it. Whose blood could it be? The victim or the perp? He bends down with a clear evidence bag in hand and pops the phone in it. He presses the button and brings the phone to life. It opens straight into the photo gallery. The most recent photo on it brings Petridis to a halt.

There it is. This is what they have been waiting for. A breakthrough that he's keeping to himself until their journey back to the station. He looks around to see where Short is. He is growing more and more attached to him. From what he was told Short was good cop. Petridis wants him to be an even better detective. Someone who will have his back. There are glimpses of that taking place.

'Short, we're done here.'

And with that Short wraps up his interview with the other plain clothed and uniformed officers and walks towards the car with Petridis. They both hop into the car simultaneously, buckle up, and take off back to Melbourne. There is silence in the car for the first few minutes until Petridis breaks it.

'You should ring home, Short. Let the family know you'll be gone for a while. Something we need to look into.'

Petridis takes out the clear evidence bag from his jacket pocket and shows Short.

'What is it?'

'The answer to this crime.'

He passes the bag to Short. On the screen is the answer Petridis was referring to.

A photo of the attack.

CHAPTER 34

Ms Grady was a well-respected veterinarian in her small, but vocal community. She lived in a little town outside Broken Hill in New South Wales called Silverton. Twenty-six kilometres north-west of Broken Hill, to be precise. In 2016 when the country had its census, Silverton was labelled one of the smallest towns with a total of fifty people living in it. There are usually fifty people involved in a murder scene, from detectives to forensics to the coroner, and anyone else enlisted in the investigation. Numbers have grown slightly over the last five years. There are now one hundred and six people living in Silverton, more than half of the properties with some sort of livestock.

Ms Lol Grady, short for Lolita, was raised in Silverton to immigrant farming parents. Lol loved working with her parents on the farm. They had all kinds of livestock. Her dad was a gem when it came to the animals, hence he was in charge of that department. Horses were her favourite. They had three horses, and Lol got the job to name them. She named them according to colour, looks, and temperament.

Stranger was the most undisciplined horse out of the three. Lol had her the longest. For the entire time she had owned that horse she always looked at them as if they were strangers, like she had never seen them before. She always played up and never listened.

The Gradys didn't have the heart to part with Stranger, something to do with a particular look she gave them. Without words, the eyes would speak volumes when you looked deep in them, a feeling of sorrow. Lol wanted to hold ownership of Stranger for that reason. She knew this horse wouldn't last a day if it were in someone else's stable. Horses get put down for being wild and disobedient. Breeders refuse to pay money for a horse if it would cost them more in the long run than what they paid for and not reap in any returns.

Then there was Indi, short for Indigenous, named for her love of the ground she galloped upon and her loyalty to her family. Lolita's parents wanted her to use proper terminology when it came to race, creed, and the colour of people. She wasn't allowed to use any racist remarks, words, or terms when it came to our native Australians, the Aborigines. Racism played a huge factor growing up in these small towns. People referred to the First Nations people in very nasty and derogatory ways. Lol knew it was wrong but was torn between the haters and the respecters. Both her mum and dad were respectful in every way you could possibly imagine, and they would argue often with family about it and eventually the families had stopped speaking to one another.

Most of the arguing came from Borce. He was by far the biggest culprit when it came to racism. Every nationality and skin colour had a name for Uncle Borce, the ones you cannot get away with today. One evening during the Christmas festive season, Lol's dad and Borce got into a heated discussion about name calling. It got out of hand, and Uncle Borce was clobbered so hard, Lol swore she could practically see the little swallows flying around his head just like in the cartoons. Lol was so proud of her dad that from that day forth she was never torn between the haters and the respecters; she was definitely a respecter. A proud moment in her life that she swears by today.

Snow was the prize show horse that won so many events and ribbons, outstanding for her beautiful coat and colour. One guess what colour she was. Her smooth silky coat and her bright blinding colour made her stand out from all the other horses. There were shows all over the state and Snow was ahead of the pack on every platform. She was the prettiest and most precious horse anyone had ever seen, and she knew it. She would wait until people were watching her before she would dip her head, arch her back, and parade around like she was on display in The Louvre, standing right next to the Mona Lisa. Photos were snapped from every angle. She was Snow and everyone loved her.

Lolita's upbringing played a big part in her life. The respect her parents showed, gave, and preached had made her who she is today. She is so respected in not only her community, but communities within a 100-kilometre radius. Lol is not only a veterinary physician, but she is also a veterinary surgeon. Lol Grady loves the animals and they love her just as much in return.

She wakes up every morning with the same routine as the day before, and the one before that, and for as long as she can remember. The alarm goes off at 6:00am. She sets two more alarms that go off fifteen minutes apart. Then she gets out of bed, puts on her left slipper, then the right. She sits on the end of the bed for two minutes. She gets to her feet and walks into the bathroom that is located down the hall. Her robe is stationed behind the bathroom door. She puts it on and then washes her face for no more than thirty seconds. She then continues to brush her teeth for a maximum of three minutes. She has a timer in her bathroom to help her keep track.

Then she walks back to her bedroom and changes out of her sleepwear and into her clothes for the day that are normally chosen the night before. Breakfast is no later than 6:45am. Two eggs scrambled on toasted rye bread, half a grilled tomato, mushrooms fried in butter, and smashed avocado on a hash brown. Same breaky Monday to Saturday since the last drought over twelve years ago. Sundays is blueberry pancakes day.

The dishes are rinsed and placed in the dishwasher for the large wash before bed. She puts her Hush Puppies on that live at the front door. She never walks around the house wearing any shoes other than her slippers. She leaves the house at 7:10am which gives her enough time to get to The Barn Store, which is the town's general store. They make the best coffee Lol has ever had. They use a coffee grain that is like no other, and a secret they keep to themselves. The store is also the post office and supermarket. They make fresh sandwiches and have home-cooked meals for those who don't or can't cook.

This morning is different.

As she prepares her breakfast, there is a knock at the door that startles her. She takes a step back and places a hand over her heart. She is a little confused at who it might be at this hour. She hesitates for a moment, thinks about whether she should open the door or play dumb. Curiosity gets the better of her. She leans in and opens the door slightly, enough to see who is there rapping at her door.

Lolita stands there with her mouth agape. She hasn't seen him for over twenty years.

CHAPTER 35

There were questions that needed answers, and answers with multiple questions. No matter how you looked at it, there was still no explanation for anything that has been going on. Who is committing the murders? Or … *what* is doing the killing?

Clifton Hill had been the starting point of this nightmarish event. Who knows when this will end? Clues went begging, victims keep popping up in the same style, the same brutality, innocent and alone.

The victim must have been taking a photo when the vicious attack occurred. It's fuzzy, but clear enough to see details. At that precise moment, the victim took a shot of what killed him. This thing was hairy, it was scary, it had bloodshot killer eyes, it had death written all over its face. No one would survive an attack of this calibre. You have a better chance surviving a Great White attack or escaping the clutches of Jack the Ripper than this.

'Where are we going?' Short asks.

'Silverton.'

'Why Silverton?'

'Did you see the contents of his wallet?'

'No.'

'His vet card for the dog says he's from Silverton.'

'What makes you think the killer is heading out there?'

'His license is missing from his wallet. The killer has a conscience, or he must be heading up there to pay his respects to the family by killing them too. I have a gut feeling about this one, Short. I've got a feeling we'll find something there.'

'But he never did that with his other victims?'

'We don't know that because we never looked into it. Maybe he had and we weren't paying attention. I need you to find all the close relatives and friends of the victims, starting with the Clifton Hill girl and ask this question: has anyone been in contact with you, besides police or media, since the murder?'

Petridis is onto something and he is not slowing down. He needs and wants answers. Short takes out his laptop and types away like his life depends on it. He emails all parties involved in the case and gives them each a name and task, and a timeline. Both Petridis and Short want all responses by the time they get to Silverton. The team has just over nine hours.

†

Petridis and Short arrive in Silverton just before sundown. They've been driving fast, changing every three hours, stopping twice for a toilet and petrol and once to stock up on food. By the time they arrive into Silverton, their eyes are red raw and tired. The sun is setting just over Mount Uhill. The regional wildlife is slowly coming out to play and the nocturnal beasts will be hungry.

Crime in Silverton is minimal. Drunk and disorderly, family violence, or fines for unregistered vehicles the only issues here. Death comes only to people whose life has expired from natural causes, or to animals with inexperienced road crossing techniques.

They drive through the short strip that consists of a number of shops. The first place as you enter is the police station. A white Holden Colorado that desperately needs a wash sits in the driveway. It's a one-man station with a building so weathered it looks like a haunted house.

Fifty metres down from the cop shop is the petrol station that offers you mechanical work, service, and a half-hearted tune-up, fuel at a ridiculous price, and a greeting that would make a lot more sense in a funeral parlour. There would be no surprises if only half the people in this town owned cars. At almost three dollars per litre, it would certainly make anyone trade their four-wheeler for a two.

Then there is a building with multiple adjoining stores. A second-hand clothing store selling everything from dresses to jeans, suits and shoes. There is a small section inside the store in the far corner which sell kids clothes and baby stuff. The general store is next to that; the town supermarket with overpriced items and shelves stocked with expired products marked with a discount sticker across the front label. People with limited money will go for discount products regardless of the use-by. A proven fact.

There is a hunting and fishing section that covers one side of the wall. The wrong person with the wrong attitude can easily buy a gun. One thing is for sure, guns don't kill people, people with guns kill people. Another proven fact.

Hair and beauty products cover the whole back wall. At least a woman in this small dingy dark town can look her best when no one is there to notice her. Sad but true.

The cash register sits on its own, taking up a small section of space. They bake their own bread there, too, the shelves behind the register are full of loafs and sliced doughy delights that would make your mouth water. The smell of fresh bread hovers invisibly through the air. White or wholemeal are the only options you have, not giving one a huge decision to make. But that might be a good thing when it comes to everyone's favourite doughy treat.

The medical centre is attached to the general store, with a walkway access between the two spaces. The medical centre is a one room, two occupant unit. The receptionist mans the front counter with Dr Sanjeev Patel as the practitioner. He's an Indian immigrant who has made Australia and Silverton his home for over twenty-two years. This centre also doubles up as a chemist. All the medication is stored behind the counter and out of clear sight from anyone entering or passing the office.

Standing on its own away from any other building in the town is the funeral home. This is the place everyone goes when they have had enough of life. The final resting place before they are put into their makeshift retirement village located underground.

Mr Derrick Hamilton and his wife, Ann-Maree, run this joint of no happiness. Passed down three generations. Mr Hamilton's father, Derrick Snr, a well-respected man in this town, took over from his father, Walter Hamilton back in the fifties. Both Derrick Snr and Walter Hamilton have been buried on the grounds, settled under a large gum tree located at the back of this quarter-acre block. Two more resting plots have been reserved and maintained for Mr Hamilton and his wife. They have no children, and Derrick is an only child and Ann-Maree the only living child. Her sister, Milly, never married and died at a young age from an illness not detected until it was too late. The Hamilton and Creswell blood line ends here.

Almost all the buildings are on the left-hand side of the town, or right-hand side depending which way you were coming into town. The pub stands alone on the opposite side, sticking out like the grand Eiffel Tower or monstrous Statue of Liberty on Liberty Island, or Uluru if you think a little closer to home.

The Silverton Pub stands grand and solid. A double-storey building with a stylish look that would make it stand out no matter where it was located. Built in the 1800s, this pub not only has character on the outside, but every evening it's filled with characters on the inside. The owner of the pub, Terry Moist, is also the barman and chooses to be that just so he can keep an eye on things. Tourists tend to flock to Silverton thanks to the Mad Max museum situated just a short drive out of town. It also has eight antiquely furbished rooms that take up the entire top floor. Each with its own ensuite and balcony.

Petridis and Short will be staying there tonight and possibly for the next three days, unless it's all sorted before that. First things first, check in and shower before dealing with emails. Petridis requested the furthest room with the largest space, while Short was always destined to get the smaller room of the two. They check in and pay upfront, and are ready to confront the workload.

Petridis opens the door to the room and yells down the hallway to Short. A simple text would have worked more civilly. Short is ready, waiting and eager to get started. All of the responding emails from the team have come through, highlighted, and marked for Petridis. Short took his surname's amount of time to get to Petridis's room, ready to work.

'Let's head down stairs to the bistro for some tucker as we continue our investigation.'

You would never have guessed that with his olive complexion that Petridis is a fair dinkum Aussie. The tanned skin, the gap between his teeth, and mole that sits under his right ear all scream wog boy. But he would tell you looks are deceiving and that he is an Aussie through and through.

Short orders the steak medium-rare with veggies and chips. Petridis goes for the burger with wedges. They both order a beer to wash it all down .

'I have some interesting feedback on what you asked for,' says Short eagerly, thinking he should start the conversation well before the food arrives.

'So, do we have our sympathetic mystery murderer visit families after the crime as expected?'

'This is probably not the answer you wanted to hear, but partly no and partly yes. He did, but only the last two. They said that they had someone come around in the days following the murders saying they were friends of the deceased and asked them random private questions. Here's where it gets interesting and confusing. When they were asked to describe the person who paid them the visit, on both times it came back as two completely different people. One tall with a thin moustache and receding hairline while the other outweighed King Kong. I just don't get it.'

'What don't you get?'

'Well, how there were two different people that had visited the family?'

'Simple, Short. He sent someone different on both occasions and didn't go himself, or he could have been one of them. He has kept his identity a secret. Like a phantom, a ghost, incognito.'

'So, where do we go from here?'

'Nowhere until I finish my burger. Then, we head over to the Geelong victim's house here and see if we can find out anything useful.'

'You mean break in?'

'No, Short, we're detectives. We do things the right way, by the law. We don't do crap like that. We will let ourselves in from the broken window at the back.'

'How do you know there is a broken window out the back?'

'I don't, but there will be.'

They eat in silence, both in deep thought; Short about the murders, Petridis about his burger. There is music playing softly, Kenny Rogers entertaining the small group of people who have gathered there that evening. The lights are so bright you feel like you were eating through an interrogation. Short makes short work of the steak but leaves the green veggies to one side like a little kid.

Now that their hunger has been taken care of, the detectives leave their dirty dishes and a hefty tip and make their way to the front counter. Terry is serving one of the regulars a beer, an old and wilted bloke in his seventies who resembles a badly constructed weatherboard home built in the settler days.

The detectives wait at the counter. Short reaches over and taps the little silver bell on the counter. Petridis gives Short a hard look, one you give your child when they have done something stupid.

'What?' says Short, breaking into a stare down. 'I've always wanted to do that. Haven't you?'

'No, Short. I haven't. That only happens in movies.'

At that exact moment, Terry looks over and gives Short the exact look that his partner has given him. He comes over with a disgruntled look aimed at Short first before turning and fixing his look on Petridis. 'How was your meal, gentlemen?'

'Great, thanks. Burger was fab-o.'

'Great to hear.'

'The gentleman at the bar,' says Petridis. They all turn towards the old fella sitting there like a monument. 'How long has he been living in Silverton?'

'Who, Bazza? Damn, Bazza is a second-generation Silverton farmer. Born and bred, and most likely die here, I say. Most of the population here are generations old. His wife died about three years ago. He spends his evenings here with the drink they call loneliness. I got that from a Billy Joel song,' he says with a smile. 'He doesn't talk much, Bazza. Just comes in, sits in the same seat, and stares at the TV screen. Friday and Saturday nights he stays longer than others coz the footy's on.'

'Does he have any other family?'

'He has a cousin here from his first marriage. They're not close. She's the town vet. Her name's Lolita. She lives about ten minutes up the road heading towards Jeepers Creek. There is a dirt track just after the bend they call Hell's Corner. Blink and you will miss it, or the corner. A pretty nasty drop if you do.'

'Does …' Petridis pauses and looks at his notes he has just written down, 'Lolita live with anyone?'

'Nah, all alone. One of her relatives lives in Melbourne.'

'We might have a word with Bazza, if that's okay.'

'Good luck. I have to warn you, he doesn't like cops that much.'

CHAPTER 36

Barry 'Bazza' Thompson is a widower and a loner. Since Bev passed away, he has taken a turn for the worse. He was once a keen farmer and even keener gardener. Looking at his garden and farm today, you can see the neglect that would make anyone feel they need to do something about it. Help the old man to get it back to its former glory days.

Empty beer cans, wrappers, and every kind of rubbish you can think of is laid out all over the front lawn. The grass has grown so long it almost covers the debris. The place has no electricity or hot water system. Even a squatter would find it difficult to live there. But Barry refuses to pay for anything other than food, which he doesn't buy much of anyway.

'I'm not paying for anything I don't need. Not lining those bastards' pockets with my hard-earned cash. They can go to hell,' is what he says to the handful of friends he has.

Barry has a dam that provides water for the property. He has cold showers and eats everything straight out of a can, cold. He has a cow that produces all the milk that he requires and he lights fires in a metal bin in the lounge room. Self-sufficient, and wouldn't have it any other way. Bev had always called him a tightarse even when things were great. They were married for over forty years, sharing one another's company for most of it. *Will & Grace* was their favourite show. Pizza and coke their favourite takeaway meal and Bev's homemade apple pie his favourite dessert. He kissed her every morning without fail when his eyes had opened for the day and every night before closing them. He loved Bev and she tolerated him. Then she died. A big part of him died with her.

'Terry … be a good lad and get me one more.'

Terry looks over to Bazza from the front counter, then back at the detectives. 'I would approach it with ease if I were you. Don't say I didn't warn you.'

Terry leaves the detectives and moves over to accommodate Barry with the beer he so desires.

'Let's leave it for tomorrow,' says Short. 'The amount of alcohol this guy has consumed could make this turn really ugly.'

'What are you scared of?' Petridis mocks. 'A drunk old man?'

'I just don't want to physically manhandle an innocent man having a quiet drink.'

'We do it now, Short. He is more likely to talk while under the influence.'

'You mean drunk?'

'I mean, whatever it takes. I tell you what, why don't you go get the car and have it ready and waiting out the front? I won't be long.'

Short is glad he got out of the possible confrontation they might have had with Barry Thompson. The man is a walking timebomb that could go off at any moment. Short doesn't want to be around for that. He makes his way to the rear of the building where the hotel parking is located, hops into the car, and brings it around to the front. He sits in it with the car idling and the aircon running, circulating cold air. Even at that time, the temperature is well into the thirties.

Petridis approaches Barry. 'Mr Thompson, can I have a word with you?'

Barry keeps his eyes focused on the bottles behind the bar. He's in no mood to chat to anyone, especially a detective.

'Mr Thompson, I have a few questions I would like to ask you. It won't take long.'

'Fuck off.'

'I need to ask you about someone who lives here in Silverton. I have his address and a potential name but I need to make sure the information I have been given is correct. Maybe you can help me with this.'

'Didn't you hear me? I said—'

'I know what you said, but that's not the answer I was looking for. I need a name and some information on this young man who lives at 11 Earl Street. Do you know him?'

Barry puts his glass down on the coaster in front of him, looks over towards Petridis, and sits there like he's about to say something. Possibly to give the detective all the information he requires. But after a few seconds he turns back and takes up his position staring at the bottles behind the bar again. Petridis's hopes shatter in a blink of an eye. Barry picks up his glass and drinks the remaining beer from his pot, then taps the empty glass on the bar. Terry knows he's calling for another beer.

'You know him, don't you?' pushes Petridis.

'I said fuck off.'

'Yeah, I heard you the first time.'

'Then fucking scram pig.'

'Not until you tell me how you know him and if anyone else lives with him.'

'Yeah, I know him, so what if I do? Everyone knows everyone here in this shitty old town. What's he done? Sucked some guy's dick in the public toilet and got caught? Fucking faggot.'

The words thrown out of Barry's mouth seem to hit a nerve. Petridis needs to keep a level head if he's going to get any information from this geezer. 'He was murdered last night. How did you know him?'

Barry looks over again, a changed look plastered across his face. Petridis can see remorse in his eyes. Sorrow fills the space between the two. 'I knew him. Good riddance, I say. One less poofter in this world.'

'I can see it in your eyes, Mr Thompson, you don't really mean that.'

'What do you know about how I should feel? You some fucking psych freak or something? You don't know me. You will never know me. Fucking pig.'

'I know that you know him and I want to know how you know him. I also want to know if he has any family living here.'

Silence fills the air. Silence is good. It's less stressful. Petridis knows Barry is thinking about what to say. 'Answer these two questions, Mr Thompson, and I promise you I'll leave and be on my way.'

'Then you will leave me alone?'

'I swear on my grandmother who I love dearly.'

'I knew him. He used to take his dogs to the same vet. He has no family here. His parents died many years ago. His sister lives in Darwin. He lives alone. Now leave me alone.'

'Thank you, Mr Thompson. You've been painfully helpful.'

And with that, Petridis stands up from the stool and turns away. That's when Barry interrupts the silence and says, 'The vet is his auntie.'

CHAPTER 37

Dear Mr Hamilton,

I would like to thank you for organising and assisting with the funeral for my beloved late mother Harriet Dawson.

She was loved by all of her children and grandchildren; she will be greatly missed.

With our grateful appreciation, we want you to have our well-loved cow Stacey as payment. We cannot afford much more but what we have is yours.

Thank you once again and God Bless.

Regards

The Dawsons

P.S She milks well

The letter was opened and read out aloud for Ann-Maree Hamilton to hear. It was not something new to the folks in Silverton for the funeral parlour to be offered a cow for payment from grieving families. It's true that families around here don't have much cash attached to their names. Livestock is the only other source of payment.

Last year when old Gracie Landers passed away, her husband gave the Hamiltons all their chickens – twelve, to be precise. They have become accustomed to these gifts, and that is why they appreciated the gift from the Dawsons. It's not easy living in a house that is attached to the funeral parlour. Corpses living on the other side of the bedroom wall. Ann-Maree has always found that creepy but after all these years she has finally become accustomed to it.

'If only someone could help these folks speak proper King's English,' Derrick says with a grin. 'A little education around here will never hurt anyone.'

Ann-Maree rolls her eyes and walks out to the backyard to hang the freshly-washed clothes on the brand-new Hills Hoist clothesline that was installed just the other day. The concrete holding it in place still shining as the sun begins to descend for the evening. The white clouds that were hovering above the town earlier have covered most of the blue sky. Still, rain is nowhere to be seen, nor does it smell like it is anywhere near. It hasn't rained in over five months. The temperature is humid and sticky which brings out the mozzies. Mosquitos kill more people in the world than any other animal.

Ann-Maree pegs up the clothes. Muffled sounds from inside the house are distracting the mood she is in. Derrick must be talking to himself or mumbling to the television. He hates commercials and tends to criticise the companies the ads are talking about. It's either, 'Oh, there is no way it costs that little! There must be hidden costs somewhere,' or, 'It's cheaper to do it yourself.' Derrick never does anything himself. He always pays someone to do it for him. Contradiction plays a huge part in his life, one after the other. And the sad part is, he can never see it when it happens.

Ann-Maree hears a noise that startles her. She looks up towards the large gumtree that is planted right in the middle of the yard. She waits in silence for a few seconds in case she hears it again. The air she's breathing gets thicker, in and then out, but the only noise she can hear is the sound of her own breath.

She picks up a pair of work overalls from the washing basket that belong to Derrick. Paint covers most of the blue fabric. She turns them upside down and inside out before pegging one leg first, then moving over to the second leg and attempting to peg that one when she hears the noise for the second time, only this time louder and clearer. Leaving the pants hanging from one leg, she walks towards the tree. Three pegs are clenched in her right hand, not feeling the pain from the wood. She takes out her mobile phone from her apron and switches on the phone torch. It has gotten dark quite quickly. The night brightens up with weak light from the torch. She shines it towards the tree. Something catches her eye; leaves rustling in the light breeze, birds singing from distant trees. Surely birds could not be making the horrible distracting noise. Ann-Maree walks closer to the tree. Her heart is pounding louder and quicker with every step. There's a pain in her chest like her heart is about to explode.

There is something lurking in the dark. Something that doesn't belong there. She thinks she sees the outline of a large figure. She looks back at the house. Should she turn back and get Derrick to come out and have a look, or continue her journey through the dark yard? Her mind says no but her feet continue taking small steps closer to the tree. A chill crosses the back of her neck like someone is blowing air from their mouth. The hairs on her arms stand on end and a funny feeling begins to run through her entire body.

Then a loud noise erupts and a flock of spotted doves erupt from the tree, scattering through the night sky like homing pigeons taking flight back to where they had come from, released from their gilded cages. Struggling to breathe, Ann-Maree manages a half-hearted smile with a snort escaping her mouth. All this panic from a bunch of doves.

She turns and starts heading towards the clothesline when she hears a growl coming from the same direction as the doves did. This growl was on the ground, not up on the tree. Ann-Maree tilts her head to try and get a better view around the tree. Someone is shining a red laser-light. She can clearly see it. Wait, there are two lights. Someone is flashing two laser-lights at the tree.

This can't be right, she thinks. The lights fade away. Then she notices something. They're not lights. They're eyes. Something has bright red eyes that are beaming towards her. It comes crawling from around the tree, taking slow methodical steps towards her. She feels the heat emanating from it, like someone has just turned the temperature up a notch. Eyes glaring, focused on its prey. Human flesh, it's dinner.

Ann-Maree turns and begins to run towards the house, but it's like when you're dreaming and trying to run from danger but your legs are moving in slow motions and you don't seem to get anywhere. Her voice has frozen, too, like the water over Lake Guy during winter.

She drops the pegs which were still lodged in her right hand. She can see the back door open that leads into the laundry. She has watched enough scary movies to know never to look back in situations like these. Just run for the open door. That's all she needs to do. Run for her life for the open door. She can hear the steps of this thing behind her, louder than her heartbeat. Its breathing is louder than hers too and she is relying on her breathing and some luck to outrun this thing and get her over the line. She is almost there, almost at the back porch. Just a few more steps to go. She can almost jump from where she is to make the bottom step.

As she reaches the first step she feels a nudge that sends her soaring through the air and crashing face first into the exterior wall. A pool of blood is forming under her left shoulder. She can't feel any pain yet. More blood is forming under her chin. She tries to move her body but nothing happens. Her body is paralysed, her jaw painfully broken. She cannot muster a word. She feels weight on her back, like someone is sitting on her. She keeps her eyes closed and plays dead, hoping whatever it is will go away. She can hear sniffing coming from behind her. Is this thing smelling her? Smelling her fear, or possibly the blood pouring out from her?

She tries to move her hand. It works. She tries to lift herself up and push him off her back. She can't, it's too heavy. She tries to muster a scream to no avail. Even if she could, Derrick would never hear it. The television is playing so loud she's surprised the neighbours haven't come over to complain. She's hoping they would. *Someone please come and help me. Please!*

As Ann-Maree lifts her head to take a breath, the thing gets off her back and grabs her by her leg. She can now feel the pain shoot up her spine. She finally manages to make some noise from her crushed neck. She yells as loud as she can. The pain becomes unbearable but she needs to do this if she has any chance of surviving. Then she is being dragged across the ground, moving backwards away from the house with great speed. Her voice fades into the night until no more sounds are heard. She is silenced. Trails of blood are the only evidence she was even there.

The night ends exactly the way it began; quiet sounds of branches rustling. The doves back on the tree doing what they do. Mosquitos buzzing in the air, searching for human skin.

The sounds from the TV stop. Derrick makes his way out the back.

'Ann-Maree, are you out here?'

Nothing.

'Maree, honey?'

He sees the clothes in the basket and only a few items on the clothesline. He turns to walk back inside to check for her when he sees the pool of blood on the porch, and the trail leading to the back fence past the clothesline. One sock lay by its lonesome self on the grass. Derrick walks towards it, then stops suddenly as he feels something under his shoe. He looks down. It's a shoe, and a foot. The foot is still in the shoe.

It's Ann-Maree's.

CHAPTER 38

P etridis receives a text from base in Melbourne.

Body part without body found at Hamilton's parlour, Silverton. Shouldn't be too hard to find. Listen out for the sirens. Lights should pave the way like a runway.

From what I've been told, we have the same beast-like amputation of a foot and traces of blood. Look into it boys.

Petridis reads it word for word and analyses the tone it's written in. Urgency and desperation. He puts his phone in his pocket and tells Short to switch off the car and remove the keys from the ignition. Short was still waiting in the car for Petridis to finish with Barry. The radio was loud in the car and Short didn't hear Petridis calling.

Petridis waves his hands frantically. Short lifts one finger to acknowledge Petridis and indicates he'll be a minute.

'We need to go, mate.' Petridis insists. 'Funeral parlour has a body part that didn't come from a corpse already stored there, your song can wait. Let's go.'

The parlour is just two blocks from where they are. Best to leave the car put and walk there. They do a quick jog to the parlour. Both detectives are fit, one in great shape. As they turn the corner, they see the chaos that awaits them.

Blue and white squad cars are parked out the front of the Hamilton's funeral parlour. The nosey neighbours are outside the front, gasbagging and being stickybeaks as usual. The lack of entertainment that goes on in this tiny dingey town makes this murder so eventful, they will be talking about it for decades. There's police tape around the outside of the property. Neighbours are kept at a safe distance by new recruits from Broken Hill.

Petridis and Short hold up their badges, and slip under the tape, let through by one of the officers. Mr Hamilton is sitting on the porch, staring blankly towards nothing in particular; zoned out like his life has just ended. Derrick stares at death every day, but now that death is a part a of him for good.

Petridis and Short walk past him, letting him mourn in peace, and enter the house. The funeral parlour is attached to the house. It amazes them how one can sleep with dead people on the other side of the wall. Morbidly strange and creepy. Derrick should charge an entrance fee to this doomed ghost house.

There's a long hallway that leads from the front door to the back, with rooms breaking off to either side. The lounge room is on the left. It has an open fireplace with a very large dark bookshelf on either side, filled with novels. Fiction, suspense and thriller, true crime. Murder, death, and espionage complete the shelves with titles ranging from classics to new releases. Stephen King novels headlines the plethora of authors.

Opposite the lounge room is the bedroom. Plain colours with plain décor. Double bed with a chest of draws. A mirror Henry VIII would be proud of, old enough to be from that same era. Petridis walks through the lounge room that leads into the dining room. Short continues down the hallway, breaking up the team momentarily. A uniformed officer stops Petridis before he can cross into the next room.

'Are you meant to be here? Who let you in? You will have to—'

Before he can finish his sentence, Petridis removes his badge from his pocket and places it on his belt. He eyes the officer and moves past him. The dining room adjoins the kitchen, which is also accessible from the hallway. The laundry room is to the right of that, which is the last room before the back door. From the kitchen window you can see the entire backyard. The bloodbath cannot be seen from the back window and is out of view from the detectives. From that distance, Petridis can see an object on the grass. He remembers the previous and most recent attacks. Nothing pretty about any of it.

He meets Short at the back door. It's already open, so they walk through it and out onto the back porch. Shock settles in, transcribed onto their faces; fear of what has gone down here. There is enough blood spilt to supply the blood bank for a week. Chunks of flesh are scattered along the concrete, more on the grass in clear sight. A grotesque, fleshy torn foot sits on the freshly cut lawn. A white sneaker keeping the cold foot warm.

'I'm heading over to the back fence,' says Short. His face is pale white. If Short hung around any longer he would have brought up the steak he had for dinner at the pub. A neighbour pops his head over with a look of concern.

'Something is in my yard. I don't want to go near it, it might bite me. It looks like a zombie.' His broad country accent blurs his words. Short is not sure what to make of him.

'You need to come and have a look,' the man says. 'I'm not touching it.'

Petridis reacts in the only way he knows. 'Don't go near it,' he says. He walks over to the fence and lifts himself up, has a quick look, and spots something lying in the neighbour's yard. It's difficult to see exactly what it is.

'It's a zombie, I tell ya,' the man insists.

'Move away from the fence and back up to your porch, sir,' commands Petridis.

'Take out your gun and shoot it,' says the neighbour, clearly showing signs of intoxication.

'I said move back please, sir,' Petridis says, extending the last three words.

The neighbour does as he's told, heading back to his ratty outdoor chair and takes his position with a cigarette stuck to his bottom lip and a beer in his hand. Petridis could do with either one of those right about now. With his hands on the top of the fence in a firm grip, he bends his knees for a better spring and heaves himself up on to the top of the fence. He puts one leg over and makes sure he doesn't crush his manhood in the process, then throws the other leg over and athletically jumps from the top. He lands on both feet with a slight bend of the knees. Perfect dismount.

The large black figure is now clearer. Shaped like a human body, only awkwardly proportioned. Petridis removes his gun from the holster and looks around for any other danger that might be lurking nearby in the dark. Nothing.

He moves closer and stops about two metres away. 'Short?'

Short looks over the fence to see what Petridis is doing. 'What the fuck is that?'

'Get over here, slowly.'

'What is it?'

'Not sure. Get around the back of it.'

'Are you serious?'

'Yes, I'm fucking serious. Just do it.'

Short gets over the fence but not with the same degree of ease as Petridis. They approach it with caution, guns ready in case it moves or jumps up. The neighbour is right – it does look like a zombie. A real ugly disfigured zombie. But then they come to a standstill. It's not a zombie, as suggested by the drunk neighbour, but a person. A person who is also missing a foot – the foot they have on the other side of the fence.

This person who is lying on the ground is Ann-Maree Hamilton.

†

It doesn't take long for the police tape to be extended around both houses. The crime scene is growing. They need more uniformed offices and volunteers brought in from Broken Hill. A call goes out to the closest officer with the task of doing that and letting Mr Hamilton know that they have found his wife.

Petridis moves his eyes from the body and looks at Short. 'We're going.'

'Where?'

'11 Earl Street. We have a house inspection.'

CHAPTER 39

Annie had finally collected her belongings from the unit she shared with Oscar and Sally and properly moved in with a friend. Her parents were unable to fly over from the States; they have their business to run, and they had no one close enough who knew how to run it for them. They offered to bring Annie back home to Ybor City but Annie refused. She wanted to see this out.

Annie has moved in with her friend, Jess Slayer. A friend she met through a friend. Not the most appropriate surname, considering what has happened. Annie refers to her as Jessica Slater to friends. No one asks any questions, so she keeps the story going.

Annie's mum had given her the standard lecture one parent would give their child at a time like this; her concern and worry for her daughter's safety was easily recognisable in her voice. Any parent would feel the same. Annie absorbed the things she wanted and filtered the rest. She is still in shock and regularly breaks down with sobs when nobody is around. She is confined to her room most of the day. She feels a lot safer in there than outside.

Since the funerals of her flatmates, she hasn't gone anywhere on her own. She has met up with Detective Natloz a handful of times and he had escorted her to Perth for the funerals. Annie hasn't seen or heard from him since the night he stayed over. Nobody has. Which is rather strange when you're the lead detective in a killing spree that has swept the State. It just doesn't add up as to why he has disappeared.

Today she is going to make a change. She needs to get out and start feeling safe again. It's been some time now since all this had happened and she's still cooped up and scared. Small steps to recovery. Annie refuses to go out at night. That will take longer to overcome. For now, a walk to the supermarket will do her good. It's only three blocks away on Station Street.

She has a quick shower and puts on some warm clothes. The weather is not that cold but there is a chill in the air. A beanie and scarf are included in today's outing fashion rags. She enters the kitchen and makes herself a coffee. Jess has one of those pod coffee machines from Aldi. Nothing like a latte from a proper machine, but this does the job regardless. Lungo and Ristretto are her favourite flavours. Jess only stocks Lungo. Annie has put the other flavour on her list to pick up.

She opens the front door and stands there frozen and indecisive, not knowing what comes next. It's like she has forgotten what to do after opening the door. Fear creeps in and goosebumps form all over her body like a porcupine preparing to get into protection mode.

I can do this, I know I can do this, she keeps repeating to herself, trying to psych herself up to leave the house. Even though she has been out many times since, she still goes through the same ritual. She didn't realise it was going to be this difficult, every time. She looks into her bag to make sure she has her house keys, her wallet, and most importantly, her phone. Jess had cut a spare for her the same day she had moved in.

Keys in hand, phone in bag, the shopping list folded neatly next to the can of hairspray for protection; something she now keeps in her bag since Sally's attack. The thought of the attack brings a tear to her eye. She wipes it away and locks the door behind her. Step one, completed. Moving to the front metal gate, she stops and looks back to remind herself why she needs to do this. Why she needs to get over this fear her body and mind is experiencing.

From the corner of her eye, she notices someone at the window. Someone standing behind the curtains, smiling. Who is this person smiling at her, mocking her fear? Her heart stops. It can't be Jess. She left for work early that morning. Had she returned and Annie didn't notice? Had she slipped in while Annie was in the shower and then locked herself in her room? No, Annie would have heard her. Jess never locks herself in the room during the day. She would have made some toast and a coffee and sat herself in front of the TV watching Netflix or Stan or Disney+.

Has this person been watching Annie while she was showering? Could he have been spying on her? She begins to drown in the gross thought that has flooded her mind. She was just inside the house, with him, and she didn't even notice him there. Has he been there the whole time?

Annie refocuses on the window and notices finally that it's not a person, but an old tall retro lamp Jess had picked up the other day from a Savers store. Her mind had been playing horrible, vivid games with her. There was nobody there to begin with. Annie's heart returns to a familiar beat. She knows it's safe to leave the gate.

†

The supermarket on Station Street is amongst a variety of stores, restaurants, and cocktail bars. The streets surrounding the strip are full of houses, but there's not a soul in sight until she gets to the corner. Cafes are lined with tables and chairs outside the façade of the buildings. Laughs and chatter fills the chilled air which makes the atmosphere relaxing and enjoyable. Annie would be happy to remain there until dark, knowing there are people she can turn to for help if anyone tries to hurt her.

Annie steps into Three Locals café and orders herself the largest latte there is on offer – triple shot with one sugar. A caffeine hit she wants to last. She doesn't want to fall asleep, as sleep petrifies her these days. Early stages of self-diagnosed insomnia.

She misses her friends. Both are now dead. One a victim to a murderer, the other possibly to something else. She hasn't been told yet and can't work it out herself. Neither can the police. She doesn't even want to attempt it.

She has fond memories of them spending many days and evenings along Station Street. The charcoal chicken place is the best in Victoria, in her opinion. Annie and her gang had mentioned that to all their uni friends. Social media posts about the chicken had eventually taking over their stories. Friends backed that theory up with their own thoughts. It was an overwhelming thumbs up from everyone.

Annie walks in to the IGA, grabs herself a basket, and heads down the first aisle. A man passes her abruptly, making her uneasy. He's looking at her and smiles. A thought about the morning with someone in her house crosses her mind. Could she be imagining this person, too? Did he really pass her, or was it just her imagination? She looks back. He is real. He's now filling a bag with Granny Smith apples. He's there for the same reason she is. Grocery shopping.

Annie takes out her shopping list, her fingers briefly brushing up against the cold metal spray can, and begins from the top. Apples are first on the list. She looks back and sees that the guy is still there. She'll go back at the end so she doesn't have to see him again or stand next to him. Next on the list are snacks. Chips, chocolate, and a bag of Natural Confectionary snakes. Grainwaves and cheese-flavoured Twisties, along with a large block of KitKat. Annie's shopping list always begins with the same contents. Apples and snacks. Why in that order, even she doesn't know.

She reaches the end of the aisle and opens the fridge door for milk. She closes the door and notices the same man right behind her, waiting for her to move. Annie almost drops her basket when she notices him there. He is that close that he'd be able to smell her perfume and freshly washed hair with coconut shampoo. Sick psychotic killers might do that. Either way, he is way too close and it's making her nervous, uncomfortable, frightened. He smiles at her again. She closes the fridge door and moves away quickly into the second aisle, out of view and hearing.

What does he want from her? Does she know him? Does he know her? Has he seen her in here before? The only answer to these questions is no, she doesn't know him. So many questions cloud her judgement that make her uneasy. Annie needs to stop them right there. She's not liking this feeling at all.

She looks around. The man is not there. He has stopped following her. She takes a deep breath and looks down at her piece of paper. Next on the list is bread. She buys Helga's Light Rye sliced bread which she loves for toasties and sandwiches. A bag of Tip Top square crumpets for breakfast. She can easily finish a packet in one sitting so she buys two. Also, a packet of sesame bagels to have with cream cheese, bacon, and eggs.

She looks over her shoulder and sees a mother with a baby in a stroller. She is placing her groceries under the bottom carriage of the massive stroller. It's almost bigger than a small SUV. Annie continues to the end of that aisle. The fruit is to her right so she heads there now. Grabbing a clear plastic bag, she starts feeling the apples. Most of them are bruised. She lifts the ones from the bottom and they look nicer. She fills up the bag and places them in her basket, then turns to head to aisle three when she sees the same guy standing with his back to her. He's just standing there in her way, not looking at her, not moving, not saying a thing. Is he waiting for her to ask him to move? Waiting for her to strike up an unwanted conversation?

Annie walks around the table with the apples so she can discreetly get around him. That's silly. Discreetly? He will definitely see her when she walks past. She glances towards him, trying not to make it too noticeable. She has him in her peripheral vison.

There is something wrong with this guy. He is not moving; he's just standing there staring directly ahead. Not blinking, not moving a muscle. Just staring into space. Annie walks past him and into aisle three. She picks up the pace, leaving behind items that she needs to buy. She moves towards the back of the supermarket where the fridge takes up the entire wall. At the frozen food section, she stands there as frozen as the dim sims and pies in front of her, nestled safely behind the glass door. Annie feels she might be safer in there with them.

She looks back towards him. He's not there. Gone, again. Could he be in the queue paying for his stuff to leave? The fear of not wanting to leave the house is confronting, confirming what she already knew – she shouldn't have left the house this morning. It was a mistake. She looks down aisle number four for any trace of this man. She is convinced he is following her. He has to be. He has popped up three times while Annie has been here. On all three occasions he has made her feel uncomfortable.

He might be gone. She can't see him. She walks past all the aisles and peeks down them. Nothing. The guy who was following her is gone. Maybe he wasn't following her at all. If he was then he'd still be here, still popping up unexpectedly but he isn't. Her nerves calm down a touch. She makes her way back to aisle four. She looks at her list and sees she needs tuna. She grabs Sirena chilli tuna, three tins, a four-bean mix, a tin of crushed tomatoes, and a packet of penne pasta.

She feels a brush of wind cross the back of her neck. She gets instant chills, her goosebumps reappearing. She quickly turns, but to her surprise there is no one there. But then it happens. Just as she calms herself down, her heart begins thumping hard and fast again. She turns the other way. Standing next to her, looking at the products on the shelf, is the guy.

Annie drops her basket and puts her hand over her mouth. What is he doing here? She wants to ask him why he is following her. He tries to pick up Annie's basket, the contents spilling out of it all over the floor. A tin of tuna rolls like a tyre further down the aisle without coming to a stop. He looks up at Annie. Her face must show how petrified and scared she is, like she has seen a ghost. He is about to say something but doesn't. Annie takes a few steps back, just as he leaves everything on the floor and gets to his feet. He turns and moves to the front of the store, disappearing from sight.

Annie looks at her shopping on the floor and moves to collect it. The tin of tuna has stopped rolling somewhere near the end of the aisle. The glass milk bottle has smashed on the floor and a pool of milk spreads under the bottom shelf. A store assistant with a name badge reading 'Liam' comes to Annie's aid. He helps her collect her things, reassuring her that everything is okay and for her not to worry.

'Did you see that man running out the store?' she asks. 'He's been following me the entire time I've been here. He frightened me, which made me drop the basket. Did you see him? He was tall and very unattractive. He looked scary. Did you see him?' Annie's panic attack has scared the young shop assistant. He hasn't dealt with a situation like this before. Fresh out of school and into the fire of dilemmas.

'No, miss. I didn't see anyone running. I was standing over there,' he says, pointing towards the front register.

'He would have run right past you,' Annie says. 'Where were you looking?'

The young assistant doesn't say anything. He is staring into Annie's scared eyes but doesn't know what to say to calm her down. His eyes become a little misty, like he is about to cry. 'I better get a mop,' he says.

She needs to get out of there quickly or she is going to scream. Sweat builds up on her forehead; she can feel a drop forming on her eye brow. She makes her way to the register to pay for the things that they collected. Not checking to see if everything was there, she places one item at a time on the belt. She wants to run home where she is safe behind walls and locked door. The register assistant, Becky, starts processing the items. The sound of the scanning beeps combined with her heart beat make an interesting tune.

Annie reaches for her purse. Just as she looks up to pass Becky her card, she sees him. He is there, holding her shopping bag for her, about to pass the bag over to Annie, and no one is saying anything to him.

'He is the one following me! He is the guy that scared me. What the fuck do you want?' Annie spits, staring directly at him. 'Why isn't anyone doing something about it? Call the cops. I want him arrested. Don't just look at me. Help me, please!'

Annie has caused a scene. Everyone in the store has stopped what they are doing and are focused on the commotion that Annie has created. Two customers behind her move away, frightened she might do something to them. The lady with the stroller abruptly leaves the store, forgetting to put her shopping that was stored under the stroller back. The security buzzer goes off to no avail. All eyes are fixated on Annie.

'Ma'am, he is …'

Annie doesn't hear the end of her sentence. She finally notices the guy's vest. Just on the inside is a name tag. 'Lenny'. He works there. He is an employee. He is wearing a hearing aid. Lenny is hearing impaired and has a learning disability that is unknown to Annie. The IGA has given Lenny the opportunity to work. He was just doing his job. Annie is jumpy and has made a big mistake – actually, a *huge* mistake. She has made this look worse than it really was.

'I'm sorry, I really am sorry. I'm so, so sorry. I …'

Annie pays for her shopping, grabs her bag, and leaves the store. She has just created a scene of disbelief and accused an innocent man of stalking. She needs serious help to get past her psychological issues stemming from the attacks that is causing this fear. She walks briskly back home, head down, focusing on the cracks in the pavement. As she gets to the front gate and fetches her keys, her phone buzzes with a text. She removes her keys and unlocks the door, drops them back in her bag, and walks in to an empty, quiet house. Before putting the shopping down, she grabs her phone to see who it is.

Her shopping leaves her hand and comes crashing down for the second time today.

The text is from Detective Natloz.

CHAPTER 40

Petridis and Short arrive at the destination. They would have been quicker if they had their car with them but it was left at the pub. A quick stop to pick it up ate a chunk of time. The little pin icon shining bright on their GPS. The street is dark and quiet. Only a handful of lights are on in a small number of properties. 11 Earl Street is even darker, not a single light on. The detectives already knew that. The owner of this house is lying in a morgue over 800km away.

They park out the front. Switch the car off. The lights go off automatically. They get out and head to the back of the car. Petridis pops the boot open and surprises Short with the contents. Petridis grabs two bulletproof vests and passes one to Short, telling him to put it on. They check their weapons and close the boot.

Petridis opens the mailbox. Letters are piled up, untouched. He removes a couple of them to see who their victim was. Jack Gumba lives at 11 Earl Street. Now they can confirm the name to go with the body. Petridis signals Short to enter via the rear. Short looks at him and says, 'Why am I going from the rear?'

Petridis looks at Short and smiles. He doesn't say anything. Maybe best he didn't.

Short heads towards the side of the house. No gate. *Thank God.* Short is pleased about that. He doesn't want to be jumping over anymore fences. Petridis walks up to the front of the house and climbs the few steps. The veranda is narrow and extremely clean. Cleaner than the inside of some properties he has entered.

A dog starts barking. It's coming from the back of the house. It's Jack's dog and it has been left on its own. Reports came in to the detectives while they were driving that a dead dog had been found not that from the body of Jack Gumba in Geelong. They had confirmed that the dog belonged to the victim by the phone number on the collar. Microchip details sealed the confirmation.

'There is a dog in the backyard,' Short calls.

'I know,' Petridis says.

'But he had his dog with him when he died.'

'I know that, too.'

'So, he must have more than that one dog.'

'That I didn't know, but now I do.'

After exchanging some more comical words, Short decides not to enter the backyard with the barking dog and proceeds to the front door with Petridis. Petridis takes the honour of rapping his knuckles on the wooden door. The house has no security door. No lights come on. He knocks again. Same result. Petridis put his ear against the door. Not a single sound. Short cups his hands on the window and looks through the glass. It is hard to see anything.

'We need to get in,' says Petridis.

'We need a warrant,' says Short.

'I got one.'

'Where is it?'

'Under my foot.'

'You mentioned a broken window?'

'I was kidding, Short. Foot is easier.'

And with that, Petridis raises his right foot and uses it as a battering ram. A perfectly placed side-kick lands on the door just under the handle. The door swings open with ease. It has a criminal feel to it that makes Short feel a little uncomfortable. He tends to follow the rules and goes by the book. Petridis has written his own book and Short is just starting to read it.

The dog is still barking at the back. By the sound of the bark, they can tell it's a fairly large canine. So much grunt behind every bark. They will deal with it later. First things first, to find out who this guy was.

Standard procedure is to call out that police have entered the premises so there are no sudden surprises. Neither party wants to be accidentally shot or hurt. No sound doesn't necessarily mean that no one is home. They could be hiding. The detectives don't take any chances with the hushed stillness, so they draw their weapons from their holsters and prepare for unexpected action. Ready, just in case.

Nothing seems out of place. A very clean and tidy house. Petridis knew that from the look of the porch. They move from room to room. Everything seems normal in there. There are picture frames on the walls with photos of Jack the way everyone knew him. Petridis and Short know him looking a little different, not as pretty as the pictures make him out to be. Jack was a good-looking bloke. There are photos of Jack with two older people, a man and woman, presumably his parents. Then some of Jack with kids. Probably not his own, as Bazza from the pub mentioned, Jack was gay. It could be his niece and nephew or family friends. They could belong to anyone. Not that it matters right this minute. Another photo of Jack with an older lady in uniform. A veterinarian. That must be the aunt that Bazza mentioned. Petridis makes a mental note that they need to speak with her sooner than later.

Short has made his way into the kitchen. He checks the fridge and pantry. All in order. Doesn't seem like anything is out of place. He did notice that Jack must either suffer from OCD or he's just a plain perfectionist. All the labels of the items in the fridge and pantry have the label facing frontward. Any item that has two or more extras are stacked up neatly with the writing matching from top to bottom, packets stacked one behind the other. Same deal in the fridge. Fruit is stacked like a pyramid, bananas nicely placed in a separate bowl so the different fruits don't touch. This guy was definitely a perfectionist.

Petridis makes his way to the lounge room. An old television is connected to a Blu-ray DVD player, a collection of DVDs on a small stand beside it. There's a small lamp on a side table, a vase with plastic flowers, and an old ashtray with butts in it. A Marlboro smoker. Petridis remembered his grandfather smoking the same brand. Petridis finds it a little odd seeing cigarette butts in the ashtray. Why would Jack leave the ashtray dirty when the rest of the house is clean? It didn't add up or make sense.

There's a drinks trolley on wheels with a couple of bottles of scotch. Vat 69 and the traditional Johnny Walker Red. Tumblers make up the top shelf contents alongside the bottles. Shot glasses and more tumblers in the two-door cupboard beneath it. A bottle of Tawny Port and Jim Beam bourbon make up all the alcohol in the house. No wine and no beer. Plain and standard drinks. He doesn't strike Petridis as an expensive kind of gay.

Both detectives meet in the kitchen and look out the back window. The dog is a Labrador and it has stopped barking. Two dog bowls are on the ground inside the laundry. Both have names on them. Trigger and Bowser. They wonder which one is outside making all the racket.

'Nothing out of the ordinary in here.'

'No, nothing. I guess he lived a simple life in this tiny town,' says Petridis.

'Where to now? I'm getting tired.'

'Me, too,' says Petridis as his eyes wander around the room, thinking about taming the rumble his stomach with a snack. His eyes become fixated on something that draws him in like the Bermuda Triangle. Petridis walks over to the far wall where a chestnut-coloured wall unit comes to life in front of him. There in plain sight is something that stands out from all the other items on it. How could they have missed it?

'What is it?'

Petridis ignores Short's question. He is lured in like he has been hypnotised by the sirens of the Seven Seas.

It's a picture frame, holding a photo of two guys. Two guys who Petridis recognises. They have their arms over each other's shoulders. One of them is Jack Gumba. The other is Willem Natloz.

CHAPTER 41

By the time the detectives had finished up with the eventful evening, every shop in town had closed for the night. The hotel provided a late-night snack for the two consisting of leftover chicken nuggets and cold fries. Petridis and Short were grateful for what they were given. Beggars can't be choosers especially when there is no other food available.

A quick bite to eat and a pot of beer were all they needed before tucking themselves in for the night. Short went straight to sleep. Petridis took a little while longer. His mind kept him up for most of the night. 3:00am and still no sign of sleep. The thoughts in his head played, then rewound, then played over and over again. The events from the night that ended in tragedy for Mrs Hamilton were the focal point in his mind. The vision of the battered body, the amputated foot, the blood splatter across the back porch, and the shocking horror of the crime itself kept the detective awake and thinking.

He gets out of bed and places his chair by the window. He slides it open and lights up a cigarette. The smoke slowly trickles out from the window, vanishing into the still of the night. The peace out there shows no sign that anything bad had happened. If asked several hours earlier what his thought of the evening were it would have been somewhat different. At the top of all his thoughts stands the photo he saw at Jack Gumba's house, of Will and Jack arm in arm. How did they know each other? He knew that Jack was gay but Natloz … was he gay? Surely not. But they were arm in arm. They were close. How close? If Natloz was gay, Petridis would have known. A gay guy will know another from a mile away. Petridis is pretty sure Natloz is not gay, and that he and Jack know each other some other way. He is actually convinced of this thought.

†

Morning breaks and the sun shines bright into the hotel room. Blinds were kept wide open, the heat from the sun beaming through the glass. Petridis can feel his body baking while lying in his bed, like being in a solarium. He kicks off the sheets and lets the rays take control of his body, recharging every muscle and heating up the already-hot European blood that is running through his veins. He glances over to his phone for the time, his eyes slowly adjusting to the light. It's 7:00am. He knows he hasn't slept enough by the way his eyes sting. He needs to visit the chemist for some eye drops before he gets going for the day.

He rolls out of bed and walks over to the window. As he looks out, he can feel the heat bouncing off his skin. He had forgotten to close the window last night. The room is cloudy with dust that has made its way inside.

Not much is happening at this time of the morning. He has a clear view of the main street and all the shops along it. Mr Wong is out the front of the general store sweeping the pavement. It's not hard to guess his name because it's plastered in big letters on the building. Wong's General Store. Dust covers the air that will eventually settle back down onto the ground. He will have to sweep again in an hour's time.

Besides the birds that have nested in the ceiling, no other noise comes to his ears. He picks up his phone and sends Short a text. He hears a ping just outside his door. Then a knock. Petridis opens the door to find Short standing there showered, dressed, and ready for a new day.

'Where are we off to first?' he asks.

'The shower for me, and then to breakfast. I'm not working on an empty stomach. Not sure when our next meal will come in this town. I'll meet you downstairs in thirty minutes.'

Petridis closes the door and removes his clothes as he walks towards the bathroom. Sets the water to hot and stands there under the faucet, allowing the hot steamy water to rain down over his entire body. Closing his eyes, he takes himself to another time, another place where nothing but empty space fills his head. Blocking all that has happened out and letting all the relaxing, heavenly music generated from the sound the water is making.

There's a loud knock at the room door that brings him back to reality. Frustration seeps in as his calm thoughts had been broken, his serenity disturbed. He had told Short he would see him downstairs. Why the hell is he knocking on his door?

Petridis turns off the water and reaches for his robe. He puts it on and makes his way to the door, water dripping over the shiny polished floorboards. He opens the door.

There is no one there.

He looks down the hallway to his right as his room is the last one on the floor. No one in sight. He closes the door and heads to the bedside table, picks up his phone, and rings Short.

'Hello?'

There's another knock at the door, this time harder.

'Is that you knocking at my door?' asks Petridis, sounding pissed off.

'No?'

'Did you knock about two minutes ago?'

'No again, it wasn't me. I haven't been upstairs since you told me to head down here. Why?'

'I'll call you back.'

He disconnects the call and makes his way back to the door. He looks out from the spy hole. He doesn't see anyone there. The view shows three metres from either end of the hallway. It's all clear.

He walks back to the bathroom, but the door is banged on again so he returns with pace. He flings open the door but sees no one, again. Looking down the hallway, he notices a shadow of a person turn the corner. Petridis bolts after them, makes the corner, and brakes in time before running into something that has been left on the floor. There is a bucket sitting in the middle of the hallway. Some sort of dark liquid inside it resembling blood. The smell is putrid.

He runs down the stairs and makes his way to the front counter. He spots Short sitting at a table in the bistro. Terry is wiping glasses at the bar. He lifts his head to see what all the urgency is about.

'Did you see anyone run down these stairs? Anyone run out of this joint?'

'I don't think I did see anyone, detective. Did something happen?'

'Possibly. Do you have cameras on the floors? Surveillance cameras?'

'Um, no we don't. What is going on?'

'Not sure yet. Send a cleaner up to my floor. Someone has left a bucket in the hallway with a vile liquid in it. Send them now, please.'

'Whatever you say, detective.'

Petridis pokes his head into the bistro. 'Short, order me the Big Breakfast, please. I'll be back down in ten. Also order me some juice, but not tomato.'

Short gives his partner a quick nod and turns his head to find the waiter.

Petridis walks back upstairs. The bucket is gone.

Damn, that was quick. He gets back to his room and as he walks through the door, he can hear the shower running. A puzzling feeling takes over his body which shows on his face. He is certain he had turned the water off when he heard the knock at the door. He is a hundred percent sure he had switched off the water. He reaches for his Glock that normally rests on his hip, but he's not wearing his holster. He is still in his robe. The gun is where he left it last, under his pillow. He is aware that placing it under the pillow can result in accidental deaths and injuries which occur when hands wander in the middle of the night whilst asleep. Petridis feels that the reassurance is greater than the risk, which makes him comfortable with it.

He walks over to the bed and reaches under the pillow, but the gun is not there. He looks beside the bed in case it had fallen during the night. Nothing. He gets down on his hands and knees and looks under the bed in case it has slipped off the bed and made its way under it. Nothing there either.

The shower is still running. He can see the steam coming out from the ajar door, making its way into the bedroom like smoke escaping from a burning building. He should send Short a text telling him to come up to his room, but his phone is now missing from the bedside table where he left it last. He looks at the entrance door and then to the bathroom door. One is closed and the other is open. He is going in without back-up. There could be someone in there waiting for him amongst the steam in the bathroom. His life is on the line. His life comes down to this one decision not to call for back-up.

Petridis sticks to the decision he's made and continues forward. His Greek stubborn heritage is going to get him killed one day. That day might be today.

Petridis is now standing outside the bathroom, no gun, no help, no protection, preparing for a grand entrance. The steam of the running shower fills the space between him and the door. He thinks of kicking the door open but that will frighten the intruder and they might start shooting randomly. He needs to be smarter than that.

Petridis puts his head through the door and looks inside. Not really smart at all. Steam has made it near impossible to see anything. His whole body follows his head and now he is standing inside. The room is not big and visibility is extremely low.

He approaches the shower, opens the door, and reaches for the tap. The water brushes against his skin and scalds his arm. The pain shoots up his spine that clealy shows on his face. Then the water is off and the air begins to clear. No one is in there besides himself. His Glock sits nicely in its holster on the bench. Next to his gun is his phone. He texts Short and tells him he is on his way. He won't mention this to Short until he works out what went on.

CHAPTER 42

Breakfast arrives at the same time Petridis does. Bacon and eggs on sourdough bread, grilled tomato, mushrooms, hash brown, and some spinach. Pineapple juice to wash this massive breakfast down. He should have asked for the eggs to be scrambled; he hates runny yolk. Short ordered an omelette with vegies, a side of potatoes, and a Latte.

'Perfect timing,' Short says with a laugh. 'Did the chef message you when it was going to be ready?'

Petridis just looks at him and says nothing. He doesn't have the energy to explain what just went down. He lets the silence between them hang for a bit before Petridis speaks.

'Some things are best not explained.'

Short stops chewing and looks over towards Petridis. Petridis's troubled expression was too hard for Short to read. Short continued eating and didn't ask any more questions about it.

†

They scoffed breakfast down like it was going to be their last meal for a while. They were done within ten minutes. Only a few words were exchanged during that time; Petridis was checking his emails on his phone while Short was flicking through current posts on the victim's Facebook account, seeing if any one might leave a hint. They leave a tip for the waitress, collected their stuff, and went on foot to the local police station a couple of blocks down.

Through the window, Petridis and Short observe Senior Sergeant Al Hitchcake sitting behind his desk looking busy. A closer look reveals what the Senior Sergeant is engrossed in. With his back towards them and the newspaper held up, they see clear as day that it's the form guide for the races at Randwick. Officially unofficial police business. After all that happened the night before, Petridis and Short thought that Hitchcake would be engrossed in the murder and not the races. They don't have the answer for that.

Petridis and Short enter the front door and make their way into the one room, one officer, three prison cell unit outside in the back of the station. The desk runs parallel across the room with a little section at the end to get from one side to the other.

There are four chairs against the left wall and a small bare coffee table. A large fish tank on the right contains four goldfish. Pamphlets and booklets on shelves hang to the side of the tank explaining who to contact about domestic violence and another which has what to do if you're caught while under the influence. It doesn't look like there is anyone else in the building besides Hitchcake. Behind Hitchcake are two small rooms. One with a sign on the door that reads 'Dunny' and the other must be the little kitchenette. Both rooms are accessible from the back door.

'Can I help you?' Hitchcake's husky, overused voice sounds dubious, but comes out loud and clear. He has lifted his head and is folding the newspaper, then places it under a few files. 'Hang on – aren't you the detectives from Melbourne? Short and … sorry, I don't remember your name.'

'Petridis.'

'Say, do you city boys know much about computers? This thing is way over the top and too high tech for this country lad. I can't seem to get it working. It's put me a little behind in my work. There is so much to write about that happened last night. Tragic, I say. I knew Ann-Maree well. Us old timers here in Silverton stick together like glue. Fine lady and a great cook.'

Petridis and Short look at each other. They know exactly what work he was looking into.

'What are you having trouble with?' asks Short.

'Everything. I'm quite sure someone wrote a book on how to use these things. A dummy's guide to computers?'

'Yeah, I believe they have. There's nothing to them once you get the hang of it, unless you're one of those dummies.'

'Maybe for you, genius. You look like you've had years of experience using computers and devices.'

'Haven't you?'

'Is this guy for real?' Hitchcake says to Petridis, nodding his head a few times over towards Short.

Petridis has an idea that could possibly work out for both parties. 'I tell you what, sir. If you help us with some information about the crimes last night, our boy Short here will give you a crash course in using this device and before you know it you'll be a genius just like him.' Petridis points over to Short with his thumb. 'I'll make sure of that. What do you say?'

Short glances over to Petridis, confused, then it clicks. He's just worked out what Petridis was up to. Hitchcake looks at Short, then Petridis. 'Deal. Fire away. What do you want to know?'

'We want to know who Jack Gumba was, who he knew, who knew him, and where he hung out. We need to know everything there is to know about this guy. If we find that out, then we could possibly find out more about the killer.'

'Wow, okay. Where do I begin?'

'From where you would normally start a story. From the start.'

'Well, okay then. Jack was born and raised here in Silverton. His parents moved away about three years ago – to Melbourne, someone had mentioned. He lived in Earl Street. His parents still owned the house. Nice little place. Nothing flash, but nothing is around here, if you know what I mean.' He finished the sentence with a giggle.

'Did he live there in the house alone?' Short asks.

'Sure did. Jack didn't like cleaning up after people. He was too much of a neat freak. He did have a young couple rent one of the rooms for a few months, drifters they were, but got rid of them quick smart.'

'Why was that?'

'Like I said, Jack was a clean freak. His house was spotless at all times of the day. Wouldn't find a speck of dust on anything. It was like walking into Marie Barone's house. Spotless. You know who Marie Barone is, right? *Everybody Loves Raymond*. Great show. Frank kills me every time.' He cracks up laughing at his own thoughts. Neither of the detectives find it funny.

'Do you know what brand of cigarettes Jack smoked?'

'Jack? Smoke? Are you kidding. He never touched the stuff. Cancer sticks he would call them'

Petridis and Short look at each other knowing that someone else must have been at Jack's house.

'Any relatives you know of in this town?' Petridis says. 'I mean, any relatives who keep in touch or visit?'

'Who, me?'

Hitchcake is definitely not the sharpest tool in the shed. In anyone's shed.

'We're talking about Jack here.'

'Oh, yes, of course we are. Sorry about that. Old head injury, makes me drift off from time to time. What were we talking about?'

'Does Jack Gumba have any relatives in Silverton?'

'Um, yes. I believe he has an auntie here and has a cousin in Melbourne. I've never seen the cousin here, though. Not sure if he has ever lived here, though. I haven't seen him in such a long time, Jack that is. The cousin might have lived here and then moved out, it's hard to keep track of everyone here. People come and go you know. I've been here my whole life, you know? Did I tell you that?'

'No, Sarge, you didn't, but thanks for letting us know. Is the auntie Lolita Grady? How far is her place from here?'

'Yes, that's her. Lovely lady. She's the town vet. Lol.'

'What's so funny?'

'Funny?'

'You said Lol, as in 'laugh out loud', Lol.'

'Oh,' he laughs, 'no not L-O-L. I'm saying Lol, it's short for Lolita. Lolita Grady is the vet's name. Everyone calls her Lol.'

Petridis and Short look at him like he was some useless idiot. He's the Senior Sergeant in this place. God help the people here. Petridis couldn't help but let out a chuckle. 'Where can we find the vet?'

Hitchcake looks over his right shoulder towards the wall clock to see the time. 'Well, at this time, she should be in her office out on Jackson's Lane. It's a dirt track that runs off the highway heading east. You can't miss it.'

'You mentioned Jack's cousin might have moved on from Silverton? Is that correct?'

'Yeah, that's right. Like I said earlier, I've never seen him but I know of him.'

'Do you have a name? Of the cousin that is?'

'Yeah, I think it's Zando or Zoldo, something like that. I can't quite remember.'

A screeching sound comes in from the back door. A high-pitched voice confirming what they needed to hear.

'Zoltan, his name is Zoltan. The cousin.'

'Shut up back there, Fletcher. Keep your mouth shut. Speak only when spoken to, you goose."

'Who is that?' Petridis asks.

'A nobody. No one worth mentioning and losing breath over.'

Detective Petridis and Short walk towards the back door. It is open, letting in a cool breeze and some sunlight. They step out the back of the station into a small uneven courtyard. Nestled towards the back of the yard is the three-cell block, housing the loud vocal local. The boisterous larrikin is chirping louder than a sulphur-crested cockatoo – almost making the same annoying sounds as the bird.

'Zoltan. That's his name,' he keeps on repeating.

Petridis takes his time approaching Fletcher, keeping his distance. Never trust a man with free spirited vocal cords behind bars.

'Fletcher? I'm Detective Petridis. Who is this Zoltan guy you keep mentioning?'

'You're not a detective. You're a pig. All cops are pigs, I tell ya. A PIG. Oink-oink, little piggy.'

'Who is Zoltan?'

'Zoltan is the guy you wanted to know about. His name is Zoltan. Didn't I tell you that already, pig?'

'Yes, you did. Is that Jack Gumba's cousin?'

'Zoltan. The cousin is Zoltan. He's a pig. A pig, just like you.'

CHAPTER 43

Derrick Hamilton was accustomed to seeing dead people in his parlour but to see his wife there was something he had never prepared himself for. He now has the unimaginable task of putting her together for an open casket ceremony. He was advised against it but ignored all the pleads; Ann-Maree Hamilton was getting an open casket service.

Derrick is flying in a team from Melbourne that will perform the almost impossible job of making her look presentable. The Hamiltons have used them before; they're a husband and wife team comprised of Dr Buzz Sawyer and Liddy Sawyer. Derrick had been a bit of a joker in the past and couldn't resist cracking jokes regarding their surname. He would say things like, 'Hey, I saw-yer just the other day,' or he would call Buzz 'Tom', as in Tom Sawyer. The jokes grew old very quickly and both couples moved on from it faster than it had started.

Now is no time to joke. The Sawyers will need a miracle to make sure Ann-Maree looks her best for the family. Her body is kept in Mortuaries and Crematoria in Broken Hill. The closest place to keep Ann-Maree until burial.

Petridis and Short make their way to the funeral parlour before they visit the vet. They want to see if Derrick knows of anyone who might have wanted to hurt his wife. They could have walked, but they had decided they would drive in case they needed to leave in a hurry. Plus, the vet's practice is out of walking distance, even for two fit detectives.

Before this murder, the town of Silverton hadn't seen a crime of this magnitude since the gold rush days. The mayor of the town, who they recently discovered also doubles as the pub owner – Terry Moist – allegedly called this event 'entertainment'. If this is what he calls entertainment then you would hate to be bored in Silverton.

Uniformed offices are patrolling the perimeter on foot, surveilling the area and beyond. A whole team of support personal have been deployed to Silverton to try and catch this thing. Forensics have worked through the night and are still there. A job that they are doing thoroughly, not to miss anything. Police tape has been reapplied as the walkway to and from the house has had quite a bit of traffic which has ripped up the original tape from its position. There won't be much evidence lying around seeing as the area has been trampled on and most likely contaminated.

The detectives slip under the tape which they have become accustomed to of late and make their way to the front door. The smell of death still lingering, the air inside and out no different to last night. An unexplainable aroma drifting and floating across the air, resting at the tip of their nose. Not a smell anyone would want to talk about. They fill their lungs with fresh outside air before entering the slaughterhouse. As Petridis and Short enter the front door, they see Derrick sitting on the couch in the lounge room, surrounded by friends and the police. His mate has flown down from Canberra and Ann-Maree's step-brother and his wife have flown in from Coffs Harbour. A family reunion to forget.

Derrick's hand is held tight by Ann-Maree's sister-in-law, Chloe. His love for the moral support is shown on his face. Bob is hovering behind the couch, pacing up and down like a caged animal. His mind is working overtime, planning on what he would love to do to the person who has caused this family heartache. He wants to hunt and kill whatever killed his step-sister.

'Mr Hamilton,' Petridis says, 'can we have a word with you please? We won't take up too much of your time. I know you're grieving and this must be hard, but we have a job to do. That job is to catch this killer.'

Derrick lifts his head but doesn't seem to acknowledge the words that were spoken by Petridis. No acknowledgement of the detective even being there. His eyes are hollow and dead. It will take a while to have any sort of life brought back into them. Those eyes will never forget what they have seen; his Ann-Maree all carved up and left for dead.

'Mr Hamilton, did you see what happened? Did you see who did this? Did you hear anything that might help us here?'

Not a single word or flinch, no recognition. Derrick is in shock and won't budge from it. This seems to be going nowhere. They won't be getting anything from him today.

Petridis and Short decide to make their way out to the backyard. Nothing has been touched. Forensics arrived late last night and the scene looks the same as it did the night before. The only difference is the sun is up and there is no need to use a flashlight to get around. The temperature is still a little crisp. The air tight in their throat. The DNA kept preserved.

Under the pergola is a dried red stain known to them. A pool of dried blood from the victim. Forensics are having a field day here, so much to do in so little time. It would have helped if they had arrived earlier, but time is still on their side.

'You would think they would have taken a chopper,' Petridis says to Short. They both ponder that thought. Evidence of a severed foot remained clearly visible. A dark patch of blood has stained the grass where the foot had once been. Now, it's probably sitting in a fridge back in Broken Hill without it being attached to a body. It isn't going anywhere and It would have freaked them out if it did. Nothing more has been added to the yard of the funeral parlour that wasn't there the night before. The body was found in the neighbour's yard. Evidence clearly shows that the thing had dragged Ann-Maree's body up and over the fence, bloody marks and broken wooden palings that weren't visible the night before is clear as day now.

Petridis notices something that stood out while glancing around the yard. There is something sticking out of the tree near the back fence. It is out of sight if you come in from a particular angle, unnoticed during the night. Once you are side-on, you can see it clearly. Scrape marks. Marks done by an animal – an animal with large claws. A wolf? Maybe. Possibly something even bigger. The claw marks are huge and deep.

Petridis walks closer and looks around to find his partner. Short is mesmerised by the blood from the foot, just seeing it last night with the sock on resting comfortably in the shoe is still bothering him.

'Short? Can you … can you come over here?'

Short struggled to break his stare away from the spot. His memory has taken a photograph of it. When he is finally able to break away, he sees Petridis standing and staring at the large gum tree. 'What is it?'

'You need to see this.'

Short makes his way over to Petridis, blinking repeatedly to get the vision of the foot out of his head. Now they're both staring at the tree, confused with what's on it. The markings tell a story; a horrid story. A story that can only be written by the killer. The final stages of a gruesome murder committed by a beast with one mission: to kill.

'What do you make of that?'

'Are they claw marks?'

'They look like claw marks.'

'Damn. They're huge. Bear? Tiger?'

'Wolf.'

'Wolf?'

'Wolf.'

'In the outback?'

'In the outback.'

Petridis takes out his pocket knife. He keeps one handy for moments like these. There is something embedded in the tree deep, way deep in the groove. An extremely large claw from a paw. Petridis digs the knife's edge into the tree, prods at it, and with some force dislodges the claw. Picking it up, he gets confirmation.

'Is that what I think it is?' says Short. 'But from what?'

'Only one way to find out. We need to visit the vet.'

CHAPTER 44

Annie had purchased her ticket for the long bus ride to Silverton. She never liked traveling on buses, especially for longer than she could manage. Anything under an hour is manageable. Anything over is unbearable. A difference she knows from experience.

Detective Natloz had asked Annie to meet him in Silverton. He had been in hiding for a while, and needed a familiar face around to discuss what had happened. Someone he could trust. Annie was that someone.

Southern Cross Station is located in Melbourne's CBD. Formally known as Spencer Street Station, this station used to be the dumps – pushed aside for its more glamorous and outstanding sister, Flinders Street Station. With its façade that could walk the runway, this other and original iconic monument has been around since 1905. More like the great grandmother than the sister. Southern Cross is still an iconic building, helped by a facelift back in 2002 that transformed it into an eye-catching wonderful structure.

Annie boarded the bus at 8:00am. Departure is at 8:15am. Enough time to get settled into her seat and prepare herself mentally for the ride. Her bag is placed in the overhead compartment, handbag under the seat in front of her, her book in hand, and her water bottle in the seat pocket. Now that she's comfortable, she looks around at the others on the bus; they, too, look around and make themselves familiar with their surroundings and the other travellers. Almost every seat looks to be occupied. She hopes no one sits next to her as the seat is still vacant.

It is time to leave. The engine starts and the door closes. Nobody has sat next to her. A relief; this could end up being a stress-free ride no matter how long it takes. Looking at the map of the journey, they should be having two stops in towns she isn't that familiar with. She had been to Bendigo once; actually, drove through Bendigo once. This will be the first time her feet will touch Bendigo's soil, or pavement. It will be a morning tea break for a quick bite to eat and a coffee. The next town after that will be Mildura, a dry desert kind of place. Always hot and bothered. More like *can't* be bothered. This town has nothing of interest for Annie. They are stopping in Mildura for an hour. That is one hour she will never get back, one hour out of her life that she has to sit in that hot, shitty town and wait until everyone else has hopped off the bus, stretched their goddamn legs, take photos of the fucking heat, and then bring all that shit back onto the bus. In all honesty, Mildura is a beautiful town with so much to see and do. There's a lot to love about this place. So much history that lays amongst this land, stories that schools in the area tend to share with students and parents alike.

But Annie is frustrated and scared. She hasn't slept well since all this began and she isn't thinking straight. She would ordinarily be gracious and excited about the prospect of visiting the town, but at this moment, everything is bothering Annie and nothing will settle until the killer is caught. She begins to sweat just thinking about it. It's bad enough freaking out every time she leaves the comfort of her place, but this bus trip will surely reduce her lifespan by years, not months. This trip will push her to near breakdown.

After a brief stop in Bendigo, the bus finally makes it to Mildura for the second planned stop. Passengers have disembarked from the bus as requested. Only Annie and an elderly woman who is seated a few rows ahead stay on board. The bus driver, Gus, recommended that they all get out and breathe in the fresh country air, fill their lungs with 'natural life support'. He used those exact words: life support. *Who in their right mind uses the words 'life support' in relation to breathing in hot dusty choking air?* Annie thinks. This guy has spent far too many unforgiving days driving and breathing in this crap air. Desert air, full of dust particles choking your insides.

Annie needs to start thinking straight and stop all this unpleasant negativity that she is entertaining. She needs to change her ways before meeting up with Natloz. She'll need to have a clear mind if she is to help him in any way.

The little old lady up ahead is mumbling something to herself. Annie can't quite make out what she is saying. Probably the heat has gotten to her. Hallucinating, seeing something or someone that isn't there, like a mirage in the desert. An oasis of water for drinking.

She gets louder and her words get clearer. Only then does it register to Annie that the old lady is talking to her.

'This weather can make you do things that are unspeakable. This heat can make you see things that aren't really there. Don't fall for it. It really isn't happening,'

The old lady's words make no sense to Annie. She continues to mumble things in a lower voice Annie can't catch.

'This is way too hot for me to be outside. This is why I'm staying in,' says Annie in a loud, stern voice, hoping the old lady hears her the first time so she doesn't have to repeat herself. A prompt response might end this conversation quickly. Annie is in no mood to talk with anyone. But guilt sets in – maybe the old lady needs some assistance, and there is no one else on board to help.

'Do you need to go out?' she asks. 'Do you need help with anything?'

Annie's words have fallen on deaf ears. There is no response from the old lady. Annie waits for her to say something, anything. But there is nothing. She might have fallen asleep. Annie can't tell from where she is sitting. The headrest is way too high to notice any kind of movement. She can only see the top part of the lady's head. Dyed purple hair at its best.

Annie lets it go and continues glaring out the window, staring at the people out there taking photos. Family photos, couples' selfies. An urge to sit out there in the heat taking photos passes through her mind briefly. So briefly, it is gone within a second. Annie stays put, as originally planned.

She opens up her book to where the bookmark is and begins to read, sipping on her cold water from the bottle handed out, snacking on the salad sandwich she had purchased from the station, costing her an arm and two legs. Before Annie finishes the chapter, the door to the bus opens, making a loud whoosh then a screeching sound. The noise makes Annie drop her book, losing the page she was on. The passengers begin making their way in and taking up their seats. Loud chatter fills the small space, talking about the scenery and things they had bought. The little old lady had company; someone is sitting next to her. Her daughter? Her granddaughter? Hard to tell from here.

Annie picks up her book, puts it on the seat, and makes her way over to where the old lady is sitting.

'Excuse me, sorry to bother you but the lady you're sitting with was saying something a little earlier on. I couldn't make out what she said. I asked her if she needed help but she didn't respond. I just thought I would let you know, see if she's okay? Maybe you can ask her yourself?'

'This is my mother. Thank you, but I don't think she would have said anything.'

'Yes, she did. I heard her talking. I think she was talking to me, but I wasn't quite sure. I know I heard her say something.'

'Sorry, Miss, but I don't think you would have heard mum talking. She was born deaf and mute. She has never spoken a word in her life.'

The ground has just opened up and swallowed Annie whole. Is she starting to lose her mind? She sits in silence for the remainder of the trip, her thoughts dominating the journey. Then, from her seat, she sees the sign.

WELCOME TO SILVERTON:
A VICTORIAN MINING TOWN

CHAPTER 45

The bus has come to a complete stop. Passengers begin moving about the cabin searching for their belongings – bags of clothes and fruit, books, and personal items. Nothing to be left behind. Take it or lose it. Annie is the last to get off with her overnight bag and a book. She had finished the sparkling mineral water she bought in Melbourne and leaves the empty bottle on the bus. Cleaners will dispose of all the rubbish before it makes its journey back.

Annie takes the two steps off the bus and clears the entrance to give herself space to think. She hears the bus driver calling for all checked-in bags to be collected. She didn't have one so she lets that slide. She is free to leave whenever she wants.

She passes the old lady and her daughter. All three smile at each other as Annie walks past. Annie stops just a little further past them and turns around, looking back to see if the old lady is watching. But neither of the women are. All is forgotten.

Annie continues onto the footpath and drops her bag off her shoulder, landing with some force on the ground. A rattle of glassware in the bag makes a noise, most likely her perfume bottle. She takes some time to look around, up and down the street. Not much going on and not much to see. Annie glances across the street to where the last of the passengers are collecting their bags.

The old lady with her daughter were greeted by relatives, huge hugs and kisses shared amongst the lot. They jump into a dirty old Ford Ute and drive off. Their holiday is just beginning. Annie doesn't stick around long enough to see what went on after that. She needs to meet with Natloz.

The bus door closes and the driver moves the bus from the street to the rear of the hotel for the night. It will stay parked behind the pub. Gus will spend the night in Silverton before loading up with new passengers in the morning and drive back to Melbourne where his shift will end for a period of time before doing it all over again in a few days. This is the life he has chosen, and he lives it without being judged. Someone needs to do it and he loves the fact that it's him. He wouldn't have it any other way.

The text that was sent to her days ago made it clear where she had to go. Another had arrived whilst she was on the bus.

> **Hi, I'm sorry to bring you out here, you're the only one I can talk to.**
>
> **When you get off the bus, make your way to the pub. Once you're in there take a seat by the front window. I'll be there not long after you arrive. We can't hang around as I don't want to be seen by anyone. Please don't tell anyone why you're here in Silverton. I don't want you to arouse any concerns or suspicions. I need to know I can trust you.**
>
> **You can trust me.**
>
> **Bye**

Annie is standing outside of the pub while she reads the message again. A quick look inside the windows shows that it is empty. She makes her way to the entrance and through the door. Once inside, she looks to the bar and sees a man wiping down some glasses, and takes a seat at a table closest to the front window. She puts her bag down on the ground and rests her book on the table.

Terry makes his way over and introduces himself. 'What would you like, love?'

'Do you make coffee here?'

'Sure do. Best filtered brew in town. Not much to compete with to be honest,' he says, then gives out a laugh which was more of a snort.

'I'll have one of those then, thank you.'

'Anything to eat, love?'

'No, no thank you.'

Terry is gone as quick as he had arrived. Moves fast for a big fella. Annie spends the next few minutes staring out the window, at nothing in particular, just gazing at the scenery which looks all dry. The heat outside is hot but bearable. Thirty-eight degrees Celsius with no wind to mention.

She can hear the coffee machine doing its thing in the background. Her phone lets out a ping. A new text. She takes the phone out of her bag and taps it to life. The little icon on the top confirms a new message. Could it be the detective? *It might be,* she thinks to herself.

She checks. It's not Detective Natloz, it's Annie's roommate, Jess. She wants to know when she'll be back and if her boyfriend can stay over until she returns. Annie's confused on why she is asking her for permission, as it's her place and not Annie's. All the same, Annie is happy she asked. Annie had told Jess that she was meeting up with friends in Bright, which is the complete opposite direction to Silverton. A little lie would never hurt.

**Sure he can stay. I'll be back in a few
days xx**

Still nothing from Natloz. She has a look at the time on her phone. Just after 6:00pm. He should have been here by now. Something might have happened. What could possibly have gone wrong in a town this small? She bets there could be a hundred things, but none of them come to mind.

Terry comes back with the freshly-brewed coffee, the aroma filling the air with a wonderful caffeinated smell. It backs up the theory of it being the best brew.

'Are you passing through or staying a few days? If you are staying and have nowhere to stay, then this place is up for contention. Give you a good rate, too.'

'Not sure yet. I'm staying for a few days but not sure where.' She almost lets slip that she is meeting someone there but stops herself before it is too late.

'Oh, alright. Let us know if you want anything. I'm also the owner here. Give ya mate's rates,' he says with a laugh.

A kid stops directly in front of the window, knocks on the glass, and holds up a piece of paper.

Meet me at the back behind the bus

'Get the hell out of here, you little ratbag.'

The tone and volume that Terry used frightened the crap out of Annie. The jolt made her leg knock the table which inadvertently caused the coffee cup to tip and spill all the coffee onto the floor and the table, soiling some pages of her book.

'I'm so sorry,' Annie says in a sad voice.

Terry thinks she is about to cry. 'No, don't be sorry. It wasn't your fault. It was that little pri—' Terry refrained from finishing the sentence. 'I'll go and get the cloth and a fresh coffee.'

'No need for another coffee. I'll come back for one, soon. I … I just need to go now. I'll come back for it.'

Annie grabs her book that is dripping with coffee and her bag and makes her way over to the door. She looks over her shoulder and notices Terry on all fours cleaning up the spilt coffee on the floor. Annie makes a mental note to pay for that coffee she spilt unintentionally when she returns, but she has other arrangements to attend to that are urgent.

She approaches the bus with caution, not knowing if the detective would be there or not. It might be a trap. That young kid could be there with an older friend or brother. They might try to mug her. She has 'tourist' written all over her. The last thing she wants is to be mugged in a foreign town, not knowing anyone here besides Natloz.

As she turns the corner, she sees Detective Natloz paying the young lad some money before scooting him away. She approaches apprehensively, not knowing what to expect. They stand face to face, staring, not saying a word. Annie makes the first move. She opens her arms and hugs him with all her might. He returns the feeling with a similar but not as tight hug. They stand like that for what seems like an eternity. Not moving or saying a word. Eyes closed and taking in all that was expected.

They finally pull away. Annie smiles. 'How are you doing?'

'I'm okay. I'm really happy you came.'

'Where did you go after you left? Did you come straight out here? Why leave so sudden?'

'I had to leave. Things began to happen to me that I couldn't understand. Things I still don't understand.'

'Are you feeling okay, health-wise?'

'No.'

'Have you seen anyone about it? A doctor?'

'No. I can't see anyone about it.'

'Why?'

'It's complicated.'

'How complicated can it really be?'

Natloz looks at Annie, his eyes are worried. He can't explain what he has been going through. She must know it's something that is pretty bad for him to skip town and stay in hiding. Something is happening to him that is out of his control. He looks tired and sick. Mostly sick.

'Where are you staying?' he asks.

'Not sure yet. I haven't organised anything. Terry at the pub asked if I wanted to stay there. Mate's rates he said, not sure what that means.'

'Okay. Okay. That would be good. Mate's rates mean he will look after you financially.'

'Oh, okay. Where are you staying?'

'There's a house I was told about that's been vacant for a while. A friend of mine owns it. No one comes around to check on it.'

'Do you have power there?'

'I do. The owner still pays the bills to make out there is someone living there. It works for me. He spends four months of the year overseas working. Most of the time he's in Port Augusta in South Australia. This place is like a getaway place for him.'

He looks at Annie and is about to ask if she wants to stay there with him but thinks better of it and keeps quiet. 'Maybe you should go and check yourself into the hotel? We can catch up a little later on. I'll order some food and we can talk about things over a meal. Let's say around 8:00-ish?'

'Yes, that sounds fine with me.' She is a little disappointed he hadn't asked her to stay with him after all they have been through.

Natloz puts his hand on Annie's shoulder and passes a piece of paper to her with the address before turning on his heel and taking off, looking around to make sure he isn't seen by anyone or followed. The house he has crashed at is not far from the pub.

Annie walks back to the pub and approaches Terry at the bar. He is serving a patron a drink. The bloke looks a little wasted, tired possibly from work as he is wearing overalls. Skin as tough as a leather bag. Eyes so bloodshot he looks like he has just crawled out of a grave. His head is down and a glass sits in both hands, a vice-like grip making sure no one steals his highlight of the evening.

The place has more people seated. She was only gone about ten minutes or so. Some having dinner, others just blabbering rubbish. Verbal diarrhea, as it is known to some old folks.

'Ah, you're back. Let me get you that coffee now.'

'Hi Terry. I might need something stronger than a coffee.'

'Right-o. One coming up. Anything in mind?'

'Maker's Mark on the rocks. Do you have Maker's?'

'We sure do, young lady.'

'I also want a room. Maybe for two nights? Do you have one for me?'

'That I do. Presidential Suite. Has a balcony overlooking our beautiful dry scenery. Give that to you for the price of a standard room. $78 a night. Is that okay?'

'Yes, that is okay. I think I can find it in my budget.'

'Excellent. I'll get my mother to set up the room.'

'Oh, don't bother her. She must be quite old and frail. I'm happy to do it. Just let me know where the sheets are and I'll collect them after my drink.'

Terry looks at Annie with glazed eyes and burst out laughing. 'Just kidding there, love. My mum passed away over ten years ago. We have maids here for that.'

They both exchange a smile before laughing out loud. Annie's drink comes fast and she downs it in one gulp. She must have looked like a serious drinker to the others.

'Here's your key. Pay on your way out in a few days. Breakfast is served in the bistro from 7:00am.'

'Excellent. Well, I better go now. Thank you, Terry.'

'No problem at all. I should be thanking you.'

Annie turns to make her way to the stairs but she notices a pair of eyes burning a hole through her. Someone is staring right at her; it's the old man at the counter she saw earlier. His hands are still clenched around his beer. She's not sure if it's the same glass or a freshly poured one. His eyes beady, lifeless, dull, and scary.

Why is he looking at me like that? What does he want? Annie's a little scared and it shows all over her face.

'Something is going to happen,' the man says. 'Watch your back. Don't trust the innocent.'

'Cut it out, Bazza. Leave the girl alone. You're scaring her,' says Terry with a serious look on his face.

'It's not me she needs to be scared of. It's that other guy. He's here in this town. He doesn't belong here. Something is going to happen and it's not going to be good.'

'I said cut it, Bazza, or I'll ask you to leave.'

'You've been warned, young lass. It's not my fault. Watch your back.'

CHAPTER 46

The surprise visit Lol received earlier today has thrown her off schedule. Her nephew showed up unannounced after being absent from her life for so long. She wasn't pleased to have seen him and he still seemed troubled to her. Something had been bothering him. They've planned to meet up in the next few days when she is free to chat, something she is not looking forward to. Her memories of when he was young have frightened her.

She was getting herself ready for an early night when her landline phone began to ring. Lol doesn't own a mobile phone so if anyone needed to contact her it was either on the phone at home or at her clinic.

Who could be calling her at this hour? She never received calls after 6:00pm. If there were any pet emergencies, the folks in this town and beyond knew to call the twenty-four hour hotline. Only then would the switchboard themselves get in contact with her. Lol doesn't want anyone having her private number. It wasn't always this way; she changed it about five years ago when she had prank calls coming through for a whole month that led to a break in. She was assaulted and held at gunpoint for money. It was a scary time for her. She was left tied up to her wall heater for more than a day. The paper boy raised the alarm when he had come around the next day to deliver the paper and noticed the previous day's paper still on the lawn. He peeped through the window and saw Lolita in distress. He became an instant hero to his mates and the town awarded the young man with the Local Heroes award that is given out annually. He did himself and the community proud.

The teens ran off with minimal cash from her purse and also walked out with her TV and DVD player. They were apprehended forty-eight hours later when a TV repairman watched the news and had seen the same stolen items in a flat he'd been called out to in Broken Hill. The kids were aged thirteen and fifteen. Even though she wasn't hurt in the ordeal, Lol had lost all her confidence and charisma, and was scared of leaving the house, even though it had happened there. She feared for her life. It took her almost two years to be able to leave her house and start treating the animals she had once loved.

She picks up the phone. 'Hello, Lolita Grady speaking. How can I help you?'

'Hello, my dog has been hit by a car. It needs help. Please help Buster. Please. I don't want her to die. I need your help,' says a male voice that was familiar, but couldn't put a finger on it.

'Did you ring the emergency number? Please ring them first to register your call.'

'I tried, there was no answer. I need you to come to the clinic. I'm waiting at the front door. Please hurry.'

'How did you get my number?'

'Please hurry. I don't know if she will make it.'

'You said she. Is Buster a female?'

'Sorry, I meant to say he. He's a boy.'

Lol thought she heard a faint cry from a dog on the other end of the phone. Her gut is telling her to hang up and call the police, explain what has just happened and get them to check it out before she goes to the clinic. She doesn't want a repeat of what happened last time.

Halfway through her thoughts, the line goes dead. They have hung up. The only thing she can hear is the dial tone. She puts the phone down and then picks it up again to dial the police. Senior Sargent Hitchcake works long hours. Most nights he sleeps there at the station. If he wasn't at the station then he would be at home or on patrol. No matter where he was, your call would reach him 24/7.

The phone keeps ringing. Lol waits for Al to pick up, but he doesn't. The call just rang out. She tries for a second time. Same thing. She tries several times but she gets the same response. She stands there, deep in thought, not sure what she should do. She walks over to the front door where her keys are housed in a bowl, puts on her coat and UGG boots, and leaves the house heading for her clinic. She's on her own. No mobile and no clue who the frantic caller is. She is purely going on instinct and adrenaline and the thought of hearing a dog in distress: three things that have changed the course of the evening. She hops into her car and starts the short journey to the veterinary clinic, not knowing what lies ahead.

†

Annie walks the short two blocks to the vacant house Detective Natloz is squatting at. The house looks like all the other houses, normal from the outside. The garden is well-manicured, the grass cut and no longer than an inch in height, and there's a small cast iron gate with a sign on it saying 'KEEP OUT'. From the outside it looks like someone is genuinely living in it, even though Natloz is living there unannounced. Natloz has all the lowdown about the house, who the neighbours are and the sticky beaks he needs to watch out for. The owner doesn't even know he is there at this point in time. Jerry has told Natloz he can use the house anytime he wants. He knew where the spare keys were kept. Jerry had kept them in that same place for as long as Natloz had known him. Jerry and Natloz went to school together back in the days, but Jerry pursued a career that was completely different, something Natloz has no interest in.

Annie approaches the gate and opens it with care. A slight creak from the hinges announces her arrival. Natloz is at the front door before Annie can even get to it.

'You're right on time. Food just arrived.'

'How did you get the food without anyone knowing you're here?'

'My little mate from earlier today. I pay him to run errands for me.'

'And you can trust that he doesn't say anything?'

'I do. Sometimes you just need to trust certain people.'

'You're brave.'

'Come in. Not much is open out here at this time. Silverton pub do make some nice fish 'n' chips though.'

'Anything will do. I never got to try the chips in Apollo Bay.'

They both smile at the comment.

'Thank you for coming out this far to see me,' Natloz says. 'I had no one else to turn to.'

'What about your partner?'

'Detective Petridis?'

'Yes. Aren't you two close?'

'We are, but I didn't want to put him in a position that would make it difficult for him to choose.'

'In what way?'

Natloz stays silent. Let's his words hang. Annie waits for a response.

'I'm not well, Annie,' he says finally. 'Something has happened to me. It's still happening to me, but not as frequent. I feel … I feel strange, like something is growing inside me. I might have had something to do with all the murders that happened back in Melbourne. I don't know what to do.'

'What do you mean you might have something to do with the murders? Detective Natloz, you're not making much sense.'

'Strange things are happening to me. I black out and when I come to, I have a hard time remembering what happened the night before. It's … it's like everything goes hazy. My memory is blocked out. I have a bad odour that lingers on my body and my breath tastes stale. I needed to leave in case I hurt someone I love. I got scared and did what I needed to do. I ran.'

'Is there any evidence to make you believe you had anything to do with the murders?'

'Some, but I can't remember anything about them. I'm still not sure about the photos and what I did or happened that night. No details. Nothing. My mind has been washed clean.'

'What are you going to do?'

'I have a family member here. She's a vet. I haven't seen her since I was a kid. I want to see her and need to talk with her. She might know something about why I'm feeling this way. I want you to be with me when I see her.'

'I think we shouldn't wait. We should go now.'

'Right now?'

'Well, once we finish our chips. I don't want to miss out again.'

After eating their chips, they both set off to see Lolita Grady.

CHAPTER 47

Lol pulls up at the front of the clinic. There is no one in sight. The place is quiet and dimmed; besides the sound and sight of her idling car and headlights, the place looks deserted. The night air has dropped and feels dead. The land is asleep, with only the sound of the distant wild animals making their natural nocturnal sounds.

She flicks on the high beam to brighten up the place a little more, trying to flush out anything that might be lurking in the dark. The building lights up like a Christmas tree. Despite all the lights being on, she still can't see anyone around with their injured dog. She switches off the engine of the car but leaves the lights on. If anything or anyone was going to pop out and try to surprise her, she would see them.

She unlocks the car and opens the door gingerly, placing one foot out and touching the hard ground. She turns her body and manoeuvres her torso to match the angle of her legs, which are now both planted flat on the hard soil. Her eyes haven't moved from the entrance to the building, focused like a sniper. She removes the keys from the ignition and hops out, leaving the door open. She pockets the keys in case she needs to make a quick getaway. The last thing she wants is to be searching for car keys if she is chased down by a killer. She scours the area before continuing on.

'Hello?'

Not a sound. The air around Lol has become thick and she feels like it has stopped completely. The building is a remote block with nothing else around it but empty land. An ideal spot for an ambush. It isn't too far out from town but too far to walk. There is a fence that borders the building with direct access from the front to the rear. She walks to the front door and with a little hesitation reaches for the handle to see if it was unlocked but no, it is locked.

She moves to the only window at the front and has a peek through it. There are no curtains, so she has a clear view inside. Everything seems to be in order in the waiting area but she notices something a little odd behind the front desk. She can see from a dimmed light in the back room that the rear door is ajar. Someone has broken in and must be in there. That phone call that she had received is all flooding back in now. It must be him. But why would he break in? Why couldn't he have just waited for her to come and open up? He must have known she was on her way … wait, did she mention to him that she was coming?

These are questions she's unable to answer, questions that could jeopardise judgement calls. It is times like these she wishes she had a mobile to ring for help. Ring Hitchcake. He'd definitely come down there right away. But she doesn't and she needs to deal with this now.

She starts her slow walk towards the rear of the building, every step with caution. Every step feels like it could be her last. Memories from her attack flood her mind. It has momentarily paused her in her tracks. Glued to the ground, her legs unable to move. Fear at its highest level. The phone begins to ring in her office. Someone is trying to get in contact with her on the landline. It rings out. She continues moving towards the back. She needs to get to the phone in the office and call Hitchcake. Whoever is in there might have taken what they wanted and left. She reaches the back section of the building and looks around the corner. She pokes her head around to see if there is anything there. No one there. Surely, they would have left once they heard the car pull up. She contemplates turning around and driving to the police station. She musters up the courage and decides against it. She stays and continues to the open door. Lol has convinced herself the place is empty.

One, two, three, she opens it with her foot. The office is dark, like a dungeon. The light from the computer the only sign of life in there. The chair from the desk has been moved from its original position. It's now sitting in the middle of the room unmanned.

She takes a step in and stops to listen for any sound. The rattle of the fridge motor is the only thing that stimulates her ears. She glances inside the clear glass door of the fridge and notices a few bottles of tranquilizer missing. Last time she had checked the bottles were all there. Twelve bottles in total. Now she can only count seven. There are enough bottles missing to put a small army to sleep.

Lol had gotten someone to install an alarm system last year after a break in that saw more damage done than what was stolen. Insurance had looked after her but it was the violation that was unsettling and stuck like glue. The thought of someone in her premises ransacking her property made her uneasy. Her belongings. Her livelihood. That thought took a while to submerge and disappear. Some days that memory resurfaces its ugly head for a short time before disappearing for a further undisclosed period of time. Luck is something that hasn't been on her side. The alarm has been switched off.

Just in case the intruder hasn't left, she wants to warn them that she is inside the building, giving them an opportunity to present themselves and so there are no surprises from either end. The last thing she wants is a startled trigger-happy teen firing unrepentantly at her. Either way, she's ready for what might be around the corner.

The courage she possessed a moment ago has completely vanished and she decides to slow her breathing down to the bare minimum, trying not to panic and make her exact position known. She enters the main room, unable to see more than a few feet in front of her. Luckily for her, she knows the layout of the room really well. It can be an obstacle course for anyone who doesn't.

Her eyes have adjusted to the darkness and from across the room, she can see a large figure sitting on the seat that's used by visitors when they bring in their furry friends for examination. Even seated, this person looks huge. Bulky and broad. Disturbing and menacing, like a bear.

Looking around the room in the dark, she can see that there is only one person there. He's some distance away from her; she can easily turn and run out the back door to her safety but she decides against it and stays. She doesn't want to be frightened out of her own place. She reaches over with her right hand along the wall, not taking her eyes off the intruder, for the light switch. She feels the switch and the fluorescent lights come up like it was the Fourth of July.

He is holding a syringe filled with invisible liquid. She knows exactly what the liquid is. The missing tranquilizer from the fridge.

'What are you doing here?' she asks. 'I was surprised to see you the other day. I thought you were locked up?'

'I was. But they can't keep a good man down.'

'You're not good. You're evil.'

'Aww, that's not a nice thing to say. I'm deeply hurt by that comment.'

'You have no feelings to feel hurt.'

'Don't say that too loud. People might hear you and make me out to be a monster.'

'They'll only be hearing the truth.'

'What, that I am a monster? Surely you don't believe that, do you?'

'I do. You are a monster. A monster that should be locked away in a cage, forever. That same cage you have lived in for the past thirty-five years.'

'Now that breaks my heart.'

'What heart? You are not capable of caring for anyone but yourself. At times you can't even do that.'

'You let this happen. You let them put me away. You're telling me that I have no heart? Take a close look at yourself there, Lol Grady.'

The mystery man's voice is getting louder and angrier. Clearly getting agitated with this exchange of words. You could almost see the steam coming from his ears, flames from his nose.

'You were out of control and become too much for your parents to handle. They couldn't handle you and your sinister outbreaks. Your mother knew you set fire to the house that killed your babysitter. We all knew it was you. She didn't stand a chance. You were born evil and there was nothing anyone could have done about it. Your mother did the only thing she could at that time, and yes, I supported her. We all supported her decision. It broke her heart. You killed everything she had lived for.'

'You fucking bitch. You are all going to pay for this, starting with you, Auntie Lolita.'

A car pulls up at the front of the clinic. Someone is here. The man panics, unlocks the door, and runs to the desk where Lolita is standing. Whoever is out there can see the light on. No need to deny that someone is inside the place. He crouches down behind the desk with the syringe pressed up against the small of her back, ready to deliver the lethal blow if anything goes wrong. He will take everyone down with him.

'I'm giving you one chance to get rid of whoever it is, or you and them will die here tonight.'

There's a creak at the door. The handle turns and opens …

CHAPTER 48

Petridis and Short head out and focus on the task ahead, visiting the vet, Dr Lolita Grady. Her place of residence isn't far from the funeral parlour. Nothing really is in this town. Silverton itself is not large. Someone will always be a stone's throw away. With a good arm, you would be able to throw a rock from one end of the town to the other and probably hit a bird mid-flight, too.

Their mission is to find out what that claw they found in the tree belonged to and how it came to be there. She knows all about animals, therefore she should know about this. If she doesn't then someone else in this town might, but she is the best person to chat with right now.

Petridis and Short head back to the hotel via the police station. Short spent some time with Hitchcake going over the basics on computers and the fundamentals. What was meant to take minutes ended up taking hours. Hours the detectives were saving for the visit to Lolita Grady's house. Petridis didn't want to go back on his word and the vet was going nowhere anytime soon.

They had a quick bite to eat and shower before heading out the door once more.

The walk had taken less than ten minutes. The house is nestled along a residential street lined with townhouses and gum trees.

It didn't stand out any more than the others did. A pretty desert villa with minimal character and lots of heart.

Both detectives approach the house and walk up to the door. It didn't look like anyone was at home but still, they did what police officers normally do; they knocked. No noise from the other side of the door. Petridis knocks once more. Same response. Crickets. Short then notices a note that has been left on the chair next to the door. The sun seems to go down a lot earlier and quicker up these parts. It's a bit hard to read in the dark, with no porch light. Short flashes the torch from his phone onto it.

The letter proved that Lolita Grady isn't at home. The letter also said that she had rushed off to the veterinary clinic on an emergency callout. If anyone needed her, they should contact the clinic. She was planning on being there a while. A phone number was listed right at the bottom. Short dials the number but there is no response.

'Should I try again?'

'No. She must be either on her way or dealing with the emergency. We have no idea what time she left here. Is that the only number she left?'

'Yeah, that's it.'

'We should go to the clinic. Let's check up on her. Make sure everything is okay.'

Without wasting time, both detectives make their way back to their car which was still parked at the Hamilton's funeral parlour. An eerie feeling brings out goosebumps on Short's skin. Something he hasn't felt since he was a teen. He feels chills and puts it down to the drop in the weather. Something does the same to Petridis, but with a slightly different effect; a strange pricking feeling in his bones. Petridis senses something isn't right. Before hopping into the car, he pops the boot open and makes sure he has all the firepower he needs ready, just in case that worst case scenario comes into play.

'What are you doing?' says Short.

'Getting things ready. I have this bad feeling that is itching my insides. Something isn't right here, mate. Just taking precautionary measures. You want your vest?'

'We're in the outback. Whatever you're feeling will turn out to be nothing. My bones tell a different story. There'll be no bear attacks tonight, mate.'

'I think you should reconsider.'

'I think I'll be right.'

The boot closes and both detectives hop in. They put their seatbelts on, Petridis's vest sitting a little uncomfortably under it. He never wears it while he drives but today is different. He feels different. He starts the car and they head off. The clinic is not that far out of town.

As they approach the clinic, they notice another car parked right in front with the driver's door open and the headlights still on. Both detectives assume it's the vet's car. They park next to it and switch off the engine. They take their time getting out. Once outside, Petridis moves closer and looks inside the open door of the parked car. There's no one in there. He switches off the headlights and closes the door. They also notice that there are lights on inside the clinic. Lolita must be in there dealing with that emergency, as expected.

'Are you ready?' says a nervous Petridis to Short.

Short senses fear in his partner's voice. 'Yeah, I'm ready. Let's do this.'

Short leads the way and reaches the door first. Through the window Petridis can see a woman standing at the desk, alone. She is looking a little nervous for his liking. It must be Dr Grady.

Short puts his hand on the door handle, turns it, and it makes a creaking sound. It's unlocked. The door opens and Short walks in. Petridis still stands by the window outside, waiting to see if anything happens.

'Good evening, ma'am, I'm Detective Pat Short, my partner is just outside. Is everything okay here?'

The look on her face says, 'No', but the word that comes out is, 'Yes.'

Petridis finally makes his way inside and introduces himself. She still looks out of sorts, a feeling you get when you are in danger.

'We have a few questions to ask you in regards to a claw that was found at a murder scene.'

'How am I able to help with that?'

'Well, seeing as you're a vet, you might be able to determine what animal it's come from.'

'Well … I'm not sure I can help you, detectives. I'm quite busy with an emergency at the back room.'

'It won't take too much of your time. We just want you to see the claw and tell us if you can identify what animal it might have come from.'

'I guess I can have a quick look for you.'

Lol tries hard not to make any sudden moves that might make the detectives any more suspicious than they already are. The man is on his knees with that deadly syringe pointed directly at her body, the tip pressing up against her skin. The last thing she wants is sudden movement that could possibly trigger a shootout. He won't hesitate in using it.

Short places the nail on the desk in front of her. Lol picks it up and has a closer look. She knows exactly what it is. 'It's hard to tell what it might be from, detective. A large animal, I'm sure of.'

'Yes, we gathered that, too,' Short says, 'but would you know from what large animal it could be? Would you be able to narrow it down to maybe one or two?'

'Hmm, no sorry. You might have to take it into town and ask someone there. I'm sorry I couldn't have been much more help to you. I really need to get back to work now.'

'Sure, sorry to bother you. We won't keep you any longer.'

Petridis turns first and heads towards the door. Short follows closely behind him. There is unfinished business here, and Petridis isn't entirely convinced she is alright. He isn't planning on leaving right away, but he'll make her believe he is. Someone else is in there with her and she made it quite clear by the way she was acting.

Short stops at the entrance and turns to face Dr Grady. 'I just have to ask you something, doc.'

Short begins a slow walk back to the bench where Dr Grady is.

'Sure, detective, what is it?'

'Do you get bears or wolves out here in the outback?'

A random and strange question, Lol thinks. One so random, it triggers something unusual in the man on the floor. His blood begins to boil, his body convulses; a specific word has definitely touched a nerve.

'Definitely not bears. But we do sometimes get wolves. The farmers tend to shoot them when they see them around on properties in these parts. They cause havoc amongst livestock, especially chickens. They tend to run scared when they're confronted.'

'Yes, I guess so. I would do the same if my stock was confronted by a wolf. Shoot it right between the eyes, I would.'

She turns her eyes downward, trying to signal to Short. Unfortunately, Short doesn't see the clue thrown at him, but Petridis does. Even then, he wasn't quick enough though to stop what comes next.

Detective Short didn't stand a chance. The man leapt up off the ground and charged Short. He had some giant claw-like weapon wrapped around his hand. His eyes glowed red and sweat dripped down his face like some crazed beast. With a thunderous swipe, the claw came down viciously across the face and torso of Short.

The claws were so sharp, Short's skin split wide open with ease. His face fell apart like slow cooked meat falling off the bone. Blood fills the room within seconds. Brain matter splatters the ceiling with red streaks.

Short's eyes are filled with fear and blood begins to pour out of his torn flesh. His legs give way as his body crumbles to the floor with a thud. His entire body begins to convulse and his heart begins to slow down to its final beat. Nothing can save his life at this point.

Everything happened so fast. Petridis didn't even have time to blink. There are screams from across the room; Lol fills the clinic with a screeching sound. Petridis comes running back towards Short's fallen body but it's too late to do anything. He draws his gun but is knocked off his feet with a kick to his gut. This man is not only tall but is also strong, built like a mountain. He has the power of a beast. That claw-like weapon makes him look like a wild beast. A wolfman. More like a werewolf, if anything.

Petridis's gun falls to the ground. The man picks it up and puts it in his jacket, away from anyone who might harm him. Petridis has a clear view of this man, but his features are distorted, the light above him making things a little hazy. Petridis can't tell who he is.

He knows they are in trouble. Short's life has vanished from existence, brutally cut short by this crazy lunatic. His lifeless body bleeds out on the floor in front of Petridis, blood substituting the varnish on the floorboards. Detective Short is dead. Lol Grady is frozen with fear. Nailed to the spot, not moving. Her heart has stopped beating, or she thinks it has. She can't hear a thing. Her inner strength subdued by fear. Scared senseless and feeling like her life is also about to end.

Petridis moves slightly further back to get away from the blood that has poured out of his partner's torso. The pool is creeping closer to Petridis's crouched body on the floor. His partner is unrecognisable.

The man's features become clearer with every movement Petridis makes. As the man moves, the light changes on his face, shadowing a different part. Slowly but surely, Petridis now recognises who this man is. His body slumps in shock and defeat.

The man is Will Natloz.

CHAPTER 49

The room falls silent, like they're standing in the middle of the Sistine Chapel in The Vatican. Only God himself or an act of God can save them. Both Petridis and Lol are staring down defeat. Beaten not by the better man but by a beast, a monster, a psychotic lunatic.

The look of despair on the face of Petridis says it all. Confusion written all over it. *Why? Why would Will do something like this? What would have made him commit this unspeakable crime?*

The man forces Petridis to his feet and makes him join Dr Grady over the other side of the room behind the desk.

'Are you okay?' Petridis asks her. She still looks like she's in shock. A nod confirms she's doing okay physically, but mentally she is struggling. This must be affecting her in a big way. The violent history she spoke about earlier with the man is being relived.

Petridis had no idea about the break in and hostage saga that had occurred at Lol's expense a few years back. Petridis also won't know about the extensive medical report on the doctor and how the incident had affected her. She had taken quite some time off to recover but those thoughts would always remain with her. The scars that have remained from the ordeal would be sneaking right in again. That wasn't an easy thing to overcome.

For the moment, both Petridis and she are prisoners in the clinic. The thought of escaping loses momentum with every minute that ticks by. They have no idea how this will end, it's almost impossible to stay positive.

Then a gun goes off. One of them is hit and they hit the ground.

CHAPTER 50

Annie has convinced Natloz to speak with someone about what he is feeling and get some advice from a professional, a doctor. They are walking to Lol's house, which is on the other side of town, a five minute walk from where Natloz was squatting. While passing the General Store, Natloz gazes through the window and stops abruptly, drawn in by something he sees. Annie hadn't noticed so she continues walking and talking at the same time. It was when she couldn't hear Natloz's footsteps did she stop and look around.

'What is it?' she asked.

'We need to go to the police station first.'

'What did you see?'

'My cousin. He has fallen victim to this crazed killer.'

And with that, they head off to the police station first. What Natloz saw in the window was the front page of the local newspaper. The heading was 'Local man killed in Geelong', along with the name Jack Gumba.

They decided to raise the alarm by heading to the police station and explaining everything to Hitchcake. They need to let him know what is going on. They see a sign on the door with the name of the Senior Sergeant.

'Why would someone name their child Alfred with a surname like Hitchcake? Sounds too much like that film director, Hitchcock,' says Annie. Natloz couldn't have agreed more.

They notice lights on in the station. He must be in. They enter the station and call out his name. There is no response. He must be in the toilet. They approach the front desk and ring the little metal bell. *Ding-ding.* The sound reminds them of a boxing match. Round Three is about to begin in the main event. Still no response.

'He must be here,' says Annie. 'His car is still parked out the front.' Hard not to notice it belongs to Hitchcake with Silverton Police written across the side of the car.

They walk in and notice Hitchcake at his desk, resting his head on a pile of books. Natloz walks around the front desk and gains entrance to the back. It looks as if he has fallen asleep at his desk. His head is down and his hands are clamped together in front of him. But Natloz is quite convinced that sergeant Hitchcake is not asleep. That's when he sees the blood. He isn't sleeping; he is dead. Someone has slit his throat from ear to ear with some sort of jagged weapon. His face slumped over a pile of papers on the desk, drowned in his own blood. Someone has silenced him for good.

Annie screams, bringing the present to life. She continues screaming all the way out of the station.

'Annie,' Natloz yells after her. But there was nothing he could have said that would have made Annie stop. She exits the station without looking back.

Natloz checks for a pulse, even though he knows there won't be one. The colour has already drained from Hitchcake's head, his skin pale as a ghost. Some papers scattered across the desk are either covered with the sergeant's blood or piled too high to be touched. Whoever did this had no intention of robbing the place; they were purely there to murder the sergeant. This was personal. The thrill and thirst of killing someone. Unfortunately, that someone happened to be the sergeant.

The rear door is wide open. It overlooks a courtyard. Holding cells are visible in the distance. Natloz can't tell if there is anyone in them. It is dark outside with only one floodlight working. Natloz steps out the back door and down a few steps. He approaches the cells with caution. There might be someone in them. It is worth a try.

From where he is standing, they look empty, but then he hears a noise come from inside the middle cell. He flashes the torch from his phone inside the cell and notices a man curled up in a foetal position, shaking, scared shitless. He must have seen or heard what happened here from his cell.

'Hey … what happened here?' Natloz waits for a response, then asks again. 'What happened here? I'm here to help. I'm a detective. Tell me what you saw.'

The man lifts his weary head. His sweaty hair is draped over his face, hiding one of his eyes. He lifts up his hand and puts it in front of his face, shielding his eyes from the bright light from the torch. Trying to build enough courage to speak. 'I … I … heard it. And then I saw it. He was crazy.'

'Who was crazy?'

The man looks closely at Natloz's face, fixated on his features. Then out of the blue, he begins screaming. The scream is so loud it would have been heard for miles. Annie comes running back in, thinking Natloz might be in trouble. She makes her way to the back where Natloz is and stops suddenly a few metres away from where Natloz is standing. The man in the cell is screaming and yelling something. It wasn't clear at the beginning, but then it made more sense when the man's voice slowed down.

'It was you! It was you!' he repeats before falling silent again, crouched in the same foetal position. Quiet like a baby who has gone back to sleep, safely rocking in his mother's arms while she tells him, 'Everything will be okay.' Annie puts her hand on Natloz's shoulder, vibrating her fear onto him.

'What was he saying?'

'I'm not sure but we need to go.'

'Where to?'

They had one more place they needed to visit to get answers. They needed to visit the vet.

CHAPTER 51

No one knew where that bullet came from.

A shot heard but not seen. A break of the window and a body collapsing. Reeling in pain and gasping for air. The man was shot.

Petridis and Lol stand close together, watching him wriggle in pain on the ground. Petridis moves quickly towards the man and pounces on the weapons, taking the syringe from his hand, the gun from his jacket, and that monstrous claw out of his reach.

The man they thought was Will Natloz in fact isn't. The scene begins to unfold in front of them and starts to make sense, the final chapter of this story taking place right before their eyes.

The door opens. Standing there with a gun in his hand is the real Willem Natloz. Two identical men in the same room at the same time. One a detective, the other sadistic killer. Petridis is standing there, confused at what has just been unveiled before his eyes. Like a magician's illusion revealed to a captivated crowd, wanting an encore and for the show not to end.

'Will?'

'Hey, partner,' Natloz says. 'Long time, no see.'

'Where the fuck have you …? You know what, don't even answer that. Do you know this guy?'

Natloz turns his head and looks over at the man who is reeling in pain. The lookalike is now leaning up against the wall, hurt. Awake and in extreme pain, no one giving a shit or trying to help him. It feels like Natloz is staring directly into a mirror. This guy is a mirror image of himself. How is that even possible? Did this guy set out to have surgery to look like Natloz? Question is, why? Only the guy can answer that.

'I don't know who this guy is,' he says.

'I do.' The words came from Lolita's mouth, floating like dust across the room. Not settling anywhere, just floating in mid-air. 'He is your brother.'

'How do you know that? Who are you?'

'I'm your Auntie Lolita.'

'Lola? Is that you?'

'Yes, it's me, Willem.'

'But … but I thought …?'

'It was a long time ago, Willem. I'm quite sure your mother told you a variant of our story, but there was one part she chose to leave out for your own good. Your mother and I had met a long time ago when she came to Australia from Belarus in the '60s. Your father came a few years later. He had to complete his registered time in the army, standard for every Belarusian male. The year your mother and father were married was the year your mother began living her life. She was finally able to start the family she had dreamt about as a little girl. She and I talked about having children for many years. You were both born the following year your parents were married.' Lolita's gaze moves from Will to his brother, changing the expression on her face when she did.

'Why didn't anyone tell me I had a brother? Where has he been this whole time? I didn't know …'

'Your surname was changed when your brother was sent away all those years ago,' says Lol.

'What was my surname before it was changed?'

'Zoltan.'

Natloz stands there in deep thought. It all makes no sense, until it does. The penny drops and he sees the clear picture. 'Natloz. They changed it to Natloz. It spells Zoltan backwards.'

'Correct. Your parents wanted to keep it similar.'

'Why did they send …?' Natloz looks over to his brother.

'His name is Igor. He was born with a disease called lupus. It's Latin for "wolf". Your brother had a rare strain of it that infected one in two million people. The disease was first noticed in the thirteenth century. Obviously back then something like this was unheard of, and anyone who showed symptoms was killed and their bodies burnt, putting an end to passing on the disease to someone else. They didn't realise that that wasn't the case. Kids were born with this rare disease; it wasn't passed on from anything else but genes.

'It starts with a rash that appears as a wolf bite. Igor started showing symptoms within two months of birth. Your parents had taken him to doctors in Sydney, Melbourne, and Perth. You were tested, too. Your symptoms weren't as bad as your brother's. The weird part is that it attacks people's immune system from ages fifteen to forty-five. Your brother wasn't even three months old.

'This disease also goes by other names you might have heard of. Some have called it hypertrichosis, also known as werewolf syndrome and Wolf-Hirschhorn syndrome. Excessive growth of hair on parts of the body that can be unexplainable. It doesn't choose a gender either, attacking both men and woman of all race, creed and colour, but more woman have been affected by it than men. It makes you very ill, affecting the brain the most, especially how you think. It is so rare they still have no cure for it.

'Your parents struggled with it and sought help from anywhere they could get it. Every year came bigger problems. Igor was uncontrollable and your mum needed to find a solution. The decision was made to have Igor move away when he deliberately set fire to the family home. Your mother was out working and you were in hospital.'

'I was? Why?'

'Igor had wanted to play soldiers with you and you said no because he was always so rough with you and you were scared. On this particular day you said no, you were both up on a gum tree at the front of the house and he pushed you off the branch. You fell out of the tree and landed head first onto the concrete, splitting your head open and smashing your nose. You were concussed. Blood poured out from above your right eye where a cut had come across four inches long. You required six stiches.'

Natloz lifts his right hand to where the scar is. He can still feel the rough skin which is now the only thing that reminds him of the accident. He looks over to his brother. Igor has a smirk on his face, remembering every detail and possibly more from that day.

'Your father said no more playing soldiers and your brother lost it. He saw red and broke out in a sweat. He became violent. Your father was trying to repair the TV that day and asked the babysitter, Sylvia from next door, to look after you while he finished the repairs. Your brother walked into the kitchen where Sylvia was making lunch holding a bottle that had liquid in it. Her back was turned and she hadn't seen him come in. She was blindsided. Igor threw the bottle that smashed over the babysitter's head. She was knocked unconscious. Igor took out the matches from his pocket and struck one up. Without hesitation or remorse, he flicked the lit match on Sylvia and watched her burn before leaving the house. Your dad hadn't realised what Igor had done and it was too late to help the poor lady. The entire house went up in flames.

Witnesses reported to police that they saw Igor standing outside next to his dad smiling, knowing all too well he had just killed an innocent person. He was sent away to Mount Gambier in South Australia the following day. Your parents didn't feel safe with Igor in the house and especially around you. Your safety was their priority and the main reason he was banished. They changed their surname and moved to the country, beginning a new life and chapter. But that didn't happen.

'Your mother moved out to Sydney for a few years chasing work. She never returned. We found out later that she had died in a farming accident. It took years for Joshua to get over what had happened. He was heart-broken. Before your mother left, her last words to me were to make sure you were looked after. Your dad wanted me to move in with you and him but I couldn't. You needed both parents and someone who knew what they were doing. I wasn't ready to become a parent. I'm sorry.'

She throws another glace over to Igor. 'About six months ago, Igor escaped from the psychiatric hospital in Adelaide. Crossed over the border and came to Melbourne. He tracked you down and wanted to make your life a living hell.'

A noise leaves Igor's mouth. His eyes are partially closed, absorbing everything he has overheard about him. Everyone looks, not feeling any pity whatsoever towards the man known as Igor, the monster. A new smile creeps onto his face, satisfied with all he has done. He still has the energy to say something. 'You all fucking deserted me. Left me to rot in that nuthouse. You left me there to fucking die, just like now.'

His voice is filled with hatred and anger, the only feeling he knows. If he had the chance now, he would kill every single one of them there.

'I should have been told about Igor,' Natloz says. 'I should have known what he was like and how dangerous he was. If I had known, I could have checked up on him from time to time, made sure he was safely tucked away.'

'He was and still is a dangerous man,' Lolita says. 'A danger to society. It has been proven he cannot be trusted. It was best you didn't know of him and of your past. But looking at the situation now, maybe it was a mistake not telling you about him.'

Igor directs his words to Natloz. 'I was made an outcast. Our fucking parents sent me away. They needed to stick by me. They knew I needed help but they fucking got rid of me. I despised them for that. I wanted you all to die. I knew then I had to do it myself. I made it my mission that one day I would get my revenge. Your parents made it easy for me by dying themselves, they did me a favour. But you, I wanted to punish you.'

Igor points at him and Natloz sees the hatred in his brother's eyes. He returns the hatred within his own. He'd seen what his brother is capable of; he'd seen the carnage that had been administered. He has seen the unforgivable killings that have spread from city to city, all just to get back at Natloz. Igor had almost succeeded in making him believe he was crazy and had something to do with the murders. Sally, Oscar, the innocent bystanders, the Sergeant, and Jack Gumba have all fallen victim to Igor Zoltan.

Short's lifeless body lies there on the floor in his own blood. His family is unaware of the horrors that await them, enjoying their evening not knowing that Short has landed himself in this predicament. How will they react when they find out? It won't be long before they do. The mourning, the grieving, the funeral, the aftermath. The hardest thing to do is to bury your own child. The Shorts are about to do that.

Natloz looks at Short, the way his body is positioned, monitoring the expression on the faces of the others. His partner Petridis, his

Auntie Lol, and Annie. All three with an expression of disbelief and gladness: disbelief it has come to this, glad it's all over.

Lolita calls the Broken Hill police station. 'I have explained to them what has happened. They're sending down squad cars and a couple of units of paramedics. This is finally over, Will.'

Natloz gives his auntie a smile. Petridis walks up to Natloz and puts his hand on his shoulder. 'I'm glad you're okay, mate. We all are.'

'Yeah, me too. I'm sorry about Pat.'

They both turn and look at him. A tear forms in Petridis's eye. He'd grown fond of the young detective. Guilt forms a knot in his throat for not being able to protect his partner. Now he's dead and there is nothing more he can do for him.

Both Petridis and Natloz make their way towards Annie who is now standing alongside Lolita when unexpectedly Igor gathers up all the strength he can muster and leaps up like a wolf to lunge at Natloz. The collision is so forceful it knocks both Natloz and Petridis to the ground. Igor's face contorts with rage, his eyes erupt in flames like a volcano. He maliciously wants to finish what he set out to do. His capture was inevitable, but he wasn't going lying down.

Igor intends to kill everyone in the room. Blood has covered most of his torso from the gunshot. He bends over and picks up the dirty claw that was taken away from him earlier by Petridis, that barbaric homemade weapon with a wolf claw, and stands over Petridis, ready to strike his final blow. He raises it high in the air with one intention – kill.

A gun goes off for the second time. Igor is hit directly in the chest. There's a pause between that and another that hits him in the right arm. Then, the final shot to his head, ending the life of the crazed monster. Igor's legs buckle and he goes down for the three count, a count that will last a lifetime. Igor Zoltan is dead.

Petridis looks over to see who fired the lethal blow. A gun held chest height in front of her; Annie found the strength to administer the final blow, the final nail in the coffin. She did it for Sally and Oscar. The final chapter to this horror show has been written and there is no one who can change it, not even Annie herself.

There is a moan from Natloz. He's hurt pretty badly. Igor had a second syringe hidden somewhere on him. When he lunged at Natloz and Petridis, he had stabbed Natloz with it before knocking them both over. The lethal blow of tranquilizer was injected, the deadly liquid streaming through his veins at a rapid pace. Natloz's eyes begin to close and he slowly falls unconscious; life slowly drawing to an end. Igor has succeeded with his mission.

Petridis moves over and begins CPR. Natloz's eyes are shut and his breathing faint. Life is starting to fade rapidly. Lolita moves closer to help Petridis, both of them working hard to keep Natloz alive. They can hear the sound of the sirens in the distance. Help is on its way. They hope they get there in time to save Natloz.

Time is running out and so is his breath. Air has stopped flowing and the sound of nothing from his mouth becomes reality. Natloz fades away and begins to drift, on his way to meet his parents in another life. His face turns blue. Air is of an essence. Pump, pump, pump, hands working frantically, trying to get his heart to start working.

The light you see when you are crossing over is all that he will be seeing now. Natloz is losing. Life is no more.

Epilogue

Seven months later

Petridis enters his office and sits down to start a new day's work. There is a routine from steps one to eight that he follows religiously. He has worked the same shift ever since that dreadful night in Silverton all those months back.

A quick glance out his office window reminds him of that night. The department has made a plaque in honour of Detective Patrick Stephen Short who was killed in the line of duty that same evening. A photo stands proud alongside the plaque in remembrance.

Sadness fills his heart, remembering the times he and Short spent together. In the little time they did spend together, Petridis felt that Short could have grown into the shoes his original partner had worn. Together, they could have become a great team. The fond memories he has always bring that smile he desires to his face.

Short was laid to rest a week after the gruesome attack. His death was hard to take in, and his funeral wasn't any easier. Seven hundred people attended the closed casket ceremony. It was a request from his family that the casket remain closed as his death was so horrific, the mortician wasn't able to make Short look any better than he was. It was sad but the right decision was made. Everyone there will get to remember him the way he looked before.

His parents and sisters had arranged a beautiful ceremony which was held at Healesville Cemetery, Short's final resting spot. Dating back from 1866, the place is surrounded by beautiful lush greenery at the foot of Mount Riddell. The cemetery is also close to where Short had grown up.

Dr Lolita Grady continued to operate as the vet in Silverton following the months of the killings. She then tied up some loose ends with the family property before selling up and moving to Brisbane. Her practice continues today as a very promising clinic in the suburb of Cowan Cowan. Life looks bright considering the darkness that fell over her not long ago. The clouds closed in on her life when she learnt that Igor had escaped the institution. She knew danger was on its way but didn't know how to stop it. The one regret she has and that will stay with her until the day she dies is not informing the authorities that she knew him and possibly alerting them to what he was capable of. Would that have stopped him? Probably not. Would that have slowed him down and saved a few lives? Absolutely.

Someone else had to stop it in the end, leaving a long trail of devastation. A happy ending to a not so happy story.

It was in the weeks that followed that she had found out that the homemade claw weapon had been stolen from a shop window. Igor had entered the taxidermist store in the foothills of Adelaide acting like a customer. He turned on the owner before killing him and cutting the paw off a large Canadian timber wolf that was on display. Igor modified the paw to make the deadly weapon that would see to so many murders; murders that sent the police on a wild goose chase around the state and beyond. It worked.

The loss of her family meant Lolita had to bury the past before she could continue with a future. Her life is finally improving and in time her scars will heal, but the memory will always be there.

Annie eventually gave up her studies to leave Melbourne and vowed never to return. She had lost her closest friends in Australia and knew it would take a long time to come back from that. She needed to be around family and the only way for that to happen was to leave Melbourne. Losing Oscar and Sally meant she had nothing else to look forward to besides her studies, which weren't as important as her friends. She has plans to write a book about her ordeal and start funds under both Sally's and Oscar's names, trying to raise money for their families to help with life in general.

Annie did have one benefit from all this. She got to meet Detective Will Natloz, or Zoltan as she later found out. She needed his company just as much as he needed hers. They grew close over time and understood what friendship meant. What she saw in Natloz was a father figure; she missed her own father and found comfort in him.

Annie flew back home to Ybor City straight after the funeral. She took with her both good and bad memories. The bad she can filter, the good will stay with her forever. She is going to miss Natloz.

After the killing of Igor Zoltan, the state wanted to use his body for research. The brain was the main organ they wanted; other parts could have been used too, but the government and Criminal Acts committee decided against the request. It was decided that Igor Zoltan's body should and would be cremated, his ashes scattered at an undisclosed location. His crimes had rocked the country so fiercely that forgetting him completely was the only option. Publishers were waiting for someone to write a book about him. Film directors waiting to cast a team to portray this sadistic killer. And there were organisations ready to stop that production.

Detective Petridis went through many months of therapy, both mentally and physically. The case had made his mental health hit an all-time low. He took leave to get himself back on track. The loss of his partner meant he would have to start from the beginning again, which would take a lot longer than he might anticipate. The powers above had wanted to promote Petridis to Superintendent, something he had worked really hard to achieve.

After the ordeal, Petridis decided that it was best he remained a plain-clothed detective, keeping in line with the request of his heart – hands-on in investigations and working his own schedule, keeping out of the limelight, and fighting crime. That's all he wanted. The request was granted immediately. Life will get better for Petridis and the memories will eventually subside but the heartache will continue forever.

A head pops in through the open door of the office.

'Morning, partner. What do we have on for today?'

As for Detective Willem Zoltan … he survived. He and Petridis are reunited and continue fighting crime, together.

ACKNOWLEDGEMENTS

There are so many people to mention with only a number of pages to use so I will make this brief.

First and foremost, I want to thank my family and friends who believed in my capability to write this book. The support and encouragement I received from my beautiful partner Annwen Kirby was second to none. She understood how my mind worked and made me believe that my way was the right way.

Thank you to my son Nicholas and stepdaughter Alessia for listening to my sentences over and over again and being honest on how they sounded. Honesty is all I wanted from them.

A massive thank you to my publishers Kev Howlett, Blaise van Hecke, and the amazing team at Busybird Publishing.

From the moment I walked into the Busybird Studio, I knew I was walking into my home – from Oscar the Labrador greeting me with a wagging tail, to Kev's smile and greeting of, 'Welcome.'

Unfortunately, Blaise passed away suddenly in March 2022, but her encouragement during our initial communication, her energy in getting a story told correctly and then published, combined with her passion for new and emerging authors and her ever-beaming smile will always be remembered and appreciated.

'Thank you to my mate Matty Evans who tipped me off about a publisher he was great mates with. If it wasn't for you i wouldn't have found Kev Howlett and the gang at Busybird Publishing. If there was ever a perfect lead then this was it.

My worries of finding a publisher was solved and the case was closed'

Thank you to my wonderful and talented editor Laura McCluskey whom from day one was as honest as one can be, and pushed me to another level. To question my work, sentences, phrases, and even particular words I had used meant that I needed to work that much harder to get this book right. I got it right.

A big thank you to my great friend and fellow author Les Zig for all your help in explaining the creativity, the writing and editing for my story. You have helped me understand so much that goes into writing a book

Thank you to Andy Griffith for helping me understand the concept behind writing. Even though our genres are on the opposite end to one another, it all made sense no matter what you wrote.

To my father-in-law Peter Kirby for letting me use his name in this book. I could have used anyone but I respect you in a big way and wanted to repay you for everything you have done for me.

To all my family, friends, and everyone else who chooses to read my book, I thank you in advance and hope you enjoy it as much as I loved writing it. This could not have been made possible if it wasn't for the people I have mentioned.

I also want to acknowledge a few people who deserve a mention for being there when I needed them the most: my mother Helen, my brother Marlon Shalevski, Kay Groves, and Karen Kirby.

ABOUT THE AUTHOR

Con Shalevski was born in Melbourne to a Greek mother and Macedonian father.

Drama, reading, and writing were school hobbies that he never grew out of. This book was inspired by a play he had written in high school. His favourite genre is crime/thriller.

He is also an accomplished professional wrestler and storyteller. He lives with his beautiful family and his pooch Arlo in Melbourne.

The Full Moon Murders is his first book.